Praise

'The brilliance of Crace's novel lies in the tension between the polished-pebble perfection of his style and the awareness that what it attempts to pin down is constantly shifting, impermanent, unfinished'
Sunday Telegraph

'Lovely, playful and imaginative. An illuminating look at "love and lovemaking, of children, marriages and lives"'
Daily Mail

'You finish *Six* itching to book a weekend break to this unforgettable city of dream and desire. Then you remember that, thanks to the singular magic of Jim Crace, you've already been'
BOYD TONKIN

'A dark, dystopian satire [with] pungent atmospherics and trenchant satire'
Time Out

'Curious, affecting'
New Statesman

'Discover Crace's brilliant mastery of suspense, atmosphere and telling detail'
Image

Six

JIM CRACE is the author of *Continent*,
The Gift of Stones, *Arcadia*, *Signals of Distress*,
Quarantine (winner of the 1998 Whitbread Novel
of the Year and shortlisted for the Booker Prize),
Being Dead (winner of the 2001 National Book
Critics' Circle Award), *The Devil's Larder*, *Six*, and
The Pesthouse. His novels have been translated into
twenty-six languages. In 1999 Jim Crace was
elected to the Royal Society of Literature.

JIM CRACE

SIX

PICADOR

First published 2003 by Viking

First published in paperback 2004 by Penguin Books

This edition first published 2008 by Picador
an imprint of Pan Macmillan Ltd
Pan Macmillan, 20 New Wharf Road, London N1 9RR
Basingstoke and Oxford
Associated companies throughout the world
www.panmacmillan.com

ISBN 978-0-330-45336-3

1 3 5 7 9 8 6 4 2

A CIP catalogue record for this book is available from
the British Library.

Typeset by SetSystems Ltd, Saffron Walden, Essex
Printed and bound in Great Britain by
Mackays of Chatham plc, Chatham, Kent

6

EVERY WOMAN he dares to sleep with bears his child. So now it is Mouetta's turn. Whispering and smudging his ear with her lipstick, her breath a little sour from the garlic in her lunch, she confirms her first, his sixth pregnancy. His sixth at least. She's 'passed the urine test', she says – an unintended play on words, which she acknowledges in the matinee darkness with half an optimistic smile. The doctor thinks she's twelve or thirteen weeks. A baby's due by May. It's early days.

Mouetta feels, of course (before the morning sickness and the backaches start, before the lifetime of anxiety and love), that her pregnancy is a personal blessing. The raven of good fortune has chosen her. It has alighted in her yard and she's been brushed by its great wing. No other, adult, explanation matters to her for the time being. She is the lucky one. This is her miracle.

They sit together in the cinema, that draughty art-house cinema down on the wharf, their elbows touching and their jackets spread across their knees, to watch young lovers on the screen, young actors making love, or seeming to. She wishes Lix would speak to her, do something more than press her forearm with his own, a kiss perhaps. But he's a film buff and an actor himself. 'Silence for the colleagues,' he usually insists. He won't ever speak, not once a movie has begun. Perhaps it's just as well, this winterish afternoon, the perfect weather for the cinema, that he will make her wait until *The End* before he answers. He wants to say he feels besieged. Another child? He only has himself to blame. To be so fertile is a curse.

LIX COULD NEVER say exactly when the pregnancies began. They always took him by surprise. Mouetta's pregnancy as well. Especially hers. He had been privy to her ovulation dates, those gaping opportunities when intercourse was ill-advised for teeming alpha-males like him. They'd not been careless, had they, at the wrong time of the month? Twelve weeks? He counted back the weeks and counted back the times that they'd had sex. Still no clues. The days were fused and distant. How could he ever tell which time, which place had fathered this new child? Mother Nature doesn't ring a bell. Whatever other noises might be made, the egg is punctured silently. If only he could call on chemistry and then biology, unsentimental disciplines, calculating, tidy and precise. They could pinpoint for him (had they the mind) that careless and productive day in his beleaguered, complicated life, could specify the hour, even.

Science has the answers every time: it was 2 a.m. or thereabouts on 18 August – the week of the Banking Riots, three dead already, the city devalued and deranged, and interest rates 'settled by decree' at a quarter of one per cent – when Lix's latest child was conceived. *Conceived*'s a charmless and misleading word, too immaculate and cerebral, too purposeful and too hygienic, to truly represent the headlong thoughtlessness, the selfishness – that night, especially – of making love. (Headlong for him at least.) It is a strangely cold and scientific word, as well. No passion. You'd think some calm technician had been employed to fit a tiny battery of genes. *Conceived* suggests a meeting of like minds, dedication, diligence, technology, and not the rain-damp, springing seats in the front of Lix's grey Panache where no two minds and no two thoughts achieved on that occasion even the briefest instant of concord or shared a common cause. That's one of the reoccurring oddities of sex, where it falls short, again, again. Opposing poles attract when lovers magnetize. His north of lust, Mouetta's south of love. Crossed purposes. And, surely, not a grand and proper way for children to begin. This child.

SOMETIMES OUR CITY, our once famous City of Kisses, with its deep parks, its balconies, and its prolific and disrupting river, like any other city, seems to have a climate of its own, a window of clear sky, perhaps, unshiftable for days, or more commonly a random storm attracted to the concrete and the bricks while all the countryside around is calm. That August night was such a night. Vague summer winds till after ten, too many stars, oppressive in their multitude, but then the concentrated, local rain, clearing the streets and pavement cafes, and breaking up the wayward, trouble-seeking crowds, few of whom had thought to arm themselves with hats or waterproofs or umbrellas. Though folk rhymes promise us that 'Storms at night/ Blow out the light/ Conceal the killer/ Blind the King', wet weather doesn't truly favour assassins and Molotovs, or fires, or leafleting. The revolution likes it dry.

The theatre had not been busy all summer. Times were hard and tickets, though subsidized, were still not cheap or fashionable. Molière's *Tartuffe*, updated as a New Age satire, with songs, dance, and video, was not much of an attraction, either, even though the cast (including 'Lix', the celebrated Felix Dern, in the lead as L'Imposteur) was 'glittering' by regional standards and all the notices – in magazines and newspapers that, against the logic of the age, had sponsored that summer's Stage and Concert season – had been dutifully enthusiastic. For once, that Thursday evening, he could leave through the foyer without too much danger of being waylaid by an autograph bibber, a theatre limpet, or – worse – an ancient friend or colleague whom it might be difficult to ignore. He was hoping for the sole company of his wife. It was their second anniversary.

As yet the rain was only light, drumming plugs of smoke and steam out of the coals of braziers at pavement stalls where kebabs and roasted beets were sold to retreating theatre-goers, but making little impact yet on all the distant mayhem in the streets. The brick-trapped wind delivered its reports of chanting crowds, the sirens of what could be fire engines, ambulances, or the police, and, occasionally, the detonation of dispersal crackers or smoke bombs. But the protests had been restricted largely to the city boulevards on the east side of the river where many of the institutions had their offices and where, if you could trust as evidence the daily lines of chauffeured limousines, the savings of the townspeople had mostly disappeared. The narrower streets, known as the Hives, on this side of the river, near the market halls, had not been targeted. No one wants to burn down bars and restaurants these days (except the police). Yet the back ways near the theatre were not their usual carefree selves. The army, armed and keen to start an argument, had been deployed to break up demonstrations. The surplus, unarmed militia, the bail conscripts (who'd chosen public service rather than the jail) and the civic police, in and out of uniform, had set up barriers throughout the city to turn back traffic, check IDs, and generally put a stop to everything. The kind of people who seemed likely protesters or immigrants or undergraduates or bitter, newly minted bankrupts were lined up at the back of army buses with their hands on their heads, like kids, and – a recent police procedure to keep a suspect quiet – their identity documents held between their teeth. Try remonstrating with a booklet in your mouth. The best you'll manage is ventriloquy.

Lix looked a likely candidate. Not bankrupt, obviously. And not a student. But artistic. Intellectual. Dressed like a writer or a lecturer, at once shabby and elegant. He was known to the militia and the police, from television work and films. Who'd fail to recognize that celebrated granite head, those expressively nervous beryl eyes, that cherry-sized, cherry-shaped, and cherry-coloured birthmark on the ridge of bone below his left eye? They waved him through. They cleared a way for him. He wished he'd brought a jacket. Then he'd turn its collar up, against the rain, and hide his famous face, his famous blemished face. It would make a change to go unrecognized, once in a while, not to be greeted on the street by strangers as if he were a neighbour or a cousin. For that, he had to go abroad these days, to theatres and studios in Britain, France, America, and Italy, where his success had not been shackled yet with any intrusive fame. He wanted the applause and the bouquets, the prizes and the statuettes, the fees, but he'd enjoy, as well, some public anonymity. For one so fertile and flamboyant, for one so arrogant in costume, Felix Dern, the showman, was – offstage – surprisingly shy and timid. That was, in rising middle age, his major flaw, his main regret – and also his saving grace.

He met Mouetta in the back room of the Habit Bar, the city's best-kept secret – or so the newspapers and radio had been saying for a year or more. He was obliged to stop and be polite at one or two tables before he'd crossed the excited, overcrowded room to hers. The Habit Bar could always boast a celebrity or two, other than himself, particularly journalists and heroes of the left and particularly when there were protests and comrades to support across town by eating out in reckless solidarity. You'd never catch a politician there or someone ministerial or military, except in disguise, wired for gossip. Even the waiters and the chefs, it was claimed, were impeccably progressive. The meals were progressive, too. No boycott goods, no shed meat, no reactionary wines, no condescending sauces. The Habit was the place to come if you were on the left and indiscreet – and, incidentally, not hard up. Its motto should have been, according to the shanty-boys who touted for scraps and coins on the terrace outside, 'One meal for the price of six'. Its nickname was the Debit Bar. And so its clientele were Debitors and not Habituals.

Mouetta was not alone. Her cousin, Freda, was sitting opposite in Lix's chair, her back against the room, but unmistakable – and dangerous. She shared an ancient, awkward history with Lix. Awkward for Mouetta, too. Her hair was up, of course, coiled and clipped in place by an ochre lavawood barrette. She had the longest neck and the heaviest earrings in the Debit, and that, for such a restaurant where short-necked diners were a rarity and jewellery was always immodest, was quite a boast.

Lix had been wondering all evening, even as he laboured through the Molière, his thirty-eighth performance of the play, what Mouetta might be wearing for their anniversary. For him. A skirt or dress, not trousers, if there was a god. And buttons down the front. And musky, ancient perfume as a sign that she had not forgotten what the night might signify. But now, as he excused himself a passage past the backs of diners' chairs, through smoke, through kitchen smells, through wine-induced curses against the army, banks, and Church, he could not take his eyes off that long, cousin's neck and when he did – he shamed himself with his disloyalty, with his nostalgia, perhaps – it was only to look down beyond her chest, her modest chest, into her lap where her fine hands were crossed and resting on, of course, what else?, her uniform: a loose black skirt.

*

Six

It was a photojournalist with *Life* magazine who, in 1979, when Lix was in his first term at the theatre academy, came up with the phrase the City of Kisses to replace the more alluring, truer title given us by Rousseau, the City of Balconies. That was the year of khaki skirts and tunic tops, when all the brighter girls were feminist, and rudely militant in bed. The photographer was one of fifty, sent to Fifty Cities of the World, to record the flavour of the place on one particular Sunday. His picture essay concentrated on our city's better-looking girls – and all of them were kissing. A boyfriend kissed, full on the mouth. A girlfriend chastely kissed in greeting from behind on the high loop of her ponytail. A grandma blessed by her granddaughter's lips. A teenage mother with a child. A puppy kissed. A couple kissing at the swimming-pool, their hair like weed. It was a city doing little else but kiss, you'd think. In a way, that is exactly how it was that year. But, famously, the photograph that truly caught the spirit of the place, so *Life* would claim, the photograph that sold countless posters and, for several years, was responsible for packed hotels and the resurrection of our red-light district, was taken at the Debit Bar. A woman in a Cuban beret applying lipstick to a glass of wine with her red mouth. Reflected in the glass, two men, their own mouths gaping and both encircled by the kiss.

Life could, of course, have photographed this essay

anywhere. They kiss in Rome and Paris, too. They kiss in Tokyo. The whole world osculates. Yet this was public kissing, and unusual for us. That was the year the post-war ban on all public demonstrations of affection, even in the theatre, was lifted. Using your lips became the simple evidence of progress. We all made up for those lost opportunities. We had the kisses that our parents missed. That was the year, indeed, when Lix first kissed in earnest – and inadvertently provided us with his first child.

There was still a framed copy of the original Lipstick poster in the lobby of the Debit on the night of Lix and Mouetta's anniversary, the first evening of the riots when interest rates seemed so much more relevant than kissing. Lix did not perform his usual playful pout for it when, a minute after midnight, he left the bar. He was exasperated. His wife and her cousin had sabotaged their anniversary. He'd planned a little hand-holding, some eye-contact, some drinks, a light exciting meal, no garlic certainly (actors and lovers should not be 'cloven-mouthed'). He'd hoped that he and Mouetta would go home to bed quite soon. Well, not 'to bed', perhaps, but somewhere on the way to bed. The car. The hall. The study couch. The stairs? The stairs had always seemed a tantalizing possibility.

HIS EVENING on stage had been, as usual, both stressful and arousing: the uncritically approving dimwit audience in their subsidized seats, the dressing up, the liberties that actors take, the swish and odour of the actresses had been a stimulant. The fear of 'drying and dying' mid-speech provided the anxiety. As did (more recently) a shaking hand, which, his doctor had assured him with the backing of some tests, was not early-onset Parkinson's as he had feared (or 'toper's wobble', as one gossip columnist had suggested) but simply nerves. Late-onset stage fright.

That evening Lix's tremor had been especially undermining. Tartuffe had held a very shaky book, and then had spilled a glass of wine. Lix was infuriated with himself. He needed to unwind. He was, of course, still partly in character even though the shaking had disappeared the moment the curtains closed. An immersion actor such as Lix cannot shuck off the emotional raiments of a play as easily as he can shed the costume. Performance always leaves its mark, for an hour or two at least. Indeed, the remains of Tartuffe's florid Pan Stik pink make-up could be seen, if you were close enough, in his eyebrows and his sideboards.

As usual, that night he'd had to kiss his leading lady twice on stage: Tartuffe seducing sweet Elmire within the text, but also Lix playacting with a colleague unjustly famous for her love affairs. Stage-kissing, obviously. Dry lips. He always relished it, however, the smell and taste of her (make-up, brandy, perspiration, cigarettes, cologne), the enticing possibility that one night their kisses might turn wet. Lix had seduction in mind. So already he had fixed his hopes on Mouetta and on stairs, the view they offered as his wife preceded him, the urgent discomfort that they promised any couple mad enough, inflamed enough to pause and kiss. He'd spent the evening scheming their impromptu, corrugated sex.

Freda, though, had other plans for him, for them. One of her students at the Human Science Academy ('an activist and very, very dear to me') had been 'listed' in the morning papers, with a photograph and phone numbers to contact with 'rewardable' information on his whereabouts. He was, they claimed, 'a firebrand leader of the SNRM, already known to the civil authorities'.

'He's such a little innocent,' she said, delighted with her protégé, a young man younger even than her own son, George. 'He printed up some leaflets and some posters, that's all. And damaged cars. Perhaps he's been a little wild. He's hardly broken any laws, but still . . .' The police would find him if he went back to his lodgings, she explained, and, depending on the level of their 'vicious inefficiency', would either teach him manners there and then or take him to the barracks yard where bright and pretty faces such as his were routinely 'spoiled'. Both Mouetta and her cousin stole a glance at Lix's cherry stain.

Six

'He's in my office now. He's hiding underneath my desk, poor little man,' Freda said. She could not stop the sudden smile, the crossing and uncrossing of her legs. 'But obviously he can't stay there.' She put her slender hand on Mouetta's arm, and sighed. Bad theatre.

Lix did his best to avoid Freda's eye. He hadn't looked her in the eye for years, and with good cause. He did not want to nod, or laugh, or match her sigh with a more ironic one of his own. He was just hoping that he could avoid the implications of the 'little man' hiding underneath her desk. That phrase, 'But obviously he can't stay there', could ruin everything. Freda's always organizing her revenge, he thought. She still distrusted, even hated him – and *with good cause* again. He acted sudden, ironic interest in the wine label, a scene he'd played before to great effect in his third film, *Full Swing*. He was not as calm as he appeared. What actor ever is? Unless he got lucky, his anniversary – just like the student's face – would be 'spoiled', no doubt of it.

Lix should, he knew, speak up at once, or all was lost. Freda frightened him. Too tough and beautiful and challenging. His cock never failed to stir itself for her. Even now, with Mouetta's hand across his shoulder, he could not contemplate the student hiding underneath Freda's desk without his cock lengthening, without jealously recasting the scene with himself, his younger self, as the protagonist: an armed policeman standing at the open office door, a seated Freda blushing, innocent, her elbows resting on her desk, her earrings swinging, catching lights, the listed student (Felix Dern, as ever, in the leading role) bunched up in the many folds of her black skirt, the audience not knowing whether this was comedy or tragedy or when the kissing – or the beatings – might begin. Good theatre.

Avoiding eye-contact, however, and dreaming the impossible provided no escape. 'My little firebrand needs your help,' Freda had already told Mouetta during Molière's and Lix's final act. And Mouetta had already agreed to offer the sanctuary of their study couch for a week or so, until it was safe to drive the student out of town, until . . . No one knew the sequel to 'until' in those extraordinary times.

'What's wrong with your place, Freda?' Lix asked, finally. 'You've got a couch to spare while George is in America, I'm sure. He can even sleep underneath your bed, with the cats.' Now he was looking at her, his leading lady for this scene, looking at her piled-up hair, her speckled throat, the clothy, hammock neckline of her top, imagining how he might stage a kiss with her. 'This fellow's *very, very dear to you*, you say.' His mimicry was faultless.

Freda, though, would not respond. She had no sympathy for Lix. How dare he even mention George?

Was he inviting trouble? She smiled at him, an icy smile that said, 'Do as I want. Otherwise Mouetta will be reminded yet again of what she has so determinedly forgotten or ignored, exactly what went on between us, twenty-five years ago when we were undergraduates ourselves. When I was carrying your child. When you were truly dangerous to know.'

She stretched her neck away from him. She'd let him talk. She'd let him puff and blow. She only paid attention once he'd dutifully proclaimed his list of predictable objections – the risk (for him), the inconvenience (for him) – and was prepared to accept what had already been agreed behind his back. There was no need to repeat herself for Lix. He was a spouter nowadays, not a sympathetic listener. Not an activist. She'd already explained herself to her cousin, how her own office and apartment at the Academy were 'always' being visited by police. Unlike Mouetta, a newcomer who'd 'married in' two years before, she'd been a citizen of this 'infuriating' town since her own student days. She was a well-known dissident, a 'bit of a firebrand' herself. While Lix, born in the town forty-seven years before, despite his posturing, was not – not now, at least – a threat to anyone. The celebrated Lix would not be visited by police, not in a thousand years. His study couch would be the safest refuge in the town. Saving this brave 'boy' (Lix winced at her transparent use of words: a cut, an edit, please!) would be a simple matter, then. They'd drive in to the campus, pick the hero up, and take him home to share their anniversary.

So Lix, defeated, left the Debit Bar, not hand in hand with Mouetta as he had planned, but as one of an ill-at-ease threesome and without a suggestion of any intimacy between them. They could be mistaken for little more than casual, frosty friends. The actor, naturally, looked grander and crosser and more thwarted than the other two, but then men always do, actors or not. They are Pierrots by nature. Smiling is for Columbines.

Lix was too irritated – and alarmed (for he was no longer an adventurous man) – even to acknowledge the greetings and congratulations from a couple who had seen his performance, on stage, that evening, a couple who had witnessed his dry kissing and his tremor from the balcony. He contemplated having Freda's callow lodger, callow lover, in his house. Her 'boy'. A week or so, she'd said. That meant three months minimum. A stranger in the frying pan. His egg with theirs. The staircase always busy with the sound of running feet. The sound of running taps. Worse even than the alternate weekends when his acknowledged children came to stay, descended on his house and his routines, his two adolescent boys, Lech and Karol (the products of his first marriage), and four-year-old Rosa (the unplanned fruit of a short, bizarre, and punishing liaison not quite before he'd met Mouetta). At least their running feet were known and loved. For, yes, despite the evidence so far, the selfishness, the sexual jealousy, the lack of courage, the peevishness on this night of their anniversary, theirs was a house of love. Lix, for all his faults, for all his fickleness, was capable of love. He had been thwarted, though, on this occasion, by the unforgiving first love, second conquest of his life.

As it happened, luck was on his side.

The rain was heavy now, disabling and hostile. It beat out its cacophonies on cars and roofs. The police had had to set up shop beneath the water-sagging canopies on the bar's terrace and were painstakingly checking the identities of anyone who dared to enter or to leave. Their mood was volatile, resentful, tired. They'd welcome the chance – were it not for the journalists present – to burst inside to tip some tables over and to crack some heads. The Debit's clientele was just the sort they hated most. Toffee-nosed and smart-arsed liberals with cash to spare, their lives ringfenced by bank accounts abroad and properties at home. Provoking women with skin like confirmation cups and catwalk clothes. Men who never had to take the tram, or wear a shirt for three shifts in a row, or work – as they themselves were working now – after midnight, in the rain, for wages that were 'held up' by the bank. A daylight robbery. Imagine how the Debitors' blood would decorate the fancy tablecloths, or how dramatically those clever, brittle heads would bruise and crack if only someone with a bit of spirit and imagination in the government would give permission for the patriots to proceed. They wanted their revenge for having to be dutiful when everyone else was having fun, for having to be young and unimportant, for being dull and out of place.

Their corporal, a towny boy though not this town, made a corridor of tables through which Debitors must pass. His comrades crowded round to take offence. Now here was someone that they recognized and did not like. Not Lix. They hadn't seen him yet. But Freda. 'Freedom Freda'. The firebrand lecturer whose rants they'd had to endure at far too many public meetings, in far too many television interviews. A critic of the army and the police, indeed. There was no mistaking this giraffe. She was a handsome woman, tall and *set*, to use the current phrase. Frisking her and requiring her to stretch her arms above her head, her fine teeth biting on her documents, was a duty and a luxury. Even Lix could see what satisfaction it was providing them, could sympathize with their wide eyes, their gaping mouths, caused just as much by how she looked as what she was saying (for she could still create a din, could shout and curse, through her clenched teeth). They'd never heard such legal threats, such posturing, such statements of intent, such growls. They'd never detained such hair before, such long and capable arms,

so willowy a neck, such arrogance, such heavy fabric
in the dress, so hectoring a voice. And what good
luck! The woman was not carrying an up-to-date ID
with her. She'd not renewed. On a point of principle,
she said. Well, on another point of principle, a legal
principle, the corporal had no alternative but to send
her to the barracks for some questioning. If only she
would show a little more respect and quieten down,
then possibly they would allow her to be taken there
'without handcuffs'. The policemen looked, and smiled,
at Freda's narrow wrists, her bangles and her amulets.
A pair of extra cuffs would finish her.

What none of the policemen or Lix had spotted was
the sudden transfer, just before Freda's hands were
raised, of her shoulder bag to Mouetta. So he was
baffled and relieved when rather than arguing for her
cousin's immediate release, as he expected, as she was
prone to do, his normally plucky wife simply took his
arm and, without a glance back or a word of farewell,
steered him through the uniforms, across the terrace,
and out into the driving rain. No one tried to stop him,
obviously. Too familiar. He was starring every Tuesday
night in *Doctor D* on Channel V&N. He was in the
advert for Boulevard Liqueur. He'd won a celebrated
Master's Medal for his solo version of *Don Juan*. He'd
gone to Hollywood, appeared in several films, and
come back almost undefiled. He'd even had success as
a singer: his *Hand Baggage*, 'The Travelogue of Songs',

recorded fourteen years before, was selling still. He was, as Freda had made clear ten minutes earlier, a threat to nobody.

The car – their large but unpretentious grey Panache saloon, perfect for the family with adolescents – was parked behind the theatre, a leisurely five-minute walk on any other night. But it was far too wet for leisure and they were far too fearful. Fearful for Freda, of course, but also for themselves. Her shoulder bag was dangerous. What might it hold? And fractious men in uniform are always frightening. Any second now and they might hear beyond the clatter of the rain the sound of running boots, the cliché call for them to stop and raise their hands. So Lix and Mouetta didn't speak as they hurried through the rain, encountering what everybody knows but needs reminding of, that speed is no protection from a storm. He ran ahead of her to open up the car but both of them were sopping and sobered by the time they'd slammed shut the doors. For a few moments, the smell of drenched clothes was stronger than the seat leather, even, richer than the perfume and the gasoline.

Mouetta – wet – looked flushed and beautiful, Lix thought. Why hadn't he noticed before how much trouble she had gone to to be attractive for him on their anniversary? A bluish calf-length skirt, a favourite blouse he had brought her from LA, front buttons even, that pretty necklace a child might wear. Cousin

Freda, the radical, had blinded him, had shouldered out his wife. She always did. She always had. There's something deadening about the vivacious company of prettier and older cousins.

Mouetta was a sort of beauty too, although a quieter sort, not theatrical but . . . well, *homely* was an unfair word. *Unaffected*, perhaps. *Contained*. She was the kind – and this was cruel – whose company was supportive rather than flattering. She'd only turn the heads of wiser men. But now that she was wet and dramatized by their short run, her beauty seemed enhanced, her perfumes activated by the rain, her hair shining like someone found soaked and streaming in the shower room, her blouse and skin a clinging unity. He should have been thinking of Freda, her arrest, what they should do for her release, their duties as citizens and their obligations as radicals. But he was not.

'What now?' he asked. They hadn't had sex in the car for months.

'We've got the keys to Freda's office,' she replied. She held up the shoulder bag. 'We'll get the guy. And then we'll have to find Freda a lawyer . . .'

'Don't worry about Freda. They'll let her out in the morning. She'll dine off this for years. "My night in chains, et cetera"!'

'Don't be small-minded, Lix. What's done is done.' She meant that both of them should always do their best to bury the embarrassment of George's provenance. 'What would the world be like without its Fredas?'

'A lot less complicated.' Lix was blushing, not inexplicably. This was not a good time for an argument.

'We still have to get her guy,' Mouetta said.

'Forget the guy!' He touched her wrist. He had the sense, though, not to put his hand onto her leg and not to ask for what he wanted most, a kiss. Not heroism, but a kiss. A kiss inebriated by the rain. A wet, wet kiss. 'Can't we just forget the guy?'

'Just drive,' she said. She never knew – or, at least, she preferred not to know – when Lix was being serious. Or when her irritation with her husband was unreasonable.

The streets, of course, were busier than you'd expect on such a night, at such an hour. In addition to the men in uniform, causing trouble where they could, and the remaining groups of demonstrators, there were civilians sheltering in the arcades and the bars, unable to get home or prevented by the road and pavement blocks and by the weather from reaching their cars. The trams and transit buses were not running: services suspended by order of the civic police. Taxis were not allowed into the central zones. You either had to walk or shelter from the rain or beg a bed from someone you knew downtown or end up as a bludgeoned passenger inside an army bus. Even those who'd reached their cars were being turned back at the Circular and were obliged to park up for the night until restrictions had been lifted. For once, the city was not dull. It was dangerous. Young men are always dangerous.

Lix crossed the river by the only open route, Deliverance Bridge, and drove round the park on Navigation Island through stands of tarbony trees and ornamental shrubs, through puddles, ankle deep, which dramatically accessorized his car with arched, silver spoilers of rainwater, until he reached the second bridge, which still allowed some access to the river's eastern banks. Beyond the bridge, the traffic was at a standstill. Even those drivers who had tried to reverse onto the pavements or turn back towards the old town's centre were gridlocked. Beyond the traffic was the Academy and Freda's office and Freda's sanctuary desk.

'We'll not get home, you realize,' Lix said. 'They're not letting anybody through.'

'They always let *you* through.'

As it happened Mouetta was wrong, or so it appeared. All the city campuses were closed to traffic, even to the stars of stage and television, it seemed. Militia volunteers, always the last to be deployed and the most unyielding, were squeezing through the traffic, ordering drivers from their cars and searching them, both the drivers and the cars. No permissions asked, no explanations given, no patience or civility. They were determined to enjoy themselves. You had either to stand and lose your dignity or argue and lose your liberty – that mischievous predicament, as old as humankind. You had to count yourself as lucky, as bags were emptied onto seats and trunks were opened for evidence of insurrection – a box of matches, say, a couple of leaflets, a fruit knife – that on this occasion the men had not been issued with their electric cattle prods. Pedestrians, mostly students trying to return to their dorms, were being turned back. They could either spend the night outside or, if they protested, or seemed too smart and arrogant, a wooden bed could be arranged for them in some dark cell. A thorough drenching would be good for them, as would a taste of prison life. Then they'd be 'graduates' indeed! They had the choice: clear off or they'd matriculate in Practical Cell Studies.

Lix raised and stretched his arms as he was instructed and let two of the young men search his pockets and his waistband and check his ID card. Unlike the other women travellers, Mouetta had not been summoned from the car. She took this as a promising sign that yet again her husband's public gift was making life easy for them. She hated it, this privilege, but she was grateful as well. She watched her husband through the hand-jive of the windscreen wipers, waiting for the look of recognition on the volunteers' faces and the invitation to go ahead.

The man who asked Lix to raise his hands did not proceed with his interrogation for very long. Nor was their car searched. Nor were they required to un-lock the tailgate. This, then, this rescue bid, thought Mouetta, would be a simple matter, though alarming in ways that she found inexplicably stirring. Her heart was jumping like a pan-fried pea. Yes, she was stimulated by the thought of having a young man about the house, a young man needing to be saved. This would be her contribution to the night, her solidarity – to steal a 'wild and innocent' suspect, 'known to the authorities', from underneath the very snobbish, star-struck noses of the police.

Indeed, her husband had been recognized. She could tell by the way he stood, by the laughter, by the parting handshake, by the way a route was being cleared for them. There was no danger, then. They'd not be caught. They could simply drive into the car park underneath the Academy, take the elevator to the seventh floor where Freda's office was, and do their good deed for the night. She could imagine the young man – painfully idealistic, sweet to look at, awkward, grateful, very scared. They could curl him up beneath the car rugs in the back and drive home through all the blocks and barricades, untouched and undelayed, because her Lix, her acting man, would have the passport of a famous face, would have the visa of a celebrated birthmark stamped onto his cheek. Then, when they were home, in their quiet cul-de-sac with its unprying neighbours, she'd make a fuss of that young man. Find towels, a spare toothbrush, some underwear. She'd cook for him at night, while Lix was at the theatre. She'd let him have the freedom of the house. She had to smile. The very thought of it. She could provide a sanctuary for both of them.

Mouetta was hospitable and motherly, two under-valued attributes, these days. Taking care of people was her public gift. One day, please god, she'd have a child. At thirty-nine she wanted very much to have a child. She'd soon be passing through the Great Stone Gate of forty, beyond which were towns and villages without babies. Stepmothering was not enough for her. Though she was very fond of George, and Lix's children from his first marriage and the 'intervening' four-year-old (she *loved* all but one of them, in fact), they were not hers, not flesh and blood and bone. As anyone with half an eye could tell. Neither was the student *hers*, of course. But, then, he wasn't Lix's either, and that made a difference. She'd drive this student mad with care as soon as her husband returned to the car and they were summoned to proceed.

So she was baffled and surprised when Lix slid back into his driving seat and said, 'There's no way through. We have to turn round.'

'They wouldn't let you through?'

'No. So it seems.'

'Not even you?'

'Those thickies don't know me. You think they're theatregoers? We have to turn round.'

'Not recognized?'

'Not on this occasion. Evidently.'

'So what do we do about Freda's student?'

'What can we do? Nothing! It's not my fault. I don't think it would be sensible to argue with those guys. You want to try?' Already he was turning the car into the space that they had cleared for him and was nosing through a crowd of appalled, thrilled students, standing in the rain with nowhere to spend the night except the tram shelters and underneath the bushes in the park. What awful fun.

'Why don't you tell them who you are?'

'I promise you, it wouldn't count.'

'What now?' Her turn to ask.

'Back home.'

A home without house guests! He stretched a hand across and rested it, palm up, in her lap. Still damp. 'You're trembling,' she said.

They'd not get home that night. There'd be no copulating on the stairs. The Circular was still cordoned off and already flooding, anyway, on the uptown carriageway, and all the other routes out to the hilltop suburbs, where Lix and Mouetta and many of the rich and famous had their houses, were blocked. There'd been a rumour that these houses where the guilty bankers and civic bosses lived would be targeted if things got out of hand down in the city. There were incendiarists about and anarchists, expert in breaching cordons. So the police protection of their home would stop Lix and Mouetta getting home. Safety at the price of freedom? Another awkward, ancient choice. Besides, here was an unexpected bonus for the uniformed defenders of the city. They could turn the rich and famous into the homeless for the night.

Lix and Mouetta had travelled twice across the two bridges of Navigation Island, annoyed and arguing, before they decided what to do. Past one o'clock already. It was a little too late and far too early to knock up friends and ask for refuge, too late to phone a lawyer for Freda, naive to think they'd find a hotel still with beds to spare. They had the keys to Freda's flat as well as her office, but that was on the campus, too, and almost certainly unreachable. And possibly unsafe. And there were cats inside and awful litter smells, which only Freda had grown used to. They could, of course, return to the theatre and raise the janitor. Lix had done exactly that one New Year's Eve, at this same theatre. They could, at a pinch, sleep in Lix's dressing room or even on stage. The Molière demanded three chaises-longues. But the chances of the janitor still being awake himself at that hour, let alone responding to someone hammering at the doors on this of all nights, were pretty thin. They did what

many other people had been forced to do. They drove
the car again onto the island and took the first gate
into Deliverance Park, looking for a parking space or
layby. Or Lix looked at least; Mouetta, disappointed,
tired, had fallen asleep already, suddenly, her body falling, as he drove, against the webbing of the seat belt.

There were no parking spaces in the park or room
for their long Panache in the already overcrowded
laybys. The park had turned into a dormitory of cars.
So Lix bumped up onto the grass, careful not to wake
his wife. He could have parked right there, just on the
corner of the lawns, next to the road, illuminated by
the headlights and the street lamps. Safe. But he had
other plans for their anniversary. He headed for the
clump of ornamental pines, the darkest planted corner
of the park, a place that he had spotted as a possibility
many times before but never used.

At first the grass, immersed by the rain, was soft
and muddy. He had to drive slowly, in the lowest gear.
He churned up ruts and wakes of earth and water. He
damaged tended grass. Soon the formal grasses gave
way to raised picnic squares and cindered ball-game
pitches, which were hard and gravelly. He switched the
headlights off and bumped forward towards the shielding canopy of trees with the help only of his sidelights.
And then – heroically – he switched the sidelights off.
The grey Panache had disappeared from view. He
knew that he was breaking Rules. That he'd be fined

if caught. Imagine what the gossip-columnists would say. He also knew that he was taking greater risks. The river had been known to swell and break its banks. In 1989, as he could testify, Navigation Island had been entirely submerged. No resident mammal had survived. But he was determined not to waste the opportunity. The sudden looming darkness and the frieze of foliage and the possibility of floods were thrilling. He'd found a spot where, even if the storm abated and there was moonlight, they'd be completely hidden from the road. Here was another chance to fix the oversight that he had failed to fix just an hour earlier: they had not had sex in the car for months, not since their Sunday drive down to the lakes that spring when Mouetta − mid-cycle and ovulating, according to her charts and her thermometer − had tried to stop him using any contra-ception and what had started out as love had ended up as argument. He would not take the risk of having one more mouth to feed (even on alternate weekends). He'd pulled the comic condom on and Mouetta had reluctantly allowed him to continue. To be so fertile was a curse.

To be so timid was a curse, as well.

Here was a predicament, then, tricky and elaborate, but so familiar to men, especially that night with so many couples unexpectedly accommodated in their cars and keen to make the most of it. Lix's wife, already irked by him, was sleeping, snoring slightly, even. Making love to her right then would require a degree of subtlety and patience that, obviously, at pressing times like these, he did not have. Sod's Law. Catch-22. The mocking Science of Perversity.

Like other men with complex and attractive wives, he'd fantasized, of course, so many times, so many tense and sleepless times, of waking in the middle of the night, Mouetta dead asleep, as innocent as a cat curled up on her side of the bed, and simply helping himself to her. *Helping himself* in both the sense of rescuing and stealing. Just reaching out and piling up his plate with her, as if she were as ready and quiescent as a slice of cake. Her body, almost naked underneath the rucked and pushed-up nightclothes, would wake before she did, as he imagined it. Or perhaps she'd wake only after he'd pushed into her, alarmed and shuddering and animated by the wet and warm conjunction of their limbs. She'd wake aroused. This would be arousal in both senses of the word for her. She had to wake aroused. That was the whole point of his dream.

Or then again, perhaps, she'd persevere with sleep despite his unignorable embraces, and he would have to penetrate *her* dreams, so that the husband would become a sleeper's chimera and only prove himself as flesh again within her slumber and her reveries. Fat chance of that. Because, of course, that was the stuff and nonsense of a dream, his dream, not hers. (Well, that's a sham. Not *dream*. This never was a dream. In men, these fantasies are conscious and contrived. They are the product of a concentrated mind, not slumber.)

Now, in this muddy and secluded place, their privacy protected by the darkness and rain, there was a chance at last – he seemed to have waited all his life for this – to make the fiction real. Except he dared not touch. He dared not seize the opportunity – though he thought of touch, he contemplated it, while Mouetta slept. He dared not even put his finger on her leg, let alone invade her skirt or slip a hand beneath the wide lapels of her cocktail jacket to pick at gaps and buttons on her blouse. He knew, of course, he was a disappointment to his wife, that waking her would wake her irritation, too. He understood. It was his fault, his never-ending fault, that Freda's student would not be saved by them, that if he always had his way then nothing brave would ever happen in their world. If only this were on the stage, a semblance of a car parked up, tilted and spot-lit on the boards where all the audience could see inside, then he'd have the nerve to act. He'd have the script. He'd be rehearsed. He wouldn't hesitate. He'd know no fear – although he'd have the tremors, possibly. That was the bitter joy of acting. It was the business of not being yourself, but knowing you could only be your best when you were being someone else.

Lix got out of the car as quietly, meekly, as he could

– he was ashamed – and hurried behind the nearest tree, beneath its canopy of rain-drummed leaves, to urinate onto the piles of peeling bark. It would, of course, be considerate, quick, and wise to masturbate. Then Mouetta could continue sleeping. He could join her, easily. He was immensely tired – and angry, too. Angry with his wife that she was not like him, not 'passionate', not idolizing flesh, not ruled and motivated by a husband's cock like women in the cinema.

His cock, indeed, was full and stiff by now. His urine, steered by his erection, made a confident and steaming two-streamed arc. He pulled his foreskin back and shook himself. It was a tempting moment, difficult to navigate. To masturbate would only rob a minute from their lives. To masturbate would make good sense. To masturbate would not annoy or wake his wife or spoil again their disappointing anniversary. But masturbation never is enough. Our populations would be decimated if it were. The joyless pleasure we can give ourselves is only dancing for the mirror. It's air guitar. It's sending flowers to yourself without the validation of a grateful kiss.

Lix required some courage in his life. He'd 'let the student down'. Betrayed the boy. He'd confirmed his lack of fortitude, his recent, growing fear of taking risks, of giving any offence. 'Dear Cousin Freda' had defeated him again. He'd lied to Mouetta and he'd disappointed her. Masturbation would not help him make amends. Besides, the rain was soaking him again. He licked the water from his upper lip. He took deep breaths. He tried to draw some daring from the air.

No one who knew him could say that Lix was bold or unpredictable. He was, as you'd expect, rehearsed and hesitant in everything including sex. Now, for once, he was an activist. What he was doing was a risk. He tucked his penis in his pants, zipped up his trousers, not without difficulty, fixed his belt, squelched through mud and water yet again, and got back in the car as noisily as he could. He turned the interior light on. He banged about. He almost hit the buttons of the radio, to fill the car with jazz and rock.

Mouetta was still sleeping, though she'd swung her body round, away from him, and was still making a pillow from the tightly stretched webbing of the seat belt. Her back was arched, her jacket high, her blouse pulled free of its moorings at her waist, two vertebrae and the top centimetre of her underpants adding to Lix's resolve.

His plan was adolescent and barefaced. He would wrap his arms around his wife to wake her, an innocent embrace, then he would say – a worthless promise, as he well knew – that he had decided they should, at first light, return to the campus to collect her cousin's student. That was their duty as progressive, decent citizens. The militia would surely have dispersed by then and, in any case, he was certain he could bluff his way through, flaunt his name maybe, offer a bribe. Signed photographs of Lix were almost currency. He'd kiss her face, perhaps. Remark how beautiful she was. Remind her that the third year of their marriage had begun. Apologize for being grumpy in the restaurant. Indeed, he'd use apologies to make her twist her body back to his.

Actually he need not have slammed the door, turned on the light, or persevered with this duplicity with such juvenile clumsiness. Mouetta had been dreaming, not sexual dreams but something frightening. Her cousin Freda had been tortured, killed; Mouetta had been handcuffed, too, and they – the police, the waiters in the Debit restaurant, her aunts and uncles, long since dead – were kicking her and tugging at her clothes. Freda's purse was pulled apart. Her body was a sack, changing shape as every toecap struck. She herself was kicking Freda, harder than the rest, kicking her for George. It was a dream too real to face alone. Lix only had to touch her lightly on the back, between the jacket and the belt, on her cool flesh, for Mouetta to respond to him. She wanted hugs and kisses anyway, to save her from the nightmare. So when her husband's hand insinuated underneath her blouse and held her breasts she was quite happy to be touched. It seemed like tenderness. He'd rescued her. She turned her face to his and they were kissing before she had a chance to say a word about her cousin Freda and the horrors they had shared.

She was hospitable and motherly at first. Her usual expertise. She welcomed him. She catered for his hands. She gave encouragement. Soon the enterprise engulfed her, too. Her heart was thunderous and jbeating on her ribs, as loudly and passionately as the rain was drumming on the Panache's glass and metal roof. She had been quickly comforted, but there was something else to satisfy. The drama of the Banking Riots and the drive across the wayward city to save the student crouching underneath the desk had animated her. How good it was to have survived the dream, to be alive and sensitive to tongues and fingertips. Her hand had reached for him, his urinous and rain-soaked lap, before he'd even dared to touch and lift the hem of her skirt. She wanted him, or somebody, at once. It wasn't long before she was in charge. She imagined she'd started this herself and was delighted and blushing. She liked herself when she was powerful. This was the way Cousin Freda must behave with men.

Mouetta was unstoppable, but she was shocked as well, shocked by the suddenness. And possibly she recognized her own opportunity, subconsciously. The chance of pregnancy. She drove her husband forward, hardly wanting him to think. Although Lix was normally the most careful and responsible of men, 'with good cause', he always said, given his already proven fertility, he would not on this occasion give much thought to condoms, although he had a packet in his trousers' back pocket, although there was a single Lubricated Shadow in Freda's shoulder bag that surely, on this night of incarceration, she could spare. So when Mouetta said, 'It's safe. It's safe,' he hurtled on. He took the risk. He gambled on the moon and on her honesty.

We are not animals – not simple monkeys, certainly – although, of all the apes, we are the luckiest, if it is good fortune and not a calamity to take such pleasure in the passions of the flesh. We fornicate in private (if we want) and that's a blessing, isn't it? We can simply mate for fun, at any time and any season that we choose, no matter if the woman's already pregnant, menstruating, ovulating, or in the middle of her lunch. The lesser apes, of course, don't suffer from the jealousy and pain or lose control.

Now they were truly clumsy in the car. She had to get her knickers off, his trousers down, the two front seats reclined, while still attending to his kisses and his urgencies and still accommodating seat belts, steering wheels, and the gear-stick. Sex in a car is never digni-fied or comfortable. The cinematic shot would edit out the jump and jerk of it, the gracelessness. There'd be a gently rhythmic car, the rain, the night, the shifting latticework of shadows from the branches of the trees, the heartfelt throbbing of the soundtrack symphony fast turning music into light, fast turning tear-gas smoke (for let us not forget what brought them to the park) into unoffending mist, fast turning darkness into a grainy dawn.

The truth of Lix and Mouetta, this night of riots and anniversaries, was even grainier. Their lovemaking, if that is what it was, was speedy and uncomfortable and somewhat disappointing for them both, though mostly for Mouetta. Human biology is unequal in its distributions and rewards. Haste cannot often satisfy any more than it can dodge the rain. It can impregnate, though. The sperm do not require sincerity before they can proceed. The eggs are not judgemental. They do not even favour love.

A dangerous ejaculation, then, for Lix. Deep in the park. Deliverance Park. Three hundred million tempest-tossed sperm, the wretched refuse of his teeming shore – and no contraception to impede them. Three hundred million! More than the total population of the United States of America, as the Planned Parenthood posters with their Statue of Liberty photograph so often remind us. There has to be a God of Mischief to over-cater so dramatically. That's why, of course, an ejaculation is known in this City of Kisses as 'a huddled mass'. A tribute to America, the land of opportunity and sex. 'Give me your tired, your poor, your huddled masses,' the torch-bearing lady says as she succumbs to suitors. Three hundred million. Oh, what a prospect, all those newcomers, each time a man dares lift his lamp beside her golden door.

It was not long before Mou (as Lix had called her in his throes, rather than the more usual diminutive, Etta) and her husband were left to disunite their limbs and clothing, to clean themselves with tissues dampened with rain wiped from the side panels of the car, and to pretend at least that their embraces should and could outlive the sex.

Mouetta turned her back against her husband once again. Lix wrapped himself round his wife, as best he could. Her mouth was bruised. She had not been compensated with an orgasm. Yet she was contented, unaccountably. Her husband had surprised her for a change. She had surprised herself. 'That's not like you,' she said, not facing him. She'd only meant to tease him, say how glad she was to have him to herself for this third year. Yet it was also an accusation, in a way.

Both of them were too tired to take offence for long and both of them had earned the right to fold up in the cushions of the car and fall asleep. Untroubled dreams. Untroubled by the activist, himself curled up but hardly sleeping underneath the desk in Freda's office, while down the fourth-floor corridor the caretaker, with master keys and soldiers at his heels (tipped off by Lix when he was being questioned by the road-block volunteers), was heading for the student's hiding place. They'd flush out all the troublemakers who'd thought they might find refuge in their rooms.

Untroubled, too, by Freda, sharing her strange cell with eleven other women, five blankets and two beds, already bruised, traduced, and undermined, fearful of the day ahead, determined, though, and proud. And so relieved that her young student lover would be saved and would by now be sleeping on her cousin's study couch.

Untroubled by those three fresh bodies in the city morgue, the youthful and impatient victims of the truncheons and the gas, the careless armoured jeep, the interest rates, the gulf between the ruling and the ruled.

Untroubled, even, by the thought of Lix's five off-spring (yes, *five* – there's one who's undiscovered yet), now sleeping somewhere in the world, produced by the only four women, other than Mouetta, he'd ever slept with. A jackpot of a sort.

So this is our opportunity to welcome Mouetta's first and Lix's sixth child into the corridor. Whom should we thank, and what, for this chance winner of the lottery? Those things that made the night so bad for everybody else? The riots possibly. The traffic barriers. The idiotic militiamen who (or so Lix falsely claimed) were not bright enough to recognize the actor in their midst? The rain with its own three hundred million random pellets, the fertile, unforgiving rain that still was beating on their car? The shame Lix felt?

These were the settings for this single conception, the only cast and scenery and props that could produce this child. Change anything and you change everything. Another place, another time produces someone else.

'CHOOSE ONE,' Mouetta said. 'Choose one. If you could go to bed with anybody here, which one?'

This was a question she'd posed to Lix a dozen times before, in public places, very often as a postscript – and not, despite her husband's best endeavours, as a prologue – to their lovemaking.

It was hardly eight thirty in the morning, Friday, not seven hours since their close encounter in the car. The early hours of her undiscovered pregnancy.

That coming night, revitalized by the drier weather, there'd be new disturbances, better organized and more venomous than Thursday's. Nine dead, this time, including three cadets trapped in a burning transporter. And, dramatically, the fire-bombing of the Bursary Chambers Club where – wrongly – it was thought some bankers and some military were dining. The wounded victims were, in fact, two waitresses, a cloakroom clerk, a fireman, and fourteen members of an investment club who hadn't had the lungs or legs to get away from their third-storey dining suite.

For the moment everything was quiet. Apart from the parked police vans and the helicopters, the city, still in debt and shock, still riotous at heart, had –

physically, at least – returned to normal. Sunshine, traffic jams, shopping and commuter crowds, and floods. Floods are normal here: the usual flooded passages and streets along the riverbanks, the flooded underpasses and the flooded gutters where, as usual, the drains had let us down. The city had been over-whelmed by rain.

Mouetta and Lix had stopped for breakfast at the Palm & Orchid Coffee House on their way back home. She held his arm across the tabletop. She pinched his hand. She wanted to inflict some gentle pain. 'Come on,' she said. 'The truth.' The coffee house – a con-verted botanic conservatory – was chock-a-block with unsuspecting women for her husband to choose from.

Lix, as usual, misread her mood. He took her question as a kind of erotic afterplay, a sign that she was still stimulated by their recent lovemaking and wanted to continue it, not physically, perhaps, but somewhere else inside her head, some secret fold. A female thing. Men recovered after sex more speedily. For women – he had said as much on stage (a play by Palladino) – intercourse was just the overture. But for a man an orgasm was – the playwright's metaphor again – 'the final, rushing note'. The music stopped, and now he could embrace the wider world again. For men (another common metaphor), lovemaking pops the champagne cork. The captive gases dissipate. The pressure is released. The pressure he was feeling now was of a different kind.

Here, for breakfast, Lix was happy to indulge his wife. He liked her question. It also made him wonder if, on their return back home, the as yet untested stairs might earn themselves a second chance. 'You really want the honest truth?' Again she dug her nails into his palm.

Lix thought he understood the boundaries and rituals of her now familiar game. He'd made mistakes before – thinking, possibly, that her invitation to search the restaurant, the bar, the hotel lobby, the departure lounge, the cast of a film, and, on a couple of occasions, the pages of magazines for someone he would like to make love to was her way of testing his fidelity. In which case, the only answer was the reassuring diplomatic one, that out of all the women he could see Mouetta was the only one for him. That was clearly not the answer she was seeking, though. He'd tried it out before and it had irritated her. She truly wanted him to look around. And choose. And tell the truth.

'Come on! Which one, if you were free?'

'But I'm not free.'

'You're free to choose. You're just not free to act.'

'I see. I am your prisoner, then. At liberty to think and look but not to move.'

'Exactly so. Like through binoculars.'

'And no parole.'

'Not till I'm dead. And, anyway, wives nearly always outlive the men. So I'll be free before you are.'

There was another lesson Lix had learned, through his mistakes. Mouetta would not welcome it if he showed too much ardour in his choice. He should not seem aroused. He should not lick his mouth or breathe too heavily. He should not need to touch himself or rearrange his trousers. She would not welcome any vulgarity either, though he was always tempted by vulgarity. He had to be dispassionate and analytical, but not too coldly scientific. 'It's just my private chemistry,' he'd said, on one occasion previously, when he'd been free to choose amongst the women at a reception they'd attended and had selected someone whom Mouetta had dismissed as 'short and plain'. By chemistry, he'd meant a little more than just the dopamine and oxytocin, or any other agents of libido. He'd meant the chance and random fusions that could occur in the test tubes of two strangers. She'd been disappointed and upset – and evidently baffled – for reasons that he never really understood. From then, he'd always found it wisest to start off with a wary, playful joke. A decoy, as it were. Then he could judge how serious she was, how easy to offend.

Lix looked around the crowded coffee hall, packed out with breakfasting commuters. Here were the city's office staff, mostly women dressed for desk work and warm weather – although the Palm & Orchid boasted that its 'atmosphere' was always semi-temperate – their make-up as yet unsmudged, their skirts and tops fresh from hangers and drawers. Still crisp and fragrant. He'd sleep with fifty women there, if life were simpler.

'The little waitress, obviously,' he said at last.

Mouetta pinched his hand again. 'Be serious.'

'I'm being serious. I like my women old and grey. And wearing sandals. I like a lived-in face with lots of chins. And I'm especially fond of bunions. You should be pleased.'

'Oh, yes? My pleasure knows no boundaries. I can get some grey highlights put in today, if that's your preference.'

'I'm joking but I'm serious. Old's fine by me. Up to a point. It means I'm not the sort to dump you for some frisky pony as soon as you begin to . . .' He hesitated, searching for a further equine metaphor. '. . . refuse the jumps.' He had to laugh, despite the warning tilt of Mouetta's face. 'The truth is, I can't wait till you're sixty – and serving me with your tray and apron. Naked otherwise, of course. Bare bunions.' Lix made his lecher's face. '"I'll have a double latte, please. And honey cake." Give me the little waitress any time.'

'Why am I less than thrilled with that good news?' she said.

Mouetta could not find it in herself to be pleased

with anything that morning. She wasn't still mentally stimulated by their lovemaking in the car, as he'd imagined. Far from it. She felt, illogically, as if he'd poisoned her. She was in toxic shock. Her temperature was wrong. Her stomach ached. The seat-belt strap, her pillow for the night, had left a ridge across her cheek that had not yet repaired itself. Her head and heart were dulled by something out of her control. She could not, dare not, put a name to it. A woman of her age and hopes who has no children yet is always nervous of an early menopause. She'd not slept well, of course. Who does, in cars? But there was something else that bothered her, something undermining and elusive that she'd squeeze out of her husband's palms with her fingernails, an answer she could only draw with blood.

It was, of course, mostly the onset of her pregnancy that had disrupted her, the gelling of the early cells, the hormone parties striking out to colonize new settlements, the stiffening of glands. How could she know at this precocious stage? How could she yet understand her sudden listlessness, the unusual and overwhelming irritation that she felt for Lix, the nagging, private voice that seemed to say her world had changed?

Mouetta was a morning person, normally. Only moody after dark, when she was tired. So this was worrying.

*

Six

SHE'D WOKEN UP in their Panache, aching and perspiring, soon after dawn. The leather front seats of a car are disappointing mattresses. Her body felt precarious, subjected to confinements and contortions for too long. She checked the dashboard clock. Five forty-six. The only sounds inside the car came from her husband's nose.

The celebrated Lix had not looked handsome with his great head lolling on one side. The angle rucked up folds of fat around his chin. His hair was unkempt and the infuriating vestiges of his Tartuffe make-up – so oddly stimulating when they were making love – were smeared from his lashes and his eyebrows across his cheek and on his shirt collar. It looked as if his cherry birthmark had been leaking its pale juice.

Mouetta let him sleep (if he was truly sleeping) and stepped out of the car in her bare feet, without her underwear, her own short hair flattened and unflattering. The ground was sodden still. Silver sheets of water spread across the park, low lit and shadowy. The mud pressed up between her toes. She wanted shelter, privacy, a pee. And then some breakfast at the Palm & Orchid Coffee House. She'd earned it, hadn't she?

Already there were signs that this could be a fine, dry day. Retreating clouds, hugging the roofs of office blocks. A clearing wind. The skies prematurely busy with geese, commuter jets, and bees. No army helicopters yet above Deliverance Park, but she could hear their chudder from across the river and – something she could not recognize at first – the drum'n'bass of flood machines, already pumping out the rain from underpasses, cellars, and low roads.

Mouetta half stood, half crouched behind the car, her legs spread like an outfielder. She held her skirt up round her waist and looked about both nervously and recklessly. Perhaps there'd be somebody walking their dog, or a jogger, or somebody else who'd slept out in the park. Well, then, hard luck. They must have seen a woman passing water before. And if they hadn't, let them look – and learn how everyday it was. How pleasurable, in fact.

She was surprised to see how deep into the park Lix had driven her the night before. The car wheels had churned up ugly and irresponsible ruts across the grass. The service road was almost out of sight, but anybody could find them there – and issue reprimands: their tracks were deep and almost unbroken. She stretched her arms and legs. She tried to warm herself, loading up on early sun. It would serve her husband right if he got caught and fined for Damage and for Reckless Parking. The celebrated Lix.

Now that her bladder had been emptied and her limbs untangled, Mouetta felt refreshed and comfortable enough to concentrate on her ill-temper. It was the product of their anniversary, that much she knew. Was it their failings – well, Lix's failings – with the student that bothered her? Perhaps, to some extent. She'd set her heart on that 'sweet boy'. On having him at home. On taking him from Freda. And, yes, her husband had been feeble, as he usually was when there was any challenge to be faced, or any risk, or any threat to his good name. Actually, the firebrand student had almost faded from her memory. What, then? The night of damp discomfort in the car? Her husband's hurried lovemaking, the sudden sated ease with which he'd dropped asleep? Not that. A woman's used to that.

Freda, then. Was she to blame? Was her arrest the cause of this uneasiness? No, that was an ancient memory as well, surprisingly. She ought to, she knew, collect her cellphone from the car at once and scroll through her contacts for a sympathetic and early rising lawyer. She ought, at least, to let her cousin know that the student had not been rescued yet. The poor boy would want feeding. But Freda's predicament had lost its urgency overnight. The detainee would have to wait, Mouetta felt, till she and Lix got home and she had showered, changed her clothes, and settled into a less disgruntled mood. Besides, what Lix had said the night before was true. Her cousin would probably be freed in time for breakfast, with or without lawyers. She'd welcome the celebrity, her 'night in chains'! Freda was too well known and well attached to stay in custody for long. As soon as they got home, they'd find a message from her winking on the answerphone, her piping, fruity voice, undulled by its experience, with her usual slogans and her provocations, her infuriating 'Ciao'. Sweet, slender Cousin Freda, oh, so brave and beautiful! And, oh, so undermining.

So now – she only had to listen to her inner voice – Mouetta recognized the truth. Freda *was* the problem she had woken to. Not the night locked up, or the student trapped beneath the desk. It was more personal – and not a problem to be fixed by lawyers. It was the certainty that she, Mouetta, was second best to her tall cousin yet again. Second best even with her husband still, even on their wedding anniversary. The small rejections of the evening before, in the Debit Bar, which normally she'd shrug away as meaningless, now seemed insufferably huge, inflated by the disappointments of the night. She could not readily forget how Lix'd stared into Freda's lap – goddammit, yes, her cousin's magnetizing lap – when he'd approached their dining table after his performance. And, yes, of course, how jealous and how sulky he had been when it was clear the student firebrand in Freda's office was her cousin's lover. She'd noticed how he'd blushed and could not look either of them in the eye while they were eating, and how oddly exasperated he had seemed when they had left the bar.

Mouetta felt defeated suddenly, defeated by the body and the face of someone else, defeated by her not so groundless jealousy and by the past, defeated by her childlessness (while her cousin had already proved herself with Lix in that regard, of course, so many years before. Freda could boast the Lovely George, *their* lovely George, whom she had raised and trained all on her own, without – she always liked to claim – 'a sniff or glance' from Lix).

Mouetta could not bring herself, despite the damp, despite the early morning cold, her lack of underwear, to get back in the car, to join her sleeping, disappointing husband. The moment that she'd married him, she'd married jealousy. She drummed her fists against the windows and the roof of the Panache. His morning call. What must she do, who should she be, to be more certain of her husband's love? The whole thing was a mystery. What urged and motivated men? Who would he truly go to bed with if he had the choice? Was it the undefeated cousin or the wife? In those first sunlit minutes of the day, she'd kicked up loops of water high across the grass with her bare feet.

So now, in shoes but still no underwear, Mouetta waited for her answer amongst the foliage and the breakfasters, her husband easily within her reach, across the teas and pastries in the Palm & Orchid Coffee House. Coffee fixes everything. She did not feel defeated any more, just baffled and impatient for his choice. She looked around the room herself. It seemed that there were beauties everywhere. 'What about the one in blue?' She tilted her head towards a group of office colleagues, two noisy tables to her right. 'She's pretty, isn't she?'

'Which one?'

'You know which one. I saw you staring at her earlier. Stop playing games.' She sighed at him, her lower lip stuck out. A famous warning sign. Mouetta sighs with that shaped mouth, and there'll be arguments.

'I mean, which one in blue? I'd sleep with anyone in blue. You're dressed in sort of blue yourself. I'd go to bed with you. When we get home.'

'You'd not choose me before all these others.' She was ashamed to set so transparent a trap.

'Of course I would.'

'Of course you would.'

They let their conversation simmer for a while and pretended to concentrate, in practised and contented silence, on their breakfasts, the Aztec coffee in the *paysanne* cups, the glacé fruits, the local – and expensive – savouries, the honey slice. The Palm & Orchid was a place where it was easy not to talk. The talkers missed the beauty of the place, the filtered shafts of coloured light, refracted and intensified by the patchworks of stained Portino glass in the conservatory roof, the sombre rhomboids of shade from the woven kites of green rattan suspended from the rafters, the massive earthenware pots of fessandra bushes, hugging crotons, lace trees, and tiger palms.

Then there was the entertainment of the birds. They roosted in the kites and in the plants at night, but during the day they gleaned vacated tables for their crumbs. Tea sparrows they were called colloquially. But they were urban finches actually, reluctantly tolerated by the owner because his customers appeared to like their noisy cabaret. So Lix and Mouetta, glad not to be talking for the moment, turned slightly in their seats, and looked beyond their coffee cups, across the break-fasters, into the foliage. Had anybody looked at them – a well-known actor such as Lix must always expect to be looked at – they'd see only surface harmony.

'Don't lie,' she said finally. Out of the blue, 'Don't lie.'

Her husband didn't dare or bother to reply, just yet. He knew this already expensive breakfast might get costlier unless he was prudent.

Lix indeed had spotted the red-haired woman dressed entirely in Picasso blue, a crisp belted linen dress with matching shoes and bag and eyes. All the best coordinates. Who could miss her? She was a beacon of high taste, and beautiful, amongst the other-wise unremarkable possibilities. And the woman in the blue, Lix knew, had spotted him as well, had recog-nized his birthmarked face, though, possibly, she had not yet recalled his famous name. He'd silenced her by staring back at her, and even smiling, once. Now she'd lost the knack of being natural in company. She'd be dreaming already, Lix was sure, of being lovely in a film.

Lix watched her, dreamed of casting her. She'd look good through a lens. No doubt of it. She'd be no intellectual, of course. No theorist. She had the body, not the mind for cinema. She had the looks but not the conversation. Her silence suited her. It flattered her, in fact.

It obviously didn't matter to her friends that the woman had fallen silent so suddenly and that her interest in their conversation had evidently ended. She held her counsel amongst her colleagues at their noisy table, as only lovely women can, barely smiling, barely speaking and barely audible when she did speak. No taking part. No looking up. No grimaces. She was auditioning. She smoked. That was not a blemish in Lix's estimation. Not when the smoker smoked so stylishly. Not when the smoker lizarded the corners of her mouth after every inhalation and seemed to love the smoke so much.

She was a study in provocation. Just like a woman in a Manet bar.

Lix could imagine making love to her, Mouetta's choice. It would not be hard to make a fool of himself with this starlet. He could – it only took a moment's contemplation – place her easily across the table in a hotel restaurant, a lucky bedroom waiting on the lucky seventh floor. He would be talking. She'd be smoking, her tongue a constant incitement. She'd kiss him in the elevator, her lips on his, no more than that. She'd not want her make-up smudged, not publicly, not while there was a chance that someone else might join them in the elevator. Lix would behave himself, as they sped through the floors, though he'd be shaking for the opportunity to lift her dress, to see if there was blue beneath the blue. In moments – once his shaking hand had got the shaking key into the lock – he'd see the room, the bed, the swift disposal of the dress, the tissues on her face, removing blusher and mascara, her showering, their double nakedness, the mirrors and the steam. Not hard at all to see himself with her. A body of that quality was rare and overpowering.

However, Lix could not truly desire the woman in Picasso blue. She was too young, for a start. Too fresh and new. Lix liked contemporaries. She was too beautiful for him, as well. And dull. As dull as hotel restaurants and hotel suites. Expensive, formalized, homogeneous, and dull. He could not imagine such a woman saying anything to make him laugh or startle him, or holding an opinion. Her smoking was her only conversation. Her only talent was with clothes and make-up. And with hair.

Her perfect body was a disincentive: that's something few women ever understand. It was not eloquent, not in itself, not even in the prospect of its nakedness. The body tells you nothing. It's not the body but a

woman's ever undressed face that most men find enticing, the undefended and arousing glance that betrays
exactly what the glancer sees in you, exactly what
she's found. The glance is more arousing than plain
nakedness because the glance betrays its promises and
pledges. The glance precipitates the futures that you
share. A body can't do that.

But this young woman's face was still expressionless.
There was more evidence in her fine face of self-
regarding display than sexual consciousness. If Lix
had sex with her, Madame Picasso in the blue, there'd
be no mischief or any joyful, human grubbiness. He'd
snub his nose, his lips, his cock on her proprieties. The
smells would all be bottled and the noises hushed and
mannered. He would be making love but not receiv-
ing it. Her sexiness was all about herself. For sure,
they'd not be having sex inside his car, beneath a stand
of peering, rain-soaked pines. She was the Princess of
Clean Sheets.

Madame Picasso's colleague, though, the little
woman sitting to her left, unwisely – given her plump-
ness – enjoying a tall creamed coffee and a plate of
brandy toasts, was much more to Lix's taste. And
closer to his age. What? Late thirties, surely, at the
very least. Mouetta's age. Glasses, hair dye, lines, a
sunburn-mottled throat, experience. Married, but
determined to enjoy herself, he judged.

Lix liked her all-black strip – jeans, jacket, tight and

nippled T-shirt – and the one dramatic statement of the shoulder-mounted silver brooch, a dragonfly, its drama somewhat spoiled by four or five white hairs, too long to be her own or even human. She was an animated talker – but a smoker, too. No niceties. Her thumb and index finger had been stained with nicotine. She laughed out loud – too loud, perhaps – given half a chance.

On those few occasions when she was not contributing to the conversation, not spilling over with her stories and her opinions, she was a goading listener with darting eyes, a touch theatrical. She reminded Lix of a character actress he had worked with, but not much liked, on a couple of occasions. Only this woman at the table was, unlike the actress, entirely without self-consciousness – and not completely drunk by breakfast time! Oh, what a partner she would make. How uninhibited and amused she would be, how eager to discover something new in anyone she met and liked.

Lix could not think of her inside a hotel room. Or any room. Instead, he placed her in a forest with her dogs. Three long-haired, silvered spaniels. (There's no accounting for the stories that men weave themselves.) And in this fairytale, the passing stranger, Lix, has stopped to pay attention to her dogs. He fondles them, their parchment ears, their wet and probing snouts. Soon, of course (the constant daydream of a man), the fondling of the dogs becomes the fondling of the woman, too. She's keen, he thinks. She's bored at home. Her marriage is in bits. I'm harming nobody.

He has her tearing at his trousers and his belt. The forest's large and tiny all at once, and noisy with the breathlessness of four impatient animals. The foliage closes in as they sink down into the cushions of the undergrowth, the almost matching smells of bracken and of sex.

IT WAS A THIRD woman at the table, though, who truly fascinated Lix. She was what Frenchmen call *une jolie laide* but in this city is more cruelly known as a Prickly Pear. A fruit that's ugly, hard to handle, but once peeled and stripped is addictively sweet and juicy beyond measure. This colleague was a woman in her fifties even, skinny and black-haired, dressed a little oddly for the office – plastic beach boots (she'd had to wade to get to work that day), white trousers, and a cardigan, half buttoned up.

Her mouth was unusually large but, sensibly, her lips were not made-up and so seemed sensuous and not promiscuous. Her hair, already slightly dulled by age, was cut to within a half-centimetre of her skull, all over. It seemed she wanted space to emphasize her good strong bones, her solid cranium, and show her earrings off: hand-tooled silver shields.

Ugly wasn't quite the word for her. It was certain,

though, had she had the chance, had she been keen to
fit the mould, she would have traded every feature on
her face for something else. The too-large nose, the
long, demanding jaw, the slightly protruding eyes too
greedy for their sockets, the Apache cheekbones, the
manly ears might all have benefited from some costly
surgery. Everything about her, except her breasts,
needed taming and reduction.

Whereas Lix could not imagine walking down the
street with Madame Picasso on his arm or even catching her without make-up, let alone yawning, sneezing,
smelling of anything other than gardenia, this Prickly
Pear with her expressive features seemed to be a woman
of irresistible, seductive disarray. That touch of coffee
on her upper lip, the unembarrassed action of her jaw
as she despatched her breakfast fruit, without the help
of her plate or the fruit knife or the modesty shield of
a raised hand, suggested a person eager to devour the
day.

A fantasy, perhaps. How could he tell anything for
certain? Her seeming eagerness might just be shallowness, an undiscerning vacancy of mind. She might be
a simpleton. Still, the visual fantasy was strong and
logical. From the much-loved bobbled cardigan to the
sea-salt residues on her beach boots, she was dressed
for action not for show. She had the footwear and the
trousers for an unexpected climb, a dash to catch her
tram, a supermarket trip, a river crossing. She was, in

fact, the woman in the room who most resembled, in everything but looks, his now frowning wife.

Lix could not help but smile while he imagined how the beautiful Madame Picasso would get on if they turned up one blustery afternoon, say, at the Cougar's Promenade on the cliffs above the long Californian beach where he and Mouetta had rented a house for their honeymoon. She'd not be able to expose her outfit and her make-up to the rain-laced wind. Her hairdo would not tolerate the weather. Her skin would not enjoy the light. Her dress would flap and wrap around her knees. Her heels would sink into the rippled sand and topple her. She would not even be able to seek the solace of a cigarette. The wind would snatch her flame away and steal the smoke. No chance either that she would agree to cut off up the beach into one of the secluded bays where they might lie down on the sand and carelessly make love.

The plumper one in black, the woman with the dragonfly brooch, might well be game in such a circumstance. But she would not belong on his imagined beach, so far from bars and restaurants. She was a woman who was determined to enjoy herself – just watch her laugh and smoke – but all her pleasures would be city ones. She'd not be agile on a beach. Too heavy, obviously, and possibly – the smoking and her weight – too short of breath to much enjoy a hike. Even Mouetta, when she had had the chance to walk with her new husband on that beach in nothing worse than misty rain, had preferred to stay inside their hired car to watch the sea in comfort.

But place the Prickly Pear on the Cougar's Promenade, suggest to her they got out of the car to brave the wind and spray, and there could be no doubt that she would soon be running down the steps, across the pebble line and tidal sand, to reach the sea. Lix could place her with her beach boots in her hand, her trousers rolled up to her knees, the waves around her calves, her short hair ruffling. She'd be convincing there. No doubt of it.

Wade in yourself, he thought. Stand next to her and feel the shingle shifting underfoot. No matter that the sea is unpredictable. Suggest to her, to that large, open face, deprived too long of flattery and kisses, that they should find a quieter spot up in the rocks. Lix was certain she would readily agree.

Two images: the pair of them embracing in the middle of the sand, her hand pushed down beyond the waistband of his trousers, his hand pushed up into the warmer regions of her cardigan reaching round to find the soft underarm anticipations of her breasts; and then the two of them, invisible amongst the rocks, fettered at the ankles by their fallen clothes, their mouths engaged, their hands employed between each other's legs. And for the soundtrack? In the film? Gulls, of course. A crashing sea. In the distance, cries for help.

Madame Picasso stranded by her footwear and the tides, her blue dress lost against the perfect sky, and no one wading out to rescue her.

'What's so amusing?' Mouetta tapped him sharply on the hand with her coffee spoon. 'I said I'm going to the washroom, Lix. You're grinning like a little boy. Were you dreaming or dozing?'

'Pretty much both. I didn't get enough sleep last night.'

'Whose fault is that?'

'I only need a nap, that's all.'

'Well, that makes two of us.'

She left the table and made her way across the room towards the toilets, even smiling at the woman in blue as she passed. His wife looked dishevelled from behind, as well she might. She'd slept in what she wore, her once-smart skirt and favourite blouse. Made love in them. Inside a car, deep in the park. She hadn't had a chance to wash or even clean her teeth that morning. So far she'd only used a comb, a touch of cologne, and a couple of tissues. No wonder she was the least crisp woman in the room.

Mouetta's absence was an opportunity, but not to contemplate his undermining shame at trading in the firebrand student for six minutes' pleasure in the car. He had to bury that at once. Rather, it allowed him to concentrate unambiguously on all the women in the room. Lix could not help himself. Besides, Mouetta wanted his reply on her return. Again he studied the three attractive possibilities over the rim of his lifted cup. He tried them out. He was auditioning. He placed them in Mouetta's seat across the table in the Palm & Orchid, imagined how they'd look and what he'd say to them, if they'd been married for two years, what might occur when they drove home, how they'd react to his determined ambush on the stairs. Again the oldest woman won the day.

He had his answer, then. The Prickly Pear. She was the one he chose, out of all the women in the room. She was the likeliest. She was the one he'd prefer if he could take just one to bed. He wondered what his wife would make of that when she came back from freshening herself. Would she believe him when he pointed to the older woman, oddly dressed, boy-haired, and overdrawn as a cartoon, and said, 'She is the one that I desire the most'?

Lix felt his cock fattening at the very prospect of it, the conversation he and Mouetta would enjoy about the woman's face and body and her clothes, how that might lead, must certainly lead, to more lovemaking when they got back home.

For surely this was Mouetta's project, to find some sexual stimulation in the answer Lix would give, whatever it might be, while still fully retaining Lix. His passions might well drift beyond recall. His body never would. Mouetta was the only one allowed. Her question, 'If you could go to bed with anybody here, which one?' was her foreplay, a scheme to get her husband talking about having sex with someone else, encouraging his imaginary couplings, his unreal consummations, so that she herself could play the role of that new woman, give herself to Lix as someone new, an actress in a fresher part. That's why she'd set him loose and left him to indulge these unrequitable but animating fantasies amongst the female colleagues at the table in the city's chicest breakfast room. She wanted him to test his dreams with her.

Isn't that what men and women did? Men and women who had shared a marriage berth for two years and a day? They'd want some shore leave, wouldn't they, to visit – in their hearts, at least – the beds of other lovers, other spouses? We need to flirt and covet strangers for the health and spirit of our marriages. They would be wearying otherwise. There'd be no love. Oh, to begin the day, each day, with fresh desires and still stay true.

Lix could quite easily, with Mouetta safely out of sight for a few minutes, catch any of the women's eye, make profiles of his famous face for them, engage one in a conversation, flirt, arrange to meet her in a bar one evening, seduce her with some tickets for his show. That's exactly what his colleagues would do, given half a chance. An actor's touring life is cut out for adultery, affairs, the weekend fling. What harm in that? And what – if he were truly someone who would cheat on his wife, other than inside his never-faithful, ever-scheming head – if he were to go up to the likeliest? If he were to step across and what? Invite her to abandon her workmates and come with him onto the long-imagined beach? What harm in that?

The harm in that for him was the misfortune – was it truly a misfortune? – that every kiss produced a child. Remember? Fertile Lix had never slept with anyone without – eventually – a pregnancy. There always was an aftermath for him.

So then: how dare he take Madame Picasso from the hotel restaurant into the kissing elevator and up into his room, the bed, the mirrors, and the steam? There'd be a child, impatient at the door. A boy, he thought. A mother's boy. Well dressed for one so small – and too obedient. The little violin case in his hand told all of it, as he stood in the corridor amid the uncollected trays, patiently waiting for his parents as they created him inside the hired room. He'd do his practice every time, be quite the little fiddler, though not quite good enough to win the prizes that his mother wanted so much – and of which his celebrated father would be jealous.

How dare he be the passing stranger for the plumper woman in the forest with her dogs? How dare he fondle them and her? There'd be a child. A pretty, well-built girl, her face distinguished awfully by the cherry mark inherited from Lix, but plucky and adventurous.

How dare the over-fertile Lix take his *jolie laide* down to the beach . . . ? Well, to all intents and purposes, that was not so problematic, he realized at once. Her age. Of course! He studied her again. Yes, in her fifties, certainly. Her fertile years long gone. Here was a woman he could safely cheat with, if he were the cheating kind. Perhaps that's why he'd felt so free in his imagination in her company. Whatever they might do, there'd be no child. It could be his first and only non-productive affair. Inconsequential sex!

His heart was racing suddenly. Here was his certain risk-free, vindicated choice, ready for when Mouetta returned. He favoured someone who could never bear his child.

Yet when she came back to the table, washed, refreshed and recologned, her hair brushed back and neatened, her skirt and blouse hand-smoothed, entirely more desirable than she had been five minutes earlier, she did not sit down to pursue the answer to her question.

'Let's go,' she said.

He recognized that tone of voice. Something troubled her. She wanted to get on. There'd be an argument. He feared she had heard somehow that the student had been arrested – and that she'd guess the reason why. She'd hate him for such wickedness. She'd be right to do so.

It was only once they'd crossed the busy Circular that his wife even spoke. She had another, unexpected question for her husband: 'Which of my cousins would you like to sleep with most?'

Lix laughed. Uneasily. He was naturally relieved that nothing worse was upsetting his wife. 'Ah, Cousin Gracia,' he said. He'd named the oldest one, a woman already in her sixties with thick grey hair, as tall and bony as an ostrich.

'Be serious.'

'Your cousins? There's not a serious answer. I wouldn't sleep with any one of them. Particularly the women.'

'And Freda, then? I'm sure you'd like to sleep with her again. She's lovely, isn't she? More lovely than before. She dresses so beautifully. Imagine if you'd never even met me that dreadful New Year's Eve, but Freda . . . well, you'd make love to her again, wouldn't you? I'm sure of it.'

'Ha ha.'

'You can tell the truth. I promise I won't mind.'

'Of course you'll mind. You've minded all along about Freda and George.' He wouldn't add his own name to the list. 'The mystery is, why do you still arrange to see the woman? Why do we still put up with her?'

'Because we must. She's George's mother anyway. She's family.'

'She's not my family.'

They drove in silence to the house, the house where they would spend the third year of their marriage, where their child – now smaller than a fingertip – would take its first uncertain steps, the house where they would love and live and row, the house where nearly all his children came to stay at weekends, in the holidays, their empty house with no firebrands asleep in their spare room.

Mouetta followed Lix through the shrubs and pots of their front yard. 'You still fancy Freda, don't you, honestly? After all these years. You fancy Cousin Freda.' *More than me.* She said it to his back.

'Not in the least,' Lix said, though there'd been moments in the car the night before and in the Debit Bar when he'd hardly been thinking of his wife. And there were bound to be some moments in the coming days, the coming months and years, indeed, as there'd been many moments in the past, when he would dwell on Freda for a while and what they'd almost, should have, shared, their George, their lost son in America, now twenty-four years old. He'd always think of her as someone he desired. Mouetta was the woman he required. This is the nature of the beast.

1

LIX LEFT IT LATE. Till November 1979. He was almost twenty-one and it was nearly midnight when he first had sex with anyone. Full docking sex, that is. Full snug'n'comfy. Like almost everybody else his age, of course, he'd had hand sex, not only with himself since he was twelve but twice with helpful boys at school and once (a birthday treat when he was seventeen) with an unsuspicious girl, one of nature's volunteers. Her first time with a boy. She'd seemed surprised at what she'd done, at what she'd made him do, and with such little exertion. She jumped back just in time, so that only her sandal and her wrist were soiled by Lix's sudden gratitude.

On that night of his induction – if it were not for the birthmark on his cheek – you would not recognize the celebrated Lix. Less heavy for a start, less grand. And much more volatile, as you'd expect of someone in his first semester free of parents and the family home. He was training for the stage at the Academy. This was a time when Theatre, newly unleashed from the censors, was argumentative and powerful. Lix truly wanted to improve the world, believed that Art was Revolution's smarter twin, that Acting and Action were equal partners. Collaborators, in fact. He'd signed up with the Mime/Scream Community Drama Collective in his first month as a student and was active, too, in Street Beat Renegades, Provocations & Co, and The Next Stage (as in Paul Roesenthaler's 'The next stage is the elimination of Captains, Chaplains and Kings'). He didn't have a repertoire, Lix said (adapting Roesenthaler yet again, our city's feted radical), he had 'an onstage manifesto'. Actors seemed to be the partisans of change back in those simpler times when appointees and the army controlled our lives even more completely than they do now, now that – to chant the cynics' chorus – theatre is unfettered and trifling, all our leaders have been democratically imposed, and Freedom has destroyed our impulse to be free.

Lix had a democratically modest fourth-floor room amongst the tenements down on the wharf, with not only skylight views across the newly named City of Kisses towards the river but also a narrow glimpsing view from his box kitchen into Cargo Street, where now there are boutiques and restaurants instead of groceries and bars and 'working folk'.

The woman who had set her heart that night on Lix stood with his binoculars (where he had stood and spied on her so many times), her back against the little stove, her face veiled by the curtains, the rubber eye-cups pressed against her lids, and focused on the late-night customers, the waitress and the owner, in the pavement bar below, across the street. His stolen daily view of her. She was surprised how large the people seemed – they filled the lens – and how unsuspecting, uninhibited they were, free to mutter to themselves, or stare, or rearrange their belts and straps, or swing their legs, with no idea that they were scrutinized. 'So!' she said. So this was where the owl had his nest. 'I've often wondered what the view would be like if I were looking down on me!'

Lix was embarrassed, obviously. Caught out. He was also frightened and aroused. For all his noisy confidence, he'd never had an unrelated woman in his room before. What might it mean? He watched her from the kitchen door, his arms stretched up to grip the lintel, his printed T-shirt riding high above his belt to inadvertently display an adolescent abdomen and the apex of his pubic hair.

She, too, seemed large – and detailed, in a way she'd never been through his binoculars. Her outfit was familiar, of course, her general shape. He recognized the fashionable 'sandinista' tunic suit with its half sleeves and 'rough-look' calf-length skirt. He recognized the matching spangled Rebel scarf. But mostly she was unfamiliar. The angle, for a start, was different. He'd mostly seen her from above, the shoulders and the head. Binoculars had shortened her. Binoculars diminish the world, reduce the senses to one. Precision optical instruments, no matter how finely ground, fog-proof, waterproof, and vision-adjusted, could not hope to convey true proximity, the candid softness of the flesh, the spiciness of scent, the rustling, independent simpering of clothes, the clink of her bracelets, the perfect imperfections and the blemishes of someone close to thirty years of age. Until that night, he'd only seen this woman from afar.

Lix, actually, like many young men, was practised in the art of watching women from afar, not always through binoculars, of course, but women he could only dream of touching, women he could only scheme about: his voice tutor at the Arts Academy, the swan-necked student called Freda from one of the science faculties, the daughter of the concierge at his apartment house, the over-scented cashier in the campus cafeteria, the tiny half-Greek actress on his course, the bursar's haughty wife in her white suits, the many tough and visionary women in his 'groups', and – let's admit the universal truth – any female under fifty simply chancing into view. All worshipped from afar. They'd all be judged and sifted, feeding his mind's eye, as casually and unselfconsciously as a sea anemone might sift the random flotsam in its reach.

When you're that young and inexperienced you take

in fantasies with every breath. You mean no harm. But then you don't expect a distant fantasy to walk up to your room. You don't imagine that the woman waiting for her boyfriend every evening after work in the pavement bar below your kitchen window will ever be so close and intimate except through your binoculars. You cannot know, might never know, that she will be the mother of your eldest child.

SHE'D NOTICED HIM standing there with his binoculars many times in the preceding weeks, behind the twitching curtains in the rented rooms. The shifting lenses caught the light and signalled to the street. As did the pale, transfixed face beyond, with its dark birthmark on the upper cheek. She hadn't minded that he was spying on her. Being watched and waiting for your lover was much less tedious than simply waiting unobserved. She did not display herself exactly. She stayed demure: crossed legs, with a newspaper or magazine to read, perhaps, or a letter to write to her sister in Canada. Sometimes a book. Occasionally a cigarette. She always seemed so self-contained and concentrated, this little information clerk in her expressive outfits. Always looking down. She had learned to watch the upper window in the building opposite without lifting her head. Men weren't as undetectable as they imagined. And she did seek out the best-lit tables in the pavement bar, the ones most favoured by the evening sun, the ones directly opposite the snooper's room. She liked this silent and seductive rendezvous.

It had occurred to her, of course, that any man so patient and persistent with binoculars, and fixated enough to waste his time staring through his lenses at her, might not be honourable or sane or attractive, even. She'd seen the remake of the classic *Peeping Tom*. She'd read the trial reports of dangerous voyeurs. There was something animal about his spying, too: faces at windows, figures in caves. She should have been more fearful and more wary. Yet she felt safe. She had spotted her admirer once, out on the street. There'd been no mistaking that birthmark, or how unmenacing he seemed. The young man was striking. The blemish on the face was beautiful, an unexpected touch of innocence for one so secretive and scheming. She was surprised, as well, at how adolescent he was. That made his voyeurism charming almost, more forgivable, appropriate. How satisfying to have magnetized a fellow scarcely out of his teens when she – a mere month off her thirtieth birthday, not married yet herself but desperately dependent on a married man – had almost dismissed herself as being attractive to no one single.

It can be no surprise then (given how her sense of worth had been diminishing) that the daily half an hour between her ending work and her part-time lover getting to the bar became for a month or so the best part of her day. She sat with a perc of coffee, out on the street, her body trim, and was desired. Desired sexually. Desired simply for the way she looked, by the young man now swinging from the doorframe only a metre behind her, with his sweet, appealing midriff and the kiss-me birthmark on his face. She did not want him for a lover. She didn't even want him for a friend. She wanted him just once, just for the hour, and just to reassure herself. A 'little interlude' to salve her wounds.

Her 'little interlude' had not been planned. She'd never cheated on a man before. Never needed to. But when the call had come through to the bar that evening to tell her that her lover had been delayed and that he'd phone her next day at her office 'when he got the chance', then she'd been troubled and offended beyond words. The small offences irritated most – the effort she had expended after work, before arriving at the bar, touching up her make-up, fixing her hair, changing into clothes he liked, the time she'd squandered during the day imagining their meeting, rehearsing their embrace – although the larger implications were unig-norable and frightening. The pattern was familiar. This was the third time in ten days that he had let her down in one way or another. This was the third cheating husband in the last two years who had disillusioned her. She took the hint. She felt the chill. Another cooling, flagging man was scuttling from her life.

She'd started out the day as a woman with some status, not bloated with self-regard like some people she could name but confident enough to know that she was valued somewhere. Whenever she was waiting in the bar – an almost daily routine for the past three months – she had a purpose and a role. She was the early half of a couple, waiting to be validated by her man – and that was satisfying. The owner and the little waitress understood that she would arrive before the boyfriend, that she would order a coffee and, occasionally, a glass of mineral water. They were used to her eager nervousness – the frequent checking in the little vanity mirror she carried in her purse, her habit of shaking her watch as if to hasten time, the way she stared into her book, her writing pad, her newspaper but never seemed to turn a page. And then, when he arrived, the lover always just a little bit too late but standing over her at last to stoop a kiss onto her cheek, they'd be familiar with his embrace, her hand bunched up across his back.

Some days they'd only stay at the table for a few moments and then depart separately. The briefest meeting, just to hug. Once in a while, they'd share a litre of beer, though clearly the man was not comfortable in such a public bar. On other days, they'd go off hand in hand to possibly a restaurant or the hotels on the wharf. Then their passion would be almost palpable. It made her beautiful, the waitress thought.

Where was the beauty, though, in being so publicly stood up? Her borrowed husband could at least have called her to the bar owner's telephone, to whisper in her ear from his safe distance with his excuses and apologies. Why would he be so cowardly to trust his betrayals to a messenger if he were not ashamed? Or lying? She'd had to smile and nod and seem wholly unperturbed when the bar owner – the co-conspirator, it seemed to her – had come to pass on the shaming news: 'Your friend said to tell you that he'll phone tomorrow, when he gets the chance.' She felt exposed. Demeaned. A woman with no purpose in that bar. She could drink a thousand coffees there and still not count as half a couple waiting for completion. She was a laughing-stock – a woman revealed as exactly what she was: unmarried, only half successful in her work, the tenant of a less than homely flat shared with two women just as unfulfilled as her, reliant on the rationed attentions of a married lying man with children and a home he'd never abandon. She could hardly hold her coffee cup without shaking, she was so angry and upset. The evening had been so promising. They had planned to spend some time together in a restaurant, the famous – and expensive – Habit Bar where all the singers and the actors went. There'd be no grubby hour in a hotel room before he hurried home on this occasion. There'd just be food and wine and romance. She'd always liked that better than the sex. Love must be fed or it grows thin.

What occurred then to turn this calamity on its head and rescue the evening? What took her up the stairs to Lix's unappealing room? An almost-stranger's room. It must have been the romance that she had already planned for the evening which made the difference. The bottle was uncorked. Sitting on her own (before her lover's phone call came) in her familiar place in the street bar had – as nowadays it often did – made her not sexually but emotionally aroused. Romantic expectation was her mood: the expectation of the stooping kiss, her lover's guaranteed tumescence, the watchful, surely jealous eyes of the bar owner, the passing glances of the many husbands going home to their dull families, the certainty that she was being spied on through far binoculars, that kissing one in this bright street was making love to two or more. Was this a mad indulgence for a woman of her age, that she was being wanted from many angles by several men at once? Perhaps this was the worst of vanities. But surely anyone could see how poised and heaven-sent she was for men.

Now what? No boyfriend suddenly. No prospect of a kiss. Not even any twitching curtains on that night. She'd checked. Just the complicit sympathy of the bar owner and his waitress and the added insult of the stiffening liqueur that they had offered her 'on the house'. To go home was impossible. How could she bear the chatter of her flatmates, the television programmes, the surrender of her hopes to all the domestic chores that needed attending to? A woman who had expected to be dining out with celebrities in the Habit Bar would be at home instead, ironing blouses, defeated by the telephone.

Still, she had to eat. So rather than order anything from the street bar – an unflattering choice of cold snacks – she went to the little Fixed Menu cafeteria, the ABC, behind the railway station where single men and women, stranded by their lifestyles and their trains, could eat without expense, and without embarrassment. She ordered menu C, the soup, the fish, the crème brûlée and – recklessly – another glass of the Boulevard Liqueur she'd been given at the bar. She'd pay for one at least that night.

She'd not got anything to read. Not even a pen to doodle with. So she could be excused for looking round the restaurant and studying the gallery of faces, the exhibition of clothes and postures. Staring was polite compared to some behaviour there, the table manners and the arguments, the lack of modesty. The ABC was the sort of place where you could stare. Nobody considered it rude. You stared and they stared back. No need to be genteel with such a cast of students, bachelors, artists, unemployed, third-class travellers.

She spent ten minutes gazing round, not really looking for her dishonest lover with another woman possibly, or with his work colleagues, or with his children and his wife, not really practising what she would say to him, in front of everyone. She studied almost every visible face, the backs of almost every other head. So she couldn't miss that half-familiar blemished man, three rows of tables down from her and walking in between the diners and their bags and cases, looking for a place to sit. The pattern on the cheekbone was unmistakable. It was her clandestine admirer. She knew at once he'd recognized her, too.

How could she be so reckless? That was not her style, not normally. She was the sort who only spoke when spoken to, in matters of the heart at any rate. A woman of that age even in those newly unshackled days did not initiate encounters of this kind. But now her fury and her disappointment seemed to shift and occupy a different space. Instead of standing boldly at the family table, the wife amazed, the children cowering, the lying husband silent, pizza-faced, as she'd imagined, she was instead half standing at her chair, pulling back the table, making room for Lix. For once she'd made a move on her own behalf. It had been easy, actually. She simply pointed at the place opposite her and said, 'It's free.' He had no choice. To walk on past, without a ready lie, would be unnecessarily rude. So he sat. He was blushing uncontrollably. The spy exposed.

The blushing, though, was irresistible. Not only was it evidence of innocence, embarrassment and shame, but also desire, arousal, fear. She'd never seen such fear on someone's face. It made her feel unusually powerful, to be able to bring on such involuntary discomfort in a man. The boot should be on the other foot. Had always been before. So this was what it felt like to be male, a hunter, predatory, to have a blushing quarry within reach, the colour in his face the flag of his arousal.

She made Lix look her in the eye by simply chatting at him like a cousin. It helped that he was so much younger than her. Perhaps ten years, she judged. It helped, as well, that she had already drunk two shots of alcohol. It let her talk. Why not? It's not unnatural – especially in the ABC – to talk when you are sharing tables with a stranger. She bullied him till he submitted to her questions. And as he spoke, about his theatre studies and his agitprop, his many opinions on almost everything, including – on that day – the good news, bad news from Iran, the coming plebiscite, the confrontation planned for Nation Day, the famine in Cambodia for which he'd organized a street performance called, he said, PolPottery, she started once again to feel contented with herself, to feel attractive, passionate, even to like the woman sharing a tablecloth with him, the unmasked peeping tom. She wasn't listening, of course. The theatre and PolPottery? Iran?

She liked it best when he was being playful, playing someone else, that is, and not himself. His speaking voice was beautiful. And he could sing. He could do accents well. Though his repertoire of American actors was amusing, his imitation of their waiter with his odd head and his strange, strangulated voice was clever enough to make her laugh out loud.

To tell the truth, though, this snooper, for all his cleverness and youth, for all his physical difference from her older, paunchy lover, wasn't her type of man. Not broad enough. Too loud and sensitive and too much of the student in his dress, his voice, his hair, too keen to change the world with his slogan T-shirt and his campaign buttons. And far too inexperienced with women. She could tell at once. He couldn't flirt if he were paid for it with gems. He didn't have the nature or the skill – unlike her own pitiless and impatient lover who used the world, and her, so roughly and so carelessly.

This inexperience was tantalizing in a way. It put her in command. She needed more than anything, on this of all nights, to imagine she was at the steering-wheel. His inexperience also made her strong enough, once they had finished eating and there was nothing on the table but their coffee cups, the bills, and their two pairs of hands, to touch his fingertips, the finger-tips that had held the spyglasses in which she was desired, and then to grip his wrists, and then to say, quite shockingly, 'Where do you live?' And then, before he had the chance to reply, 'I know exactly where you

live. The fourth floor above the bar along the street.'
How wonderful to see him blush again and squirm.

She could not stop herself. The night was beckoning
and she was dressed for it. But if there was any hero
in her sights, the young man (now hurrying with her
out of the ABC and into Cargo Street, four flights of
stairs ahead of them) was not the one. She herself
was the only person she observed in her mind's eye.
The clock reversed. Again she was the woman, half
a couple, waiting at the street bar. But magnified.
Enlarged. Desired. The blur of men passed by and
liked her hair, her dress, her face, her legs. How better
she must be than any wife, they thought. Half of the
city wanted to sleep with her. She was the woman on
the poster for *Life* magazine, the lipstick and the glass
of wine, kissing everyone. Her mouth. Her tongue. She
only had to lift her face and look around and smile for
them, for all the men. The telephone could ring and
be ignored. She'd not be caught. Four storeys up, the
winking lenses could only catch the light.

'So,' she said again, 'it's quite a view you've got up
here.' She meant it as an undemanding invitation for
the man, the boy, to step across and wrap his arms
around her waist. Somebody had to close the gap
between the pavement table and the room. Surely
that was partly his responsibility. She soon knew, as
seconds passed like struck bells, the binoculars still

heavy in her hand, that this young man would never take the single step across the kitchen to press against her at the windowsill, his lips against her neck, his cock lengthening against her leg. He was too scared and innocent. She'd have to make the move herself.

The act was simple. She reached across and touched the bare torso above his belt, the boyish plume of hair. 'So!' she said again. The word seemed unavoidable, as did the pouting moue that delivered it. Then, 'You're quite the little spy.' She wanted him to talk before she kissed, before they made their way to his untidy bed in his unruly room. She wanted to discover what she looked like in the lens. 'Tell me ... why you look at me.' She nodded at the street below, the almost empty bar, as if she were still sitting there.

Lix did not consider himself to be a spy or a snooper, of course. His frequent reconnaissances from behind the kitchen curtains were just routine for him, something for the wasting moments of the day, which at least allowed him to imagine that he had a part to play in all the kissing that was taking place that year. What else was there to do when he was home – an empty home – except put on the radio or choose an album for the record-player, then browse the street with his binoculars? This was the closest he could get to contributing anything to *Life*'s portrayal of the city.

The woman from the bar, now standing with her fingers wrapped around his belt, was wrong if she imagined she was special. He did not only have eyes for her (though it was hard, for the moment, to think of anybody else while she was pushing up his T-shirt). He was indiscriminating in his interests, so long as his attentions could be held by someone female and attractive. His eyes were robbing women from the street as non-judgementally as a mugger. And his excuse, should he be caught? And his excuse, now that he had been caught and challenged by the woman breathing in his face, so close that he could smell her perfume and her scalp? It was his duty to observe, of course. Watch people in the street, his drama teachers had instructed his group. Watch how they behave. Follow them, even, to see and learn what people do when they are innocently on their own. He was only studying, through his binoculars.

'It's just part of my course,' he said. 'You're always there. I always watch, that's all.'

'It's something more,' she said. 'I know about you men.' She wanted him to tell her that he'd always wanted her, that he had thought about this moment many times before. She wanted him to say, 'I was excited when I caught you in my lens.'

Instead he said, 'I'm finding this embarrassing.'

He meant that the impulse that had taken him to seek arousal at the kitchen window was hardly targeted. He was not seeking consummation with a woman with a name but only giving vent to haphazard randiness, that wild anarchic master of the unattached. He only meant to satisfy himself. Now he faced the fear and the embarrassment of achieving the impossible, of doing something he had never had to try before. He must transfer his universal and unfocused longings for any woman safely chancing by at a distance to this particular and all too present woman.

She slipped her shoes off, kicked them across the kitchen floor, becoming short and vulnerable without her heels. 'Kiss, kiss. Are you allowed to study kissing, too? Come on.' She shocked herself, on tiptoes, in bare feet, her tongue surprising his, her hands pushed up inside his shirt as if he were the woman. She was in the mood for shocks. She'd had a shocking and unhappy day and she was hoping for some pleasurable revenge.

She should not, though, have kissed his birthmark quite so readily. She should not have held its short soft hairs between her lips. He gasped and tried to pull away. 'I'm sorry,' he said.

'For what?'

'For this . . . the blotch.'

His birthmark would unman him all his life, he'd always thought. This red and hairy naevus would repulse the girls. It would be the obstacle denying him a wife. He'd never met a single female who had not stared at it for a moment when they first laid eyes on him or who, otherwise, had battled with themselves to fix their attention elsewhere. He felt that people's eyes were darting constantly, judgementally, to his cheek-bone, that it fascinated and repulsed them like a harelip or a wall eye, like some unsightly boil. He felt as if his body had no other purpose than to haul his flaming cheek around. His burning cheek, his everlasting blush. His boyhood friends had teased him for it, called him Smudge, indeed, a pitiless nickname which he had foolishly adopted and still allowed when he went home, just to show that the blemish did not really bother him these days. But, oh, it did. It shaped the way he was.

Lix had developed the habit while still a young boy of holding a hesitant hand up to his eye when he spoke to strangers as if shielding it from sunlight. It drew attention to the birthmark, of course, rather than hiding it, and gave the boys something more to tease him about at school. He had tried to keep that hesitant hand in his trouser pocket, to be – or seem – relaxed about himself. Too frequently he also felt obliged when making new acquaintances to introduce himself as Smudge and then point out the cherry-coloured birthmark as if it had not already been noted and ignored. He made jokes about it at his own expense. He was over-insistent, in fact, and made some old acquaintances so uncomfortable that they started calling him Felix and looking fixedly at their feet when they conversed rather than give offence by flickering a glance at his face.

What Lix could not accept, would never realize, but which the woman from the street bar had recognized at once, was that the naevus was attractive rather than ugly. How tender it had been to kiss him there. It was like kissing someone better on a bruise, or kissing someone's eyes to stop the tears. Here was an invitation to be tender. The birthmark was the sweetest part of him. It lent to an otherwise inexpressive face a sardonic and whimsical note, a touch of innocence and beauty. What small romantic successes Lix had enjoyed in his teens had been encouraged rather than hindered by what the mark did for his face. Lix did not understand. All his personal and public failures he blamed upon the stain.

Perhaps that's why Lix grew to love the cinema so much. It was a refuge where his birthmark was not seen, where everybody faced the front and no one stared at him. It does not explain, however, the oddly self-exposing decision he had made that he would be an actor, someone stared at for a living. Or, possibly, as his best friend cleverly observed when Lix announced that he had won a place at theatre school, 'He's looking for a job where he can cake himself in make-up.'

If only his best friends could see him now, a woman on her tiptoes kissing him, again, again, on his birthmark as if the cherry stain were fruit. Here was proof for them at last that love – or passion, anyway – was blind, that it could overcome, ignore, forgive the blotches and the blemishes.

She kissed him there again, prevented him pulling back. He was a timid soul, birthmark or not. Another man, most other men, would not conceal themselves behind the curtains of an upper room. They'd be out on the streets themselves, consummating their desires. Another man would not require cajoling and encouragement. But here, still at the kitchen door, still with her lips pressed to his cheek, she recognized quite soon, was someone who, if he (just like the city) had hardly kissed before – and that seemed possible, to judge by his hesitation – then almost certainly he had not made love before either. He was more than inexperienced. A virgin, then? She felt more purposeful.

Thank goodness someone there was purposeful. Lix was all at sea. His only physical contact with women – other than that one startled volunteer – was on stage or in his acting classes when there was a drama coach or stage directions to guide him: *Take her arm* or *Seize her roughly* or *Embrace*. And he obeyed the script. And she – whichever student actress it might be that day, instructed to be his Blanche, his Juliet, his Beatrice, his Salome – responded by the book.

These were the licensed touches of the theatre, unconsummated congresses, studied passion – love technique that's only there to dupe the audience.

Of course, the flesh he handled was not fake. Those

onstage partners in his embrace were genuine women, ready with the action and the words. These were real lips. Those hands he took to kiss or shake, those costumed shoulders he enveloped in his arms were not from Props. The peasant's dress that dashed against his ankles when they danced was fraudulent, just dressing up, a play. Yet when his hand supported her – the girl in his stage group, whoever she might be that week, his partner – for her cartwheel, then those glimpsed legs were alarmingly real, as was the heady smell of bottled perfume from Chanel, as was the bra strap, textured and insinuating against his palm.

None of them were quite as real as she'd become, the little shoeless woman from the pavement bar who now was backing him out of the kitchen, across the wooden boards of his small room, until his legs were pressed against the endboard of his bed and he was toppling.

She knew enough about young men to please if not utterly satisfy herself before she let him ejaculate, although their lovemaking had been so urgent and frantic that neither of them had removed a single item of clothing. Not one, except her pair of shoes, abandoned in the kitchen. His underpants and trousers were round his thighs. Her underclothes had just been pulled aside. Her brassiere, still fastened at the back, was riding underneath her chin. Thank goodness for the sandinista 'rough-look' skirt. She could go home by tram and look respectable, and not appear unbecomingly dishevelled. Despite her tears. For there'd be tears as soon as she descended from his room.

THE WOMAN hadn't yet revealed her name to Lix. She was feeling guilty, actually, and would have lied if he'd enquired what she was called or solicited her phone number or suggested that they make the ABC their occasional rendezvous. But he had not enquired, solicited, or requested. Having sex had doubled his embarrassment, not eradicated it. His tongue, so active just a few minutes before, was now entirely tied. No matter. She didn't think they'd meet again anyway. She didn't even think she'd go back to the street bar any more. Her future, clearly, was elsewhere. Her catch would have to find another friend for his binoculars.

They lay in bed, his narrow bed, for far too long, looking at the posters on the ceiling – rock groups she'd never heard of, demonstrations and campaigns she'd never join, experimental plays she'd hate, and on the facing wall an illustrated slogan by Roesenthaler, which declared that 'The Artist is the Armourer'.

'What must you think of me?' she said.

'I don't think anything. Well, nothing bad.'

'Am I your first?'

'First what?'

'First one in bed.'

'First what in bed?'

She shrugged. Men always disappointed her. 'Where can I wash?'

'They've got a shower down the corridor. I use the kitchen usually . . .'

Lix followed her into the unlit kitchen and waited at the door (a host at last) while, finally, she began to take off her clothes, a silhouette against the darkened window, and drape them over his radiator. She tied the towel he gave her round her waist.

'I've got some coffee if you want.'

'I do need coffee, yes.'

Lix leaned across her at the sink to fill the saucepan with water. Her breasts were hard and cold against his arm. 'I'll have to boil some water for you too, if you need to wash,' he said. 'There isn't any hot. Not from the tap.' The gas flame dramatized the room. 'I have a question.'

'Go on.'

He wanted to ask, 'Am I OK in bed? Can I be confident with girls? What should I know that I don't know?' She was an older woman, after all. It was her job to put his mind at rest. Instead, he said only, 'What's up?'

'"What's up?"' Already she could see how irritating he could be.

'You know, I mean, what's going on?'

She leaned against the window frame and looked down on the street below without the aid of his binoculars. Nothing moved. It was past midnight. The street bar had been packed away, its shutters drawn, its chairs and tables folded and padlocked. 'I came with you,' she said, 'because the guy that I am always waiting for, down there, did not show up. That's why.'

'Let's go to bed again.'

She was astonished, not that the object of her 'little interlude' didn't seem to care about her lover dumping her – Why would he care? Nobody cared – but that this innocent had been transformed so quickly into something more familiar to her, the predatory man forever wanting to make love, demanding it, cajoling it. She'd been a fool to take her clothes off while he watched and then to stand half naked in the semi-dark, her body silhouetted in the street-lit window frame. It had been a provocation, obviously. He was provoked. Quite clearly so. His body, his erection, flattered her. She almost welcomed it, this second visitation. How could she not? She was, she believed, its single cause. His body was awakening again to her close presence in the room. It validated her and no one else. Lix, though, was not intent on flattery.

This time it was not left to her to close the gap between the pavement table and the room, to take the single step across the kitchen. He was no longer scared and inexperienced, it seemed. He pressed himself against her at the tiny sink next to the window. He pushed his trousers down.

She was a little nervous suddenly. She'd lost control. This was, when all was said and done, a stranger's room, a dangerous place. 'We've done it once,' she said.

'You're beautiful.' Already he had one hand on her breasts and the other was pushing up the towel. 'Let's lie down in the other room.' He shouldered her towards the door. The sycophant became the psychopath in seven seconds flat.

Where was the tenderness in this? It was, of course, too much to ask for love, in these odd circumstances. But tenderness? How kind was Lix with her? Perhaps it was too soon and he too young for tenderness. The heart and brain are slow to play their parts when men discover sex. We can allow him some excuse: he meant no harm; he'd seen too many films and thought that making love was an aggressive act; he wanted to redeem himself, in his own eyes. And we should recognize this tender and forgiving truth: in later years Lix proved to be a man who was not cruel or casual in his consummated passions but, with one costly exception, only copulated with the woman whom – for the moment at least – he adored.

Cupid is by nature mischievous, irrational and irresponsible. By now, even without the kindness and the tenderness, she was aroused herself to tell the truth. The words 'You're beautiful' will always do the trick. There was something else that had alerted her and quickened her: the window frame, the windowsill, the curtains still not drawn against the prying night, the empty street below, and his binoculars still hanging from their peg.

'Let's do it here,' she said. 'Be quick.' She turned her back on him and braced her arms against the window frame. She stuck her bottom out, a silent fat-lipped purse of soft flesh, and reached behind her legs for him, to guide him in. 'Come on, come on.' Her senses were all genital. She hardly felt his fingers on her back, she hardly heard his breathlessness, the kettle boiling on his stove, the rattling woodwork of the window frame, the division and adhesion of their skin. She pressed her forehead up against the glass but noticed no one passing in the street below, no cars, no revellers, no cheating husbands too late to meet their patient mistresses, not even any cats to catch her eye. Lix might be lost in her. But she had half forgotten him. She'd not delude herself. She was not passionate for this probationer. She was the subject and the object of her own desires. She lost herself, four storeys up, in only what was happening to her, a woman in so many places all at once, it seemed, the bar, the bed, the ABC, the gloomy street-lit room, the city's dark, conspiring boulevards, a woman who had only meant to reassure herself.

So now, at last, we've reached the early moments of Lix's oldest child. A girl, in fact. A girl called Bel. She'd have a vestige of her father's naevus on her cheek, the slightest smudge. By now she'd be, what?, in her mid-twenties and still waiting for the moment when she'd want to, dare to, make the phone call to her unsuspecting 'dad'. She'd phone one day. She'd write. She'd send a photograph. The ball was bouncing in her court. For the moment, though, on that midnight of induction in 1979, in that year when we began to kiss, Lix had no idea how this encounter would prolong itself . . . so physically. He felt the kettle's hot steam massage on his back. But he could not remove himself from her just yet. His legs were suddenly as weak and boneless as the towel that had unravelled from her waist. He had to gasp for oxygen. Otherwise he'd never felt so free and ready for the world. Courageous, too.

2

THEY WERE IN LOVE, the unblemished student actor and the swan-necked girl. Theirs was a clumsy love, admittedly, rushed and bodily and bruising, as first loves often are. It was (to use the country phrase) a jug thrown by the potter's toes', ill formed.

We excuse the lovers for their gaucherie. They were scarcely adults then. This was only 1981, the first – and only – year of what we called at the time (depending on our politics and age) either the Big Melt or the Laxity, when, having practised kissing for twenty months or so – life after *Life* – and having benefited from the unexpected tourist revenues and the unforeseen attentions of some foreign capital, our city governors withdrew into their meeting rooms and chambers, their dining clubs, to concentrate on getting rich and getting laid. Thus letting all the rest of us get on with life.

Remember it, how brief it was, the melting of the civic snows, the urban thaw? Remember how, for not-quite-long-enough, even the policemen let their sideboards grow and let their patience lengthen also, how foreign books, LPs, and films came in, uncut, unmarked, the shock of glamour magazines, how we *Last Tango*ed and *Deep Throat*ed amongst ourselves as if the untried ardours of the cinema could light the way to Paradise?

It's hard to credit now our absurd light-heartedness, our determined disregard for any law and regulation (the pettier the better), our contempt for grammar, and proprieties, and common sense, and modesty. All the things our parents should have cared about (if they'd not been melted by the Melt themselves) were flouted on the street, without a care, with appetite.

It was possible, without much fear of being challenged, to walk around without IDs, to pilfer food in the spirit of democracy and beg for cigarettes, to make a din at night and hang out in the squares all day, to ride the trams without a ticket, to park our parents' cars on prohibited pavements, and to boulevard ourselves as brashly as we wanted to, as drunk, as stoned, as underdressed.

How effortlessly modern and valiant it seemed, after all those years of being sensible and neat, just to dress badly. An hour of impulse shopping at the new black-market gutter stalls that sprang up everywhere that year equipped you for the revolution. The streets were full of gypsy partisans, denim clerks with hairstyles from the LA seventies, wiry Bolsheviks in fat-man overcoats, white aboriginals in T-shirts with slogans calling for the replacement of god with punk, and government with Panarchy, and women in skirts of every cut and cloth and colour, displaying lengths of flesh or tights that previously had only been approved for foreign visitors and imported magazines. Even Navigation Island was prised free from its wardens for a while and turned into a non-stop festival of music, drugs and picnicking. Woodstock Nation – finally. Our city had some catching up to do.

Remember all the litter and the buskers in the streets, the open windows and the jaywalking, the sudden obligation to sample newly tolerated taboos in bed, the suicides, the debts, the pregnancies, the jazz, the reggae and the rock, the blissful loss of self-control, the arguments, the endless, carefree jousting with the couldn't-care-less police? Ah, yes, the Laxity that only lasted, only could be tolerated, for a year, but which briefly made us Free At Last, free to speak our minds, free to organize and demonstrate and not be 'disappeared'.

We understood and we forgave the lovers, then. Forgave them for their arrogance and foolishness, the risks they took when risks were safe to take. They were only the excited products of their time, no more responsible for how they were than lungs are guilty for the air.

That December Thursday was their twenty-seventh

day together, the high point of their reckless, infinitely short affair. A day of intercourse and action. Never in their lives again would *Fredalix*, these two guileless doctrinaires, feel so apprehensive and elated, so nauseous with fear, so poised, so eager, and so licensed to escape into the refuges of flesh once they had done their foolish duty for the world.

LIX CAN'T BE SURE even to this day whether it was his shared infatuation with this lofty campus beauty (shared with anyone who laid their eyes on her), or merely a desire to prove himself a decent partisan before both the Laxity and his student days were over, that had prompted him to stand up at the November meeting of the Roesenthaler Comrades Co-operative (so named mostly to achieve the acronym RoCoCo) and suggest, as if he were proposing nothing more perilous than leafleting, that they kidnap Marin Scholia.

His idea had been a crudely simple one, and only mischievous. That was the Spirit of the Times, his public contribution to the Big and famous Melt. He'd meant to draw attention to himself, to say what he had guessed the firebrand Freda would like to hear. He'd not intended to be taken quite so seriously.

The Arts Academy where Lix was in his final year of Theatre and Stagecraft Studies had been endowed the semester before with nearly $7 million by Meister-

Corps, the electronics and engineering giant from Milan, Berlin, Boston, and Hong Kong, to pay for a new bar, a theatre, a concert hall, a gallery, and a cinema on the campus, all in one custom-built star-shaped complex. A pentacle of creativity.

These were tainted millions, actually – or so the more progressive of the students judged. They'd not be seduced by the prospect of new facilities and subsidized alcohol, especially as their own studies would be over by the time the pentacle was built. These dirty dollars, they claimed in the student freesheet, had been made from low wages in the Far East, 'the blanket marketing of shoddy and environmentally damaging products in dishonest packaging', arms-for-timber deals in Africa, and from stock-market trickery (to which many of their parents had fallen victim).

Now, on Thursday the seventeenth of the coming month, just as the students would be going home for their winter vacation, MeisterCorps's American chairman, Marin Scholia, would be visiting the city to open the company's new central offices in the tower block that we have known since then as Marin's Finger and to pass on (or so the rumour-mongers claimed) his yellow envelopes of thanks in thousand-dollar bills to our finest councillors and planning commissars. He was a worthy target, certainly.

Lix stood before the nineteen students in RoCoCo, then, with something safely moderate in mind at first.

It's always best to stand, if you are tall enough, to concentrate an audience. He held a photocopy of a news report he thought would interest them. He read it out in his trained voice, reducing to a whisper almost when he reached the part about the chairman's final appointment of the day.

Lix knew, of course, that he was being watched by everybody in the meeting room (stagecraft again) – and that included Famous Freda Dressed in Black, the campus beauty with the sculptor's head who could have been a model had she chosen, who could have slept with anybody there, then dined on them, and still had volunteers, who could have been in films or (on our news-stands finally) stapled into *Playboy* magazine. At 5 p.m. or thereabouts, Lix read, Scholia planned to 'drop in' at the campuses to lay the first stone of what is still the MeisterCorps Creative Centre for the Arts, or MeCCA. (Though MeisterCorps itself, of course, is no longer with us. It finally buckled to its creditors in the Labor Day Freefall, the 'Wall Street Dive of Two Thousand and Five'.)

'We'll have to organize a vigil,' someone said. Exactly Lix's thought.

Then Freda spoke, not bothering to stand, not bothering to raise her voice. A typical riposte, uncompromising and seductively extreme: 'Pickets are a waste of time. You know they are. The police just box you in.'

'A moving picket, then!'

'A picket or a vigil, what's the difference? Somebody, please, suggest a petition. Or a delegation! Or a letter-writing campaign. Just as ineffectual.' Freda had discovered that she could say exactly what she felt. Her beauty licensed her. Nobody dared to take offence, especially if she spoke as softly as an infants' teacher or a nurse. 'A line of little placards or a bit of paper with some signatures isn't going to trouble MonsterCorps, is it? Correct-me-if-I'm-wrong.' A little singsong phrase. She raised her eyebrows, waited for a moment, looked around the room. 'No, we need to give Marin Scholia a surprise. And shake him up a bit. Something memorable. If what we do doesn't put us on the evening news, then what's the point?'

Her unruffled escalation shut the meeting up, or almost did – for out of somewhere, wide of script, entirely unrehearsed, ad-lib, Lix saw an opportunity, a rash and sexual opportunity. He said, to her, 'Why don't we grab him? Lock him up. Give Meister Scholia a chance to . . .' To what? Lix hesitated for the words. He wanted to seem breezy and ironic. He'd almost blurted out, too solemnly, 'We give him the chance to quantify his crimes.' Surely Freda would approve of that. Instead, he said, in the perfect accent of a tenth-generation Bostonian, 'You've dined, old man – and now it's time to face the waiter and the bill.' Rescued, flattered even, by a legendary movie line. Burt Lancaster.

He noticed Freda leaning forward as he spoke. She'd had to twist her madly lengthy neck to stare at him along the row of student radicals. Her earrings hung as heavily as pears. Her bangles clacked as she pushed back her hair to clear her view and show her throat. Lix was, for once, pretty certain that she was not staring at the blemish on his face. Her mouth was open, and her eyes were bright. She was admiring him. She'd hardly even noticed him before.

'Then what?' somebody asked. 'It's risky, isn't it? Kidnapping millionaires is only officially authorized in Italy. What do we do with him, anyway?'

'You grab the millionaire. You grab the headlines, too. That's it.' Lix was performing like a love-struck teenager, unable to restrain himself. 'And then you have to let him go, of course. Eventually.' He hardly recognized himself. He'd transformed for her. Picasso syndrome, it was called: the artist's style of painting changed for every woman in his studio or bed.

'We let him go, but only when he's signed an Admission of Responsibility, an Admission of *Liability*,' said Freda, not bothered whether or not she sounded breezy and ironic. 'That would look good in the newspapers. That'd be front page.'

'He won't do that. He wouldn't even sign the Seven Principles. Even GlobeOil signed the Seven Principles.'

'Even Nescafé.'

'We keep him till he does.' She craned her neck again and smiled at Lix.

His neck rushed red for her. He came out in a sudden sweating blush, which seemed to fill his eyes and drench his hair. His pulse had quickened, and his mouth was dry. Men fall in love more speedily and much more bodily than women. It was for Lix a joyful, new experience, this unexpected triumphing of self. How brave he must appear to her – and must continue to appear. And how he wished he'd never said a word.

So it began, the kidnapping, the love affair, the making love, the life of Lix's second child.

AS IT HAPPENED, theirs was little more than flirting talk at this stage. RoCoCo was not truly dangerous any more than the Laxity was truly a revolution. It was only striking poses in the names of Liberty and Love, with no more consciousness of the consequences than a T-shirt has for its silk-screened slogans. RoCoCo's members were soft and inoffensive youngsters, essentially, freshly baked survivors of the teens, trying to sound less mild and dreary than they really were, and only wanting to be a part of this great city's quest for romance and advancement. They could alarm nobody but themselves. RoCoCo walking down the street, all nineteen of them in a gang, despite their voices and their hair, their leather belts and wallet chains, would not cause anyone to step aside. A bunch is no more chilling than a single grape.

Theirs was the sort of reckless moment, then, that could not hope to flourish in maturer company. A wiser group would quickly audit all the pros and cons and realize that kidnapping could only backfire on the kidnappers. The headlines would be roasting. Their protest would bear bitter fruit. The only lasting victims would be themselves. So, the prudent ones at the meeting sank into their chairs, voted to support the 'action' but did not volunteer themselves. They sat with faces like a Chinese Monday hoping not to catch sweet Freda's eye. They knew how prevailing she was, and how seductive just a glance from her could be. And dangerous. A kidnapping, even if it were shortlived and justified, could put them all in jail, despite the Melt, or jeopardize their academic grades or disappoint their lecturers. Their parents would not sympathize. Not all their parents could afford to buy them out. Their job prospects would be undermined. Travel visas would be denied them, long after the events. Anyway, they were not sure (though silent on this matter in such company) if kidnapping was 'right'.

So in the end, in this most skittish time, there were just four from RoCoCo prepared to spread their wings beyond a picket line and stand with Freda: a glumly cute, gay woman from the Language School (who wanted more than anything to disappoint her lecturers and undermine her job prospects), two tall and overweight post-Maoist anarchists from Freda's science faculty, and Lix, all of whom it was soon apparent aspired to more than comradely contact with their dazzling colleague. They were the four comrades most unhinged by her and most ardent for her approval. The heart controls the head and makes us mad and brave and radical. The revolution rides the lustiest of mares.

Five volunteers would never be enough for the swarming ambush that Freda had in mind at first, her show of force, her mighty kick against the pricks. She'd seen the glorious newsreels from 1968, the year of barricades, with the columns of police rebuffed by mobs of students, armed only with their banners and some cobblestones. Never by as few as five. Again the city had let her down, she felt. Only thirteen years previously, Peking, Paris, Prague, Chicago, Santiago, Rome had all been pulled apart by people less than thirty years of age. It must have seemed to Freda that Youth could be truly powerful in every corner of the world, excepting ours. She kept a press photo from 1968 in her wallet: a Czech, wild-haired and young and biblically beautiful, his jacket pushed back on his shoulders, his shirt pulled open, was baring his chest, his rack of ribs, a centimetre from the barrel of a Russian gun in a gesture that, for Freda, was sensual and thrilling. It always made her think of 'The Fox's Lament', 'Stop me, shoot me, if you dare / For I'm too far and fast to care'.

She wondered sometimes, was he still alive, this semi-naked man. Was he still a radical? He looked, she thought, a bit like Lix. She'd noticed it when he'd been standing up so pompously and so theatrically at the RoCoCo meeting. That birthmark, certainly, made his face seem challenging. She'd wondered what his ribs were like and how his hair would look if ruffled up a bit by her. Would it look more like the Czech's? What could she do to make him look more Czech?

It was at that moment, peering across the room at Lix, his eagerness to please, she decided she'd accept him as a lover for a while and even that she would allow herself a period of being in love. She had not flushed like he had flushed for her. Her pulse had not increased for him. Her feelings were not bodily. She was calmly concentrated on the chance that Lix had offered her of pushing back the jacket, pulling open the shirt, and making politics with kisses on a comrade's rack of ribs. Freda always needed someone in her bed when the optimistic ghost of 1968 invaded her. Her body and her spirit demanded company. But not just yet. She'd let his role intensify as all the action of the coming weeks intensified, as they prepared to pull the cobbles loose and press their chests against the police and MeisterCorps. She'd save their best encounter for the aftermath of Marin Scholia's kidnapping. She would defeat him on his bed. That was her long-term urgency.

Time to begin. Freda followed blushing Lix out of the meeting room and made him talk to her as they walked across the campus to their almost neighbouring academies of Human Science and Theatre Studies for their evening lectures. She was, she said, again in her soft, fiercely reasonable voice, 'irretrievably disillusioned' with RoCoCo. Marin Scholia was being virtually delivered into their hands. And they could only muster five. 'Some throng.' They'd need twenty-five at the very least to rush the chairman off his feet, she said. They could not expect the head of a leviathan like MeisterCorps to stride into their university unaccompanied, like some delivery boy. There would be the usual dignitaries and luminaries surrounding him, men and women in their best clothes who would be easy to intimidate. There'd be private guards as well. Americans were paranoid whenever they left home. They moved around in skittish flocks, 'like trigger finches', never trusting anyone. 'Americans are terrified of streets,' she said. And there'd be armed police, perhaps, despite the recent ruling that the campuses were off-limits to any unauthorized civic forces. There'd be the television and the press, of course, and beefy businessmen from MeisterCorps, who maybe, emboldened by their lunch and their genetic hatred of the young and studious, would be quick and eager to deploy their shoes and fists.

Besides, even if RoCoCo had volunteered en masse and were a hundred strong, Scholia would avoid a crowd. He'd steer clear of anybody seeming faintly aggressive. Anyone approaching him would have to look absolutely safe. He had his share of enemies who would be glad to land a punch on his old Yankee chin, or splash an egg across his suit. (Making 'tat that didn't last and enemies that did', she joked, was Meister-Corps's contribution to the world.) She'd heard that men like Scholia never walked closer than five metres to a building, in case some demonstrator on the seventh floor was standing by an open window on a chair ready to spit or urinate. 'Or dump,' suggested Lix. They laughed together for their first time.

'We need,' Lix said, already seeking ways of reining in his Mad Idea, but reining in, as well, the female of his dreams, 'a strategy that's more in keeping with the Melt.'

She snorted in reply and stretched her neck and shook her hair. A frisky thoroughbred. 'The Melt's a cheap diversion. They'll let you change your clothes, but just you try changing anything that matters.'

'Well, then, something smaller-scale at least. You can't beat men like Scholia with force, anyway. There's five of us. And three of them can't run. No, you have to beat a man like that with weapons that he hasn't got.'

Lix was not speaking from experience. Nor was he speaking in a voice he recognized from his wide repertoire. He was someone new and unrehearsed, the over-cheerful, over-careful supplicant, who wanted desperately to keep this woman at his side. His voice had softened, matching hers. He tried and didn't quite manage to sound as uncompromisingly logical. He could feel his body change just from being close to her, within her odour range. Close enough already to have brushed her hand with his and for their shoulders to have collided several times. He might risk a friendly parting kiss, he thought, like comrades do, but that was far more daunting than the kidnapping, even. He found that he was almost dancing as he walked. He must have seemed childishly exuberant to her, to anyone who spotted him, but he'd never experienced such escalating changes of his mood and did not know how to restrain himself. His stride had lengthened and his arms were swinging loosely. He let his knuckles brush her skirt, her fabric and his skin producing startling ecstasies. She didn't seem to mind.

'Like what? What hasn't Scholia got?' she asked. 'The man's got everything.'

'He hasn't got a sense of humour. And he isn't young,' Lix said. 'We have. We are.'

Again, he'd earned some smiles from Freda – though he was too besotted and disarmed to glimpse in these approving and addictive smiles something he would only be able to articulate once their affair had ended, and was in jagged pieces: that he could never be exactly the irresistible, magnetic target of her desires. She was the target of her own desire. She was entirely dazzled by herself. Who wouldn't be if they were her? The most successful people are most dazzled by themselves. In seeking love, accepting it, she was polishing a mirror, all the better to see herself. The best that Lix could hope for was the opportunity to provide Freda's arm – and her reputation for flying in the face of convention – with a compliant accessory. There were, he would have thought, less satisfying roles in life.

What Freda and her four admirers planned over the next few weeks (once Lix had been installed on Freda's arm, her new man-friend, her latest co-belligerent) was eventually, as Lix had hoped and engineered, far removed from honest kidnapping and shows of force. Little more than just a prank. This was not 1968. It was instead the playful year of Laxity. They were not Baader-Meinhof or the Red Brigades. Still, they could pretend they were. That was the whole point, wasn't it? To truly play the part, to cast themselves as dangerous but then, if it backfired, to declare themselves as little more than kids, excited students overstepping the mark. Only Youth and Humour attempting politics.

They met in different bars each night, swathed by secrecy and smoke, huddled round their glasses and their cups like five improbable bullion-robbers, to finalize their tactics, fired up by cigarettes and alcohol. They were as furtive as possible and theatrically well behaved in public. They never spoke about their 'mission' on the phone. They had code words: 'the posse' and 'the prey'. They took no notes. They kept no minutes of their meetings. They had to memorize their allocated roles, their spoken lines, their stage directions. They were the anti-heroes in a film and, like the anti-heroes in a film, they felt adorable. Excitement made them better-looking than they'd ever been before, and better students, actually.

The language student's task, in this unlikely plot, was to 'look absolutely safe' in her disguise (which meant, in her case, no boots and jeans, no hand-rolled cigarettes, no sappho-sappho shirt, but the camouflage of glasses, make-up, and a stage wig) and then to stop the chairman as he passed the rank of recessed external elevators in the narrowest part of the campus concourse on his way to his foundation stone and his brief duty with a trowel. All dignitaries walked that route; it was the only one not begging for repairs, the only one with winter flower beds and murals, and – perfectly, for RoCoCo's purposes – the only one where visitors would have to walk in single file.

Now for the simple sting. The vanity hook. She'd ask Marin Scholia to sign a copy of his 'inspirational' autobiography, *Trade Winds*, with its front jacket photograph of the chairman on the deck of his ostentatious sloop, also called *Trade Winds*. Her line was this: 'Fantastic book, Mr Scholia! Truly fascinating. Can you sign it for me?'

It was easy to disarm such men with unwarranted flattery. If a young woman praises a businessman for his creativity, applauds a writer for his cooking or his sporting skills, congratulates a politician for his sense of humour, or a banker for his figure, then she has immediate command of his attention. It seldom fails. The chairman would be charmed and startled. (None of the reviews had praised his book, after all. They'd judged it dull and self-serving – and overpriced.) The chairman's open hand would flick up by his cheek. He'd wave his fingers until an acolyte produced a fancy pen. And the language student would request a time-stalling dedication to a person with a name not easy to spell. 'For Alicja Lesniak', Freda had suggested. Her private joke. A recent foe.

The two heavy anarchists from Human Biology (also disguised and 'absolutely safe' – they'd even promised to sacrifice their beards and put on the jackets they'd reserved for Graduation Day) would then join the sycophantic queue of book-lovers, holding further copies of *Trade Winds* (which, as a matter of principle, they said, they'd steal not buy from the academic store). When their turn came for signatures, while they fumbled with pages and their pens, their cameras, even, toadying to the chairman with their thanks for his insights and his philanthropy, the linguist would step back to call the service elevator – not already in use, touch wood – and hold open the door.

A simple plan: the posse makes its understated contact with the prey.

Now came the part that nearly always works with startling simplicity in films but where they'd most likely fail, where Lix at least was hoping they would fail. The flattered chairman, concentrating on the frontispiece of his own book, would be a metre from the open elevator. Two steps, two shoulders, two litres of good luck, and he'd be bundled into the metal box by his weighty, grateful readers. Every author's fantasy. His retinue of beefy businessmen and minders might well have time to see they had been tricked and thrust their polished boots between the closing doors. The elevator might not oblige and come when summoned. The chairman might be nimbler than he looked. If he was, if they could not persuade him through the elevator doors, then all RoCoCo had to do was shrug the whole thing off. Exuberance. Misplaced excitement at the man's philanthropy, the prospect of his palace of the arts. An author should expect the rough and tumble of his fans, et cetera. They'd only meant to take the great man for a drink. A student stunt, that's all.

If the doors were quicker than the boots, then Marin Scholia would be safely theirs. There were no basement stairs on that side of the building. So no one could give chase. One floor down, five seconds later, and they'd be in the utility corridor, amongst the heating pipes and generator leads, the cobwebs and the under-powered bulbs, the cleaning trolleys and the laundry rolls, the smell of leakages and paint. *Film noir.*

The kidnappers had timed and measured their escape. A foretaste of the fun they'd have. Rehearsals are more fun than true performances. Forty paces to the right, past storerooms and the boiler-house, the ground-staff's kitchen, would lead them to an exit door. They'd pin a careful statement to the door, signed by their noms de guerre, Lix's adolescent soubriquet of 'Smudge' and once again the name 'Alicja', which outlined their grievances against MeisterCorps but guaranteed safekeeping for the missing millionaire and promised his release, once he'd been 'entertained'. 'You'll have him back in time for dinner,' they'd write, in the hope that this would be enough to dissuade his minders from calling in the police.

Beyond the doorway, in the parking bay, the latest lovers in their hired van would be waiting for delivery.

*

LIX AND FREDA wanted Scholia to themselves, of course, a private accessory to their new affair and its total consummation later on that day. It would not be wise, they argued, she insisted, for their three, and by now (despite the wigs and graduation suits) possibly identified, accomplices to join them in the van for their escape once the chairman was in their hands, no matter how 'absolutely safe' they looked. If the police were summoned and they were quick enough and had the gumption to search vehicles for the city's newly missing guest, then they'd be looking first for two large students and an unassuming, short-haired girl (and one whom they believed, with any luck, was called Alicja).

Freda and Lix, however, were unknown faces so far, and could more safely complete the last leg of the kidnapping on their own, an innocent young couple, not short, not overweight, with nothing odd about their van except − (as you'd expect) the blaring music on their radio-cassette. They'd chosen Weather Report for their escape. A stylish touch, for what kidnapper ever draws attention to himself with raucous, horny jazz? This was during the year of the Melt, remember. In a recent immoderation, meant to make the streets more jubilant, many drivers keen to prove their solidarity played their music loud through open windows. Something for pedestrians. Freedom was Amplification, in those expressive days. Noise could hide a multitude of sins.

They'd blindfold Marin Scholia as soon as they had slammed the van's rear doors and sent their three comrades off by foot, in three directions. They'd tape his mouth if it were necessary. Be practical, they told themselves. A man like that was bound to make a noise if given half a chance. He'd call for help, perhaps, but not be heard. The panels of the van were triple-clad, metal, wood, and fabric lining. Weather Report would drown him out. If he struggled while Lix was driving off, then Freda could cope. She was a tall and healthy woman after all, and Marin Scholia was a man in his late seventies and as weak as a blown egg, by all accounts. He wore a hearing aid. He used a walking-stick. He'd had a minor stroke. His bones would be like breadsticks. Freda could probably knock him over with her earrings.

Within a moment of accepting their delivery, the lovers would be circling the park with its year-long revellers on Navigation Island, driving sensibly once they had crossed the river (by the perfectly named Deliverance Bridge) into the old city, their music slowly muted, just one more unremarkable vehicle in the mid-afternoon rush-hour queues. Then they could proceed on the quieter bankside roads until they reached the little Arts Laboratory on the wharf.

Lix had arranged an exclusive matinee performance for his elderly charge. An outing to the theatre was never wasted time, especially for a man who, two years previously, had bought the Boston Playhouse, demolished it, and built a gaming mall. The four surviving and determined members of the Street Beat Renegades, the agitprop group that had so consumed him during his first terms at the Academy, would be waiting with their stilts, their light and smoke machines, and their accordions, and with a tripod camera, ready to begin the old man's entertainment: *Meister Scholia's Dirty Dollars*, their hurriedly improvised morality play in the medieval style, based on the fable of the Fat Man and the Cat, with Sin and Virtue unambiguously portrayed for their dull-witted audience of one, and dollars denoted by a bowl of cream (and cream represented on the stage by half a litre of white distemper). They'd give him Music, Tumbling, and Dance. Stilt-walking and Puppetry by 'members of the cast'. The script? By Felix Dern himself. Forty minutes (mostly mimed, as Scholia only spoke American). No interval.

Theirs would be an alliance, then, of stage and campus, the intellect and the imagination, politics and pleasure, hope and desire. 'Silence for the comrades, please!' RoCoCo Renegades.

How could the chairman not be charmed? Marin Scholia would not truly be their 'captive', after all, and not their 'prey', but just their involuntary guest and only for the afternoon. Was that unreasonable? They'd turn him loose as soon as it was dark, outside the zoo where city vagrants gathered for their soup each night

– another clever touch, they thought. They'd make him eat some soup. They'd take a photograph for the press and for their own scrapbooks: the animals, the dispossessed, the humbled businessman, the steaming bowls. Then he could get a taxi back to his ostentatious hotel in time for dinner. No damage done – except perhaps the blunting of his appetite for soup, and bruises on his backside from forty minutes on a wooden chair. Otherwise, no harm could come of it.

The RoCoCo Renegades hung on, then, to this colossal self-delusion and the courage it provided them: Marin Scholia would be charmed by them, their nerve, their play, their youth, their sincerity, and he would shrug the matter off as he might shrug off the peccadilloes of his own three sons, none of them (according to the gossip press) exactly beyond reproach. Better he'd had children who engaged in politics, who had their say, than those three party animals with their unfastened ways.

The nine conspirators could imagine him, back home in Boston in a week or two, recounting his experiences on a television chat show: 'These young people taught me something valuable that I might never have realized otherwise. And I am grateful to them for it.' Studio applause.

So Marin Scholia had been transformed in their imaginations, before they'd even laid an eye or hand on him. The more they pictured him, delivered into their brief care, the more they redefined him as a sort of willing guest, an eager volunteer in their debate about the future of their city and the world. At best, they were the sons and daughters he'd never have. They were his natural heirs. At worst, RoCoCo and the Renegades would have provided him with an interesting and an improving interlude that he would want to think about, digest, and not dismiss completely. No worse than that. No need for police or any prosecutions, then. He was endowing an arts complex, after all. And what was this but art? A happening. An offspring of the Melt. They'd make him understand before release, before they delivered him into the back seat of his taxi, that theirs had only been a bit of heartfelt fun. Where would we be without the creeds and dogmas of the young?

'FOUR MORE DAYS until our first anniversary,' Freda reminded Lix, reaching forward from the back of their hired van to rub the side of his best cheek. 'A month! I haven't stayed with anyone this long before. What shall we do to celebrate? What would you like to do?' She beat out the remaining days, with playful toughness and her knuckles, on the bony hump behind his ear. 'One. Two. Three. Four. And then you're in my record book.'

'That can only hurt.'

'I like to hurt you.' She pressed her face against

Lix's and blew into his ear. He'd suffered her lips, her knuckles, and her fingertips that day, bruising indicators – or so he'd found in those four weeks – that Freda was feeling anxious rather than amorous, despite the promise of her words.

For once she liked the way he'd dressed. He'd dressed for the occasion. The linen scarf tied at the throat had been her choice, her first and only gift for him. It made him look a touch more dangerous and jaunty than usual, more like the Czech she'd so often fantasized about, more like the kidnapper he'd prove to be within the hour. An ear of cloth stuck out beneath his chin like the blue touchpaper of a firework, hoping to be lit. If things went well with Scholia, she'd light this lover up herself later, release the chairman at the zoo and then release her lover's linen scarf, release him from his trousers and his shirt, release herself from all the prospects and the tensions of the day, with kiss and punch and stroke.

Freda was captivated by Lix. Her feelings were not insincere, though she'd deny it for the most part of her life. She was not captivated by his looks. Or by his questionable energy. But by his fear and reticence, which she mistook to be the saintly attribute of patriots and revolutionaries like Nyerere, Cezar, and Mandela, a kind of granite sweetness, which showed no malice and no alarm, which never raised its voice without good cause. He had what she would never have, she thought, the Gift of Sympathy.

He loved her, of course, like everybody else, though love like his defied analysis. To contemplate it was to stare into a maze, and volunteer to lose yourself. It was uncharted, inexplicable. He loved her with a perseverance and an abandon that would startle anyone who knows him now. He'd take the maddest risks for her, he could persuade himself, eat glass and fire, walk coals, obey, obey. She was his driving force. This kidnapping would mark the proof and climax of their love.

She tugged his kerchief ears, and said again, 'Come on then, say. What would you like to do, Comrade Felix Dern? To celebrate our thirty-one days?'

He'd like, he thought, to spend the day in bed with her; he'd like, indeed, to put their madcap plan on hold and, instead, clamber right then, at once, into the metal-ribbed and windowless asylum of the van's carcass to seek out something fresh and new with her, one of those many deeds he'd heard about and seen in films and read about in American novels and even simulated on the stage but not yet tried.

What shall we do to celebrate? he asked himself. Let's *soixante-neuf*. Let's see what sex is like for colonizing tongues and lips. Let's snuffle in between each other's legs.

Or bondage possibly. Some blindfolds and a gag, the ones they'd set aside for Marin Scholia, should he prove to be a problem, would be irresistible on Freda. Not that Lix had much appetite for deviations of that kind, and never would, but his four weeks with her had been appallingly frustrating. Sometimes, it seemed, she loved him with her fingernails and teeth but little else. And so his imagination had been running wild. They'd not had any intercourse so far in which he had felt free to give expression to himself. Not proper intercourse. If *proper* is the proper word. Penetration was 'for men', she'd said, and though they'd consummated their relationship in the legal sense, penetration had become either his last and unencouraged port of call, allowed when she'd lost interest anyway, or just a station to the cross of Freda's pleasure, the cross he had to bear. What bodily encounters they had regularly indulged in – mutual masturbation mostly, and oral sex, unreciprocated – served her 'right to orgasm', she said. She'd not be used by any man. For militants like her, 'The front line is the bed.' Lix understood how right she was. He understood and sympathized until those moments when his brains went south and he required and hoped – just once – to be in charge of her.

He'd like to love her standing up, for instance. A memory revisited. Or fuck her on the kitchen floor, for goodness' sake. Uncomplicated sex. No politics. Or make love to her out on the river in a rowing boat when she was wearing something other than black. He'd seen the couples making love in their hired thirty-minute skiffs, in their white summer shirts, lapping at each other in the shadows of the bankside candy trees. He'd like to join the gang. Or him on top, for a change: she'd always straddled him when they'd played almost-sex, when she – climaxed herself – finally permitted him to come into her. She always liked to be the playground bully who had won the fight, her full weight on his shoulders or her hands pressed down against his wrists, inviting penetration but only just allowing it. Submit to me. Defer, defer. Not mainstream cinema at all. Perhaps they'd never truly fornicate in ways he wanted to. Though he could always live in hope. And hope was justified. She'd said she had a treat for him, once Scholia was released. At last, she'd promised it. Something for 'the man'. As soon as they had finished with the chairman, she'd come back with him to his little room, above those once-trod stairs. She'd be his captive for the night, she said.

So Lix had not only rehearsed for *Meister Scholia's Dirty Dollars*, he had also prepared for the Afteract with Freda. He'd cleaned his room, tidied up the scattered, careless clues to the compromiser that he really was. Binoculars, a German magazine, products from companies that he ought to boycott, postcards from his mother, tubs (unused) of naevus-masking cream, pyjamas from his teens. What kind of love affair was this, that he felt safer when he hid himself from her? He'd bought new bedclothes, too. Blue sheets. He'd primed the gramophone with music that he knew she liked. Not Weather Report, with Wayne Shorter crazy on the sax, but Souta's *Chinese Symphony*. He'd purchased decent coffee and a pair of pretty cups. No bread and beans for her. No vagrant's soup. He'd got fresh maizies and fruit preserves, and joss-sticks bunched together in a metal vase. He'd scrubbed his dirty little sink. He'd torn the corner off a pack of contraceptives and slipped them underneath the bed. He wouldn't want to battle with the cellophane, in case his moment passed.

Lix's moment, actually, was perilously close. Their appointment with the chairman was for three fifteen. He'd not be late. By five fifteen, *Meister Scholia's Dirty Dollars* would have been premièred and the charmed and blindfolded captive bundled back into the van. By six, the chairman would be home for tea. Fredalix's madcap afternoon would soon be in the past. Like 1968.

'What are you thinking about, right now?' She broke into his fantasies.

'Umm, 1968. To tell the truth.'

She was startled. 'Me, too,' she said. And then, 'I'm waiting for your answer, anyway.'

'What answer's that?'

'Our little anniversary.'

Six

What could they do to celebrate, then? He had his answers, but he dared not say. He said, 'You choose.' There was no point in voicing his desires, he thought. They were too shoddy and infantile, and dangerously mature to speak out loud. Besides, in twenty-seven days of love, he'd learned that Freda always called the shots.

He'd learned, as well, to his surprise, that in extremis Freda had a timid facet to her character, not that she trembled with alarm when any hazard offered itself – like it was being offered there and then, with Marin Scholia on his way – or would even take a single, compromising sidestep to avoid a conflict or a test. No, her apprehension took a more reactionary form. She turned into a sort of harebrained girl, a teenager, a chatterer. Perhaps this was the vestige of the privileged daughter that she had once been and was frightened of becoming again but needed to hold on to like a child might need its comfort rag. This was how she drove off doubt and fear: with chattering.

Small-talk was Freda's way of steadying herself. She'd learned to smother her worries with blankets of trivia. So now – awaiting their heroic moment in the van – she pressed herself against the back of Lix's driving seat, a hand on his shoulder, and babbled on about their 'anniversary'.

Lix twisted his mouth towards her hand and kissed the sinews of her multi-bangled wrist. He kissed her bruising knuckles, too. The sweetest liberty. She smelt of soap and coat and nicotine. Familiar. As were her favourite black wool skirt, her blonde meringue of pinioned hair, her walking boots with yellow laces, her smoker's throat. Nothing she was saying was typical of the Freda that attracted him. In fact, there'd been no evidence all afternoon – not since they'd collected the van from the hire centre in their false names (Alicja Lesniak again, and Smudge), half hidden behind their high, disguising scarves – of her trademark stridency, her usual impatience at any trace of sentimentality ('Our anniversary', indeed!), her absolute conviction that her views were unassailable. Her voice was hesitant. Her hand was shivering – not from his kissing, surely, and not only from the cold. (It was cold, though. Our city always is in mid-December, that Thursday no exception – and especially throughout that winter of 1981–2, when storms and wind and multinationals came into this neglected and contented city to fill our empty spaces and all our current troubles started.)

No, it was the prospect of their perilous adventures that shook her usual confidence, that dried her throat, that raised her pulse into the nineties in ways that her love for Lix never could, that made her want to urinate as often as a dog. 'We ought to celebrate,' she said. 'We must. What can we do that's big enough?'

Lix was familiar by now with this single vulnerability, the self-inflicted comfort of her prattling. After all, they had been passionate and inseparable comrades in almost a month of politics. He'd stood beside her on the picket lines supporting Sakharov and Bonner, two Russian intellectuals he'd only heard of when she mentioned them but who were on a hunger strike and were worthy of support for reasons he had not dared to ask. She and Lix (on their first date as Fredalix) had joined the unlicensed procession to the Soviet consulate. The closer that the police lines had got with their reverberating shields and their crowd sticks, clearly forgetting for the moment, despite their sideboards, that they were in the middle of the Big Melt, the less Freda had sloganized and the more she'd talked about a holiday she planned in Greece, if only she could bribe a visa for herself. She had not ceded a centimetre to the policemen's sticks. Instead, she'd switched the danger off, relit her thoughts with Adriatic sun and chattering – and, surely, that was valiant. And worthy of support.

He'd wept with her in clouds of tear gas and Mace when police had tried to break up the 'Geneva Solidarity' disarmament march on the Combined Defence Consulates. This time she'd taken blubbing comfort from recalling, word for word, a conversation she'd had that afternoon with her Natural Sciences tutor. It seemed that they had parents from adjacent villages. Lix, the novice at so many things, had been one of the first to flee that demonstration. His eyes, stomach, and lungs had not been trained to cope with nausea, blistering, and pulmonary oedema. So he'd abandoned his first love on a traffic island and had only rejoined her twenty minutes later when he rediscovered her in exactly the same spot, standing almost alone, enveloped in the fog. The gas had dispersed but she had not. She'd taken comfort from 'adjacent villages'.

He'd held her shaking hand when they had paraded by the barracks jail with their lit candles in the midnight vigil for detainees – and conscripts coming off their shifts (for laxity can cut both ways) had dealt out kicks and punches to the men and shouted in the faces of the women: Bitch and cow and whore and bitch again.

Freda was not used to being anything but loved by men. Nor was she used to tolerating raised voices other than her own. She'd treated the loudest and the crudest conscript to one of her dismissive routines. She'd invited him to go home to Mummy and not come back to town until he'd learned to tie his own laces and to button up his own shirt and to zip up his own mouth. He'd responded with some shocking, vulgar menaces. She'd trembled then, a mixture of theatrical distaste for vile and vicious men and some honest, justified distress for herself. Soldiers raped in every corner of the world, and would ever do so, with impunity. Our city was no different. You only had to see the porno magazines that had so recently arrived along with the Laxity. You only had to watch the men in bars. You only had to hear the venom in the conscript's voice. She felt that, finally, she'd become a citizen, she'd said – and let us not forget her age, her admirable naivety – of the Commonwealth of Universal Womanhood, the Femetariat. She was truly horrified for all the sisters in the world, the bitches and the cows and whores, the wives, who soaked the bruises up.

That brutal night of menaces, only two days after their romance had begun, had been the first time Freda and Lix had shared a bed. A significant moment for any lovers: admission to a woman's bed, in those uncomplicated times, was an admission that her privacies were ready to be breached. Sex in the car or on the settee was for irregulars and opportunists. But to share your pillow and your nightie with a man, the body-worn sheets ornamented with your own dead hairs, the linen batiked with your saliva, sweat, skin cream, and make-up, was to offer up a tender invitation to be loved again, again, again.

They had not shared many privacies that night. They'd simply hugged like camping pals, like cousins, in fact, with Freda wanting nothing more than the solaces of touch and only Lix expecting greater things. It was a pity to leave such an opportunity *unused*, he had thought. Well, *unexploited* was a truer word. To share a bed, to share a pillow, even. To be so close to her and yet disarmed. Yet he was wise enough by then (despite so far having only that single – or was it double? – full experience of binocular sex two years previously) to know that a woman who'd been spooked by threats of rape, and had only recently joined the ranks of Universal Womanhood, would not be in the mood for happy-go-lucky sex. He'd had to bide his time, resist the impulses to push his hands beneath her clothes or tug her buttons and her zips. He'd had to treat the cousinly hugging as an opportunity to show his finer love for her, to be diffuse, and not display his physical desires too obviously.

So, Lix had hugged his lover in her rented room as anodynely as he could, as indirectly as he could, his body arched to shield his treacherous tumescence. And he had listened to his Freda handling her fears by chattering about – bizarrely – the American actress Natalie Wood who'd drowned a couple of weeks previously and who, together with the bare-chested Czech and Che Guevara, had been 'a sort of icon' for teenage Freda, the biddable and dutiful family girl she'd once been.

Lix had held her in her wrap of shawls, curled up around her on her bed, until his lover's body had dropped asleep and she'd been free to wake again as certain of herself as ever. And they had masturbated each other for the first time and then shared breakfast on her sunlit, dormitory bed.

*

SO HERE THEY WERE in place, RoCoCo and the
Street Beat Renegades, waiting with their *Trade Winds*
and their flattery, their blindfold and their charm, their
instruments and circus skills, their well-intentioned
thoughtlessness, for Marin Scholia to arrive and lay
his foundation stone. Their day of heartfelt fun had
come. The chairman's limousine would, any minute
now, come curling round the campus service road, past
the Masters' Lawn with its bad statues and its frosted
beds towards the University President's official resi-
dence. There'd be official handshakes and smiling faces
from the reception party, naturally. A $7 million gift
would brighten anybody's face.

At most, it would take ten minutes for the chairman
and his group to reach the elevator doors. A rich old
man never wants to hang about, particularly on days
like this when every breath he'd take would carry a
chill. In fifteen minutes then, or less, the exit door
beyond the service corridor would open on the wind-
torn parking bay, where Fredalix, as tense as athletes
on their blocks attending on the discharge of the pistol
shot, were waiting, and planning their evening out –
such innocence – their anniversary, where they might
dance (for Lix was quite the hero of the discotheque:
the darkness suited him) where they might eat, what
play or film they could investigate to mark their love's
longevity. No talk of making love.

The vehicle was shaking, not as it might seem to

Lix from Freda's shuddering but partly from the wind, which slapped and pressed their van's high sides, and partly from the fast and heavy traffic speeding past their parking spot on the highway ramp behind the campuses. It was a biting afternoon, with gelid blueness, spiteful gusts, and forecasts of snow. Disruptive snow, intent on injury. The City of Balconies did its buttons up.

You might have thought if you had encountered Fredalix for the first time that afternoon that it was Freda who, for once, on this occasion, would prove to be the quitter and that Lix must be the braver of the two. Of course, that was not just. Or likely. For all her trembling, for all her trivia, Freda was fully resolute. They'd go ahead with their barmy plan because she said they would. No turning back. They'd take the risk. They'd face the consequences. Talk of their coming anniversary was only Freda's way of saying, 'We will be free next week. We'll not get caught. We'll not be robbed of our certificates. Our parents will not be informed. In just a couple of days, exactly as we've planned, we will have earned our little place in folklore, campus history. Our hidden faces will be on the front of newspapers.' Her constant naive mantra was (would always be), 'I am in charge.'

Lix, deceiving Lix, deceiving both himself and anyone he met, the master of disguises and of masquerades, despite his outward calm, his steady hand

and voice, his best attempts to remind himself that what they were attempting was not so revolutionary, was intensely apprehensive. Just twenty-two years old, and already he was in the tightening grip of his major flaw, his main regret, his saving grace – timidity.

He should – and could – have kept the company of gentler souls than Freda. Alicja for one. She'd also set her heart on him. Yes, Alicja Lesniak, the unsuspecting and innocent dedicatee of Marin Scholia's *Trade Winds*, the girl who'd be (so Freda hoped) the prime and named suspect of his kidnapping. She was that year's plump but clever president of the student caucus. Indeed, Lix had, a few months previously, against his better judgement, accepted an embarrassing approach from her, an innocent invitation to a film but made while she was touching the back of his hand with a single finger. Only their shoulders had touched in the cinema. On another occasion, she had held Lix by the elbow in the campus bar, on some pretext, and turned her unpretentious face too readily to his.

Alicja was Polish by descent. The Lesniaks were one of our city's richer families, and she was keen to prove her political independence from her inheritance. She was, of course, active that year in Poles Abroad for Solidarity and Lix had last met her when she had spoken three weeks earlier to RoCoCo, seeking its support for her daily vigil outside the Polish Trade Mission.

'The Lesniaks are Ruling Class,' was Freda's view, recognizing Alicja as a rival in more ways than one. 'Never trust the daughters of the Ruling Class! Besides, Wałęsa is a Catholic.' So Lix (because this blonde and slender stem of womanhood was his ideal of womanhood and he wanted to be well regarded only by her) allowed Alicja – his wife-to-be, the mother of his boys – to turn her face away, to take her hand away for almost eight more years.

He'd missed his safest opportunity.

He could have stood in line at Alicja's side, in her dull, responsible campaigns, her fleshy hand in his, sensibly dispersing when the police required them to, retreating from the tear gas and the batons, and not provoking rapist conscripts with her looks. She'd still provide the chattering, this plumper girl, but save him from the danger and the fear, preserve the little courage that remained in him – for Lix had realized when he was just a teenager this shaming fact, that courage was a finite commodity, as nonrenewable as fuel, and that he had almost exhausted his own supply. Since he'd been sixteen, seventeen, he'd sensed the timid years ahead. He'd hoped a woman like Alicja was waiting for him in the shadows, with promises of uneventful days.

Instead, Lix had stood in line with Freda and scared himself to death. However, he already had the knack – how else would she be fooled by him? – of dropping all his fear into his toes. An actor's phrase. An actor's knack. A breathing exercise. Control the lungs, control the dread, and then step out into the lights to seem unflappable before an audience. Technique and practice.

So you could – as Freda had – mistake this young man with the birthmarked face for the most resolute of activists. As calm and stubborn as a rock. You could expect great things of him. She felt it now, behind him in the hired van. He'd hardly moved when she had rapped him so firmly on the bone behind his ear. He was so still and unperturbed, his hands clasped neatly in his lap, his breathing soft and regular, his comments cool and rational while she, she knew, was talking like a fool. She thought – and this was genuine – that she and he would be comrades for eternity if only she could stay as unwavering and dispassionate as him. He'd be a useful foil for her loud ways.

She kissed her fingertips – that resurrected little girl again, that Natalie! – and touched the bone behind his ear. A damp caress and an apology.

'You OK?' she asked, feeling more physically excited as the minutes ticked away.

She felt him smile and nod.

'I'm fine,' he said, though had he the choice, he would gladly start the engine of the van and drive away from what they had arranged to do. Lix only had himself to blame. Again. After all, it was his plan, his entertainment, that would go so oddly wrong that afternoon. Three prospects frightened him: the kidnapping, the Street Beat premiere, the lovemaking. He'd need to navigate the city streets for her, then be an impresario, then steer their risky course to bed. He would have to be uncharacteristically calm and strong.

Marin Scholia's limousine had surely reached the campus gates by now. Lix concentrated on settling his nerves by breathing only through his nose and focusing on the woman in his driving mirror, the shrunk and silvered planes and facets of her shaded and reflected face. He was mesmerized by her but almost queasy with misgivings at the certain prospect of the ardour and the kissing that was promised him. He practised breathing, his feet braced against the floor of the van. He bedded Weather Report into the radio-cassette. He checked the ignition on the van – this must not turn into a farce. The engine turned and purred at once. The petrol tank was full.

'Not long now,' Freda said. Again she leaned forward, reached across his shoulder to stroke the side of his cheek. Not long for what? Not long before they'd trade the chairman for an orgasm?

THEY COULD HAVE WAITED there for three more months before the chairman showed his face. His foundation stone was finally laid in the March of 1982, when the Laxity had ended, the city streets were calmer and predictable, and once again we truly had good cause to demonstrate if only we could demonstrate. But Marin Scholia never crossed the river to the campuses that December afternoon. He did his duty at MeisterCorps's new central offices then flew out, in his own jet, ahead of any snow, to Rome.

Lix and Freda concentrated on the exit door for forty minutes. It owed its only movement to the wind. Of course, they feared the worst: kidnappers arrested and a bungled afternoon, their comrades spilling all the beans, their futures ruined by their foolishness.

Finally, more than an hour after their appointment and not a sign of Marin Scholia, Freda got out of the van, fiercely angry with herself and everyone, and walked around the campus blocks to hunt for their three accomplices and to check if anything was happening. It was. The Poles.

Alicja Lesniak – so much to answer for – had wrecked RoCoCo's plans. That very morning in Gdańsk, troops had opened fire on demonstrating workers. Seven dead. At General Jaruzelski's hands. The news had reached the small clutch of demonstrators, plump Alicja included, who gathered every afternoon outside the Polish Trade Mission opposite the campus gate to protest against their country's martial law. And some mad Pole, who'd never been to Poland once, as it turned out, had fired a hunting gun and chipped the paintwork on the Mission's door. The streets around the Mission were closed at once. Armed police moved in, with snipers, horses, and armoured vans. The Pole was shot in the leg, then bitten by a police dog. Military bullets chipped a lot more paint and shattered windows in the Mission as police 'secured' its safety for the afternoon. Anyone who looked remotely Polish was rounded up, including the building's employees and the Head of Mission himself. Alicja Lesniak was shoved into a cell and kept there until midnight when her father phoned his 'good friend' in the Ministry and she was chauffeur-driven home in snow.

The two shaven anarchists and the tidy lesbian, bizarrely dressed and late for their appointment anyway, were trapped behind the barriers, two hundred metres from their Scholia ambush site. What could they do (but thank their lucky stars)? And Meister-Corps (which had considerable shipbuilding interests in Gdańsk) had been advised to keep their chairman safely in the quiet parts of the town. The campuses were undisturbed.

'That fat-wit idiot,' Freda said, as she and Lix drove off in their hired van in the last light of the day. She held Alicja Lesniak, her bourgeois rival for Lix's heart, entirely responsible for the failings of the afternoon. She meant to, had to, settle scores immediately, revenge herself both on the woman and the farce. She wanted 1968.

*

FREDA AND LIX should, of course, have gone first to the Arts Laboratory on the wharf where their four edgy and – by now – baffled actor comrades would be killing time waiting for their audience and for the curtain to go up. Lix, unquestionably, should at least have phoned them. He was almost a professional actor himself and a tense one. He must have discovered in his two-plus years of training how intolerable first-night nerves could be, even when the expected audience was only one old man, dragooned and obedient. He must have recognized how jittery they would be feeling, not fearing critics exactly but more the unpredictable attentions of the police, especially when they would have heard the sirens from across the river and the thrumming whirr of helicopters, and finally the crack of gunfire.

Yet by the time he and Freda had traversed Navigation Island, in brewing silence, and crossed Deliverance Bridge into the old part of the city, they were focused only on themselves, their personal distress, their unreadiness for admitting yet to anyone – even to each other, indeed – that they had made themselves a laughing-stock. They could not, would not, show themselves to Street Beat Renegades without the chairman in tow. It would be humiliating, for Freda because she would dread acknowledging so farcical a failure, and for Lix because he would not want to expose his immense relief. They'd let their comrades simmer for a while.

Besides, who could guarantee that one of the other three farceurs from RoCoCo had not already made the call or even dropped in at the Arts Lab with their narration of events that afternoon, how seven dead Poles had robbed the chairman of the Fat Man and the Cat, how one plump girl had ruined everything. So Freda and Lix felt if not exactly *free* then at least *excused* to turn their backs on the blemished afternoon and indulge the moment and the still unblemished prospects for the night.

The chairman had eluded them, but all their other plans and passions were in place. They needed shriving, urgently, spreadeagled like two crosses on the bed, to rid themselves with body sins of all the punctured virtues of their politics. Their blood was up. There were more urgent things to do than hunt a telephone. More urgent than the minor needs of friends.

They hardly spoke, of course. The vibration of the van, the parabolic headlights of the passing cars, the blare of people going home, the very first snowflakes provided all the commentary and all the stimulation they required. Everything's symphonic and arousing when the object of your journey is a body and a bed. Sometimes in matters of the heart words are not required. Are ill-advised, in fact. A misjudged word deflates. She'd only had to say, 'Take me somewhere,' and push her fingers underneath his linen kerchief and touch his earlobe once for Lix to be in no doubt what was required of him. These were the clearest stage directions he could hope for.

So let the acting comrades wait. The lovers had to hurry first to Lix's rooms – and then, when they were finished with each other, they could perhaps drive down to the theatre with their disappointing news but fortified and rescued from humiliation by their love-making.

Not telling their comrades sooner about the shambles on the campuses, having them waiting with their stilts and their accordions, was part of the excitement. For Freda anyway. It made her irresponsible and negligent when her more public attempts at being irresponsible had so recently been aborted 'by that idiotic Pole'. She liked to keep men waiting and men guessing, anyway. She liked to see their lungs dilate, their nostrils flare, their vocabularies shrink just because she'd passed extremely close to them. It showed their weakness and her strength. How mystified and paralysed they seemed to be by her. Perhaps that's why she'd chosen harmless Lix in the first place, because her choice would mystify the waiting men, the self-satisfied, better-looking ones who'd done their best for the past seven terms to sleep with her – and failed.

By choosing slightly blemished Lix she had confounded all the rules. She was declaring what she truly felt about the mass confusion that seemed to value looks above the hidden virtues. Of course, she'd been a victim but also, she knew, a beneficiary of the confusion. Still, it was satisfying to think that when she'd make love to Lix that afternoon, she'd not be making love to all the other suitors in her life, the other handsomer men whom she'd imagined making love to her, whom she'd rebuffed in dreams. She'd wanted them, but they'd been turned away. The corridor was crowded with these men. Only she and unexpected Lix were in the room. Not making love to many men was what made making love to one so flavoursome.

By the time they had finally found a place to park their empty, unproductive van and walked – not even holding hands – the half a kilometre against the homeward-rushing crowd and chilly winds through narrowing streets and climbed the stairs to Lix's rented room, Freda had already formed a plan for their lovemaking. Her nerves were shot by all the waiting in the parking bay behind the campuses but not so shot that the sexual subtext that had always underscored their plans to kidnap Marin Scholia had been wiped out. Embracing tension as she did in politics was her pathway to arousal. To be so purposeful and incorruptible on the picket line or in the ruck of demonstrators or up against the chests and chins of police was to dance the tango of pressure and release.

By now – they'd reached the shabby, postered door to Lix's room – it seemed as if the kidnapping was history, successful history, airbrushed, rewritten, and perfected. They'd caught-released the chairman, nudged the tiller of the world, and now could celebrate amongst and with themselves. Their fear and bravery had only been a prelude, an act of preparation, for the sex. Passion of the soul, and passion of the genitals.

Therefore, a frigid woman ('fat-witted' Alicja Lesniak) could never make a true and unbowed revolutionary, in Freda's view, any more than a timid leafleteer ('that idiotic Pole' again) could prove to be convincing in the sack. You had to feel it big to give it big, in other words.

So then, she had decided, by the time her Lix's shaking hand had got the key into the lock, that their lovemaking would be a little reassuring drama of a sort, two comrades pumping courage into each other once they had pumped some courage into the world. Her usual mantra, then? 'I am in charge.' She knew exactly what she wanted from her comrade on the far side of the door. He must not change his clothes, undress, when they got into the room, for a start. He must not take his kerchief off. She'd break his fingers if he tried to loosen it. The jaunty knot was part of what she wanted from the man. Nor must he slip into some open-throated bourgeois sentimentality, dutifully whispering sweet platitudes, proclaiming love instead of solidarity. She wanted camaraderie of spirit, not romance of the soul. Romance was for life. Romance was too soft and feeble to truly satisfy. She wanted the drama of the streets relocated in between the sheets. They'd be two partisans and they'd be making love between the detonation and the bomb. It didn't matter what he wanted out of her. She was in charge. This was her needy afternoon.

His room was tidier than she remembered it, a disappointment of a sort. The sort of tidiness to mark a mother's visit or an inspection by the concierge. The bed was made up like a dormitory bed. Lix tried to put the light on, but Freda held his hand. 'We have to hurry up,' she said. 'Come on.' She fantasized the clatter of militia boots, fast running up the stairs. 'I want you now.' The *you* was not quite Lix and not quite nobody. The Czech was trapped between her legs, wild-haired and beautiful. She straddled him, and pushed his shoulders back onto the bed and pushed his shirt up onto his shoulders, and kissed the bare and perfect rack of ribs, her lips as urgent as a Russian gun.

She was too fast for him. He held her head and tried to kiss her on the lips. She turned away. Too intimate. It was not intimacy that she required. The opposite. She wanted urgency and alienation, the meeting of two strangers united only by a single cause. For once his instant penetration was required, allowed, demanded. She put her hand between his legs and felt through the cloth for that part of him that could convey the whole of him. 'No kissing, Comrade Lix. It's counter-revolutionary.' A joke of sorts, of

course, but one intended to inform her lover what her
desires truly were.

He was quick to understand. He was an actor, after
all, well versed and trained in improvisation and pick-
ing up on what a partner hinted at with her ad-libs.
He said, '*The Rebel and the Mutineer*,' the title of a film
he'd long admired. 'Too insubordinate to kiss.'

He tried to pull her coat off her arms but she shoved
back his hands. 'Today,' she said, 'the woman is in
charge.'

Again, he let her be in charge.

WHERE HAD IT all gone wrong, this briefest love
affair? It had gone wrong that afternoon. He knew that
much. Marin Scholia flew with it to Rome. General
Jaruzelski gunned it down. It couldn't last beyond
that afternoon. It was as if that afternoon had been the
only destination for their love. Thereafter, they were in
decline.

Lix often spooled it through his memory, that hour
in that little room. He could not identify the point
of separation. Or specify his guilt. He'd let her be in
charge, despite his fantasies. He'd let her hurry him.
He had not tried to hurry *her* – for he well knew that
Freda was a young woman who dismissed that under-
pinning law of physics, that an action of any energy or
force should only result in a reaction of equal energy
or force. Anything mildly unwelcome, the breeziest of

pressures, she would greet with the fury of the seven spinster winds. So, certainly, she would not tolerate an overzealous lover, too keen to dominate her on a bed, too eager to have his way. She'd called the shots, the modern woman making up for all quiescent females in the past. There'd been benefits in that for him, of course. Uncomplicated penetration for a start, though under her and not on top. She'd been audacious and abandoned because the politics and history said she could.

In fact he had been glad, aroused, that she had pushed him back and held his wrists. Like that, he was too trapped and too engrossed by her urgent passion to make his own mistakes. As she hovered over him, directing him – how would he ever come with her on top demanding that he come? – he had not seen much evidence of romantic love in Freda, or in her sudden interest in his ribs, his kerchief and his shirt. She hadn't spoken his name. Or even looked him in the eye. Yet her passion was all too evidently real. Passion's something that truly can't be faked, not even on the stage or in the films. An actor never quite captures the randomness, the disarray. So there can be nothing more honest and reassuring – in the short term – than a partner's lust. These are the moments in your life that are sincere. You mean it, absolutely mean it, until the moment's absolutely gone.

Lix absolutely meant it, too. Some cultures claim

that, when lovemaking has reached perfection, the earth has moved, or that the yolk has separated from the albumen, or that the clocks have chimed in unison, or that the lovers' bodies have dissolved. Here we say, 'The Bed Grew Roots.' The bed grew roots that afternoon for Lix.

The universe was suddenly minute: its all-consuming detail pressed against his face, snagged at his toes, the linen and her skin almost impossible to tell apart. If anything or anybody but this long-necked girl, her breasts and earrings swinging like a hypnotizer's watch, had crossed his mind that snowy evening, then it was only briefly and diffusely. A car horn from the street below, perhaps. The tock of high heels on the wooden stairs, as someone else came home. The clink of cups and bottles from the street bar below. And possibly, but only for an instant, the ageing memory of that little information clerk, their bruising minutes at the kitchen windowsill – and then her tears illuminated by the cruel and sudden timer lights as she, that troubled stranger, fled. And now, the rattle of his bedroom window frames as what was forecast – wind and snow – announced itself across the city in gusts of frozen air.

WE LEAVE THEM lying on his bed, intimately awake, relieved from their desires, engaging with the calm that only sated fervour can provide, and looking forward to some time alone. Not quite tranquillity, but self-possession. The farce of MeisterCorps had ended without too much embarrassment, without too many tears or bruises. They could forget it easily or portray their happy failure as something heroic. Nobody from RoCoCo had been shot or dragged away. Nobody had been compromised. They were the victims only of bad luck and bad timing. Finally, though, they'd got it right: exactly as they'd hoped and planned, Lix and Freda had honed and blunted all the sexual edges of their day. Now was the time to disengage. Withdraw.

Let's not forget, though, that this bed in Cargo Street was cursed. This narrow student's cot with its new sheets and its cheap coverlet had played its ancient trick on Fredalix. The roots that it had grown were tougher, deeper than they'd bargained for. Some mischievous coincidence had made this little room high above the wharfside district dangerously fertile, an efficacious city version of the Vacuum Cave in fairytales where couples spent the night to guarantee a pregnancy (and risk pneumonia). Lix had already produced a child in it, a girl – and now that he'd been mad enough to take a second woman there, another child had been implied, a son, a George, an heir.

The explanation is mundane. The contraceptive Lix had readied and slipped beneath the bed had let the lovers down and either Lix had spilled his semen, or Lix had pulled on the sheath too late. Or their lovemaking might have dragged the contraceptive loose, shortened it and buckled it, like ankled popsocks, cold and corrugated on his shrinking penis end. Or they had stayed with it just half in place for far too long after he'd ejaculated, allowing his emissions to leak and seep and fertilize.

So Lix and Freda might *imagine* that their day of lunacy and passion had let them off scot-free, no police, no blame, no aftermath. Except? Except that Freda had become some moments earlier the unexpecting mother of his child. It was a pregnant woman now who slumped down on Lix's chest and concentrated only on the pumping of the once-loved lover's lungs. It was a pregnant woman, too, who hugged the actor to her chest and whispered that she had to wash and dress, who peeled herself away from him, separating their adhering clothes, despite the vents and furrows of their skin clinging on with semen glues and sweat. It was a woman quick with child who was already imagining the pulling over of the sheets, her journey home, the getting on with life and no regrets. It was a mother who pulled aside the window blind in Lix's room and looked down on the office workers, overworked, as they made muffled progress to their trams and took on the trembling rearrangements of the weather-laden wind, the scrim of falling snow, which seemed to make our city both lighter and darker at once.

Cargo Street was full as ever at that time of the evening on a weekday, but more tentative than usual.

The fallen and impacted snow had made the pavements treacherous. So everyone was concentrating on their balance, their collars up, and either heading home where it was safe or making for a bar or restaurant where it was dry and welcoming and full of other weather refugees. Nobody was aware of Freda watching them, four storeys up above their heads and hats.

This was a night of pregnancies, and not just Freda's pregnancy. The snow is sexier than sun. The cold encourages us to get to bed and hug the person we love. Our folklore says it's so. As does demography. The snow is consummate. Fine weather brings the birth rate down. So this was only one of many rooms that benefited from fertility that night, and Fredalix was only one of many pairs. None of them as yet was counting on the cost, the cost of lovemaking, the cost that lasts for three score years and ten. Nobody thought, when all the hugs and kisses had been finished with, to tell themselves, *Things never end. They only stretch ahead from here.* We have to thank our lucky stars for that.

3

A HIGH APARTMENT with a river view would be ideal, they'd thought. Three or four rooms facing east, with a small balcony in the City of Balconies where they could taste the air. The water and the sunset seemed important then. So did remaining close to the city's ancient, motivating heart, near neighbours to the bustle and the stir, of course, but also close to graduated couples like themselves who'd once been untroubled students and were now more compromised. Couples, that's to say, who wanted permanence but were not prepared quite yet to celebrate that fact. They were still young, but not so immature as to imagine as they'd once done that marriages could prosper in cramped, cheap rooms. They required somewhere they could stay until they were ready not for children but for a single child. Five more years, perhaps. Somewhere big enough and bright enough for privacy and rows and lovemaking.

Alicja and Lix had not been made of gold when they'd moved in together. His meagre, irregular fees from the stage and, more frequently, from busking in the local restaurants, and her low wages as a consultant-volunteer on the night shift at the Citizens' Commission were not enough to rent a river view.

Their income wasn't quite enough, even, to pay the rent on the more modest, unbalconied apartment they'd finally settled for, their two ill-kept low-ceilinged attic rooms in Anchorage Street, a busy neighbourhood – too much bustle, too much stir – nine blocks from the grander embankment residences that they'd aspired to. It was hardly larger, though more expensive, than Lix's old fourth-floor student room-'n'-kitchen near the wharf. They fell in love with it as soon as they pushed back the sloping door in the bedroom alcove and found that they could step out on the roof. Still no river view. But somewhere to smoke and drink a beer, their urban version of the rural stoop. Somewhere to grow their herbs and vegetables in pots. Somewhere to be expansive and look out across the city, through the pylons and the tower blocks, the aerials and radio masts, beyond the leaf-fresh suburbs and the new commercial parks, across the plains towards the faint, uncivil hills.

This 'private roof patio' was the landlord's justification for the scarcely manageable rent. They'd had to borrow from the bank and make do at first with thinly furnished rooms. They had a bed, an electric stove, two bamboo chairs, a pair of bicycles, a fly larder, and little else to make the first months of their marriage comfortable, except their books, their gramophone, and what Paul Knessen has called 'the conciliating rigours of the flesh'. Well, they had love, of course, the most essential furnishing of all, especially when poverty and hardship share the home. It was a calmer and less threatening love than Lix had had for Freda but a thorough love, nevertheless, and one that would not soon be ripped apart by passion.

They could have had a river view quite easily and a fully furnished apartment on the embankment. The Lesniaks were made of gold. Alicja's parents, despite their mistrust of Lix ('Actors never pay – and actors never stay!'), would have cleared the rent and swallowed all the decorating bills, rather than have their daughter share a staircase with waiters and shop assistants in a street unfashionably 'mixed'. They had a friend who ran an import/export enterprise and who, if leaned on not too gently, could sort out some stylish furniture. ('And no bamboo!') A new business colleague, eager to impress, might well be happy to provide a television and a fridge. 'You want a telephone and no delays with the connection?' her father asked. 'For me a working telephone is just a call away. I only have to whisper in a friendly ear. I only have to say our name.'

The Lesniaks would pay to have Lix's cheek 'spruced up' as well. A fashionable surgeon was in their debt. How could their son-in-law expect to succeed on the stage when he was branded like that? Besides, a birthmark such as Lix's spelled trouble and adversity for anyone who came too close. A Polish prejudice, perhaps, but never wrong. It seemed a pity that their pretty daughter had ended up with such a curiosity. Every problem could be fixed, however. Mrs Lesniak would make the phone calls; Mr Lesniak would write the cheques. Alicja only had to nod and she could have an apartment and a husband, neither of which would offer much offence to the eye. The Polish parents are the best.

Alicja, despite her husband's counsel of caution, turned down every coin. 'I like things as they are,' she said. She meant she loved the man she'd married, would not want to change a cell of him. More than that, she wanted freedom from the Lesniaks, a chance to flourish as herself and be resolute on her own account. Finding a husband such as Lix would set her on her way. Her married name, Alicja Dern, provided instant anonymity. Anonymity was exactly the base upon which she was determined to construct her successes and achievements – for this was something hidden from the world: buried underneath her sweetness, her patience and her eagerness to please, Alicja was driven by a need to climb and conquer a different, higher summit than her father.

Lix's ambitions, however, were not concealed. How could they be concealed? To be an actor, even one who's not in work, is to declare a public dream and purpose. But he had not yet got his call from Hollywood. He'd not recorded his first album. He'd not been cast as Don Juan or hosted any television shows. In his late twenties now, he'd ended up a table singer, as dependent on tips as any waiter, and – no more the Renegade – a minor, disappointed stalwart of touring theatres and the city's lesser ones, famous only in his dressing room. So Mrs Dern could still be judged mostly by her own achievements and campaigns and by the impacts that she'd make on platforms of her own. She took up causes in the neighbourhood, chased complaints, investigated failures of the city government, but never made a nuisance of herself. His sweet, plump, tireless wife, Lix said unkindly to her face, when they'd been stopped once too often in the street by troubled locals, was 'a problem magnet'. She'd be upset to know his nickname for her was the Quandary Queen. Yet she was more respected and well liked than any Lesniak had ever been. That was more important than a sunset and a river view – and harder to acquire than foreign furniture.

Now only three months later, finally, they had a river view without the help of Lesniaks.

On the same day that they gained their river view, they conceived their son, as well. Five years ahead of time. Much sooner than they'd planned or wanted. We can be sure it was Alicja's first child. She was a virgin when she first met Lix, a lapsed but well-trained Polish

Catholic, fearful of the wrath not so much of God as of her all-seeing, all-knowing, and all-powerful mother. It was true that Alicja had 'sacrificed herself' to Lix, 'surrendered herself, immodestly' while the family was 'dining' (her mother's later version of events) before they'd married. But only a month before. She was hardly dissolute or precocious. Despite her hidden appetite for change, she would not consider sleeping with anyone apart from the man she married for three more years at least.

Lix was not a virgin, as we know. Already he'd had sex, penetrative sex, with Freda (even if the penetration had only been a short PS on all but one occasion). Nineteen times, in their not-quite-a-month of passion, on and off the picket line. And twice with the nameless little clerk, who back then would have been about the age Lix was now, approaching thirty.

This would not be his first child, or even his first son. It would be the timid actor's third mistake. His first – his birthmarked daughter, Bel, the product of binoculars – was undiscovered still, undiscovered by Lix anyway, though very nearly nine years old already and full of life while Lix's life, to tell the truth, was emptying. The vessel full of dreams and plans had sprung a leak – no wad of fame to plug it.

Several times the girl had been within a hundred metres of her father. This city isn't all that large. You meet and pass and meet again. They'd shared a crowd, a tram, a shopping street, a flu virus, they'd strolled the same catalpa avenue in Navigation Park one Sunday afternoon, bought nutcake from the same vendor. And recently, when she'd been in the Play Zone by the zoo, her mother had seen Lix walking past, beyond the roses. Unmistakable. Not a face she could forget. If it hadn't been for the round-faced woman on his arm, she would have found the courage to go up – for Bel, her daughter's sake: a blemished child has a right to meet the author of her blemishes – and introduce the pair of them, acquaint their family naevuses.

His second grand mistake – Freda's six-year-old son, George – was still an awkward and rancid secret that Lix had kept from Alicja. What was the point in telling her? He never saw the child himself, had not even been identified as its father by anyone other than its mother. Alicja had hated Freda, anyway, and Freda despised her, 'Lix's dreary compromise'. A little clear-skinned boy, especially if he had his mother's neck and hair, would not appeal to his wife, nor would it delight any of the Lesniaks. So Lix was happy to keep his past secret and resigned to being not so much an absentee parent as an evicted one. It had been Freda actually, when she was six months pregnant and her relationship with Lix long dead, who'd commanded him to stay away: 'The child is mine, not yours. My pregnancy. My body. My responsibility. My private life. My kid!' she'd said, rapping out her arguments on the palm of her hand with knuckles that had once shown love for him. 'You understand?'

'Five very eloquent *my*s,' he'd said, as mordantly as he dared. Her throat and earrings tortured him. This had been the dream once – to be with Freda and his son, a sort of neo-family. 'Consider me as good as dead.'

And that had been it – at least for the time being. Fredalix split in two. Then three. They went their separate ways. She had – and raised – his unacknowledged son.

COULD LIX have any idea yet that there was a curse on him, a more insistent version of the happy curse that falls on almost everyone, that if they persevere with sex, then chances are – not quite as sure as eggs is eggs, but close – a pregnancy will follow? Certainly that one mistake he knew about had freighted all his fantasies and practices of sex with Cargo Consequence. Had he become afraid of making love because of Freda and her son? Before Alicja, he'd not had intercourse with anyone since he and Freda had split up in 1981. That was seven years. Key years for young men in their twenties. His month with her had been a costly farce and a disaster from which he'd not recovered yet. How pleased Freda would be if she discovered how she'd blighted him and all the women in her wake, even – especially – Alicja.

Six

Certainly, Lix had been slow on the night a month before they'd married to respond to Alicja's unLesniak initiatives. She'd never been that intimate before or so daring. She'd seemed excited that her parents were downstairs with dinner guests and hired staff, immediately below, separated only by a rug, the ceiling joists and plaster. The wine they'd smuggled into her room had helped. As had the cannabis. She locked her bedroom door and put on music as a soundtrack and to disguise the noise they might make. The actors always made a lot of noise in films.

He'd not encouraged her. Because he understood the dangers better than she did? Because he feared the consequences? Because she was not Freda? Because there wasn't a single condom in the house? No, actually, because he had not yet succeeded with an erection. Nervousness was playing havoc with his potency. Fear despatches its adrenaline to the lungs, the muscles, and the heart, and undermines the blood flow to the genitals.

Alicja, however, had thought his reluctance considerate and endearing but had surprised herself by pressing forward with inflamed resolve and – always the ones you remember – inexperienced but persuasive hands. Finally, Alicja was 'graduated', as they say. She and Lix had made the light shade swing above her parents' table. She liked to think she'd peppered everybody's soup with ceiling plaster. But Lix's imagination had almost let him down that night, and let her down as well. His fear of those five mys was not an aphrodisiac.

THIS WAS THE season of his third mistake.

Although their marriage was already three months old, he and Alicja still had no table, or any reason to join the city's morning rush-hour. Lix had no rehearsals at that time, and it would be another year before his fortunes changed so magically, and so disruptively. So neither of them needed to leave the apartment until the afternoon.

In those days, their marriage was an embarrassment of time and poverty and self. In other words, if it was free or very cheap, then they could do it all day long. So they would take their breakfast and their books out onto the roof during that late spring and sunbathe with their backs against the slates in their nightclothes, the matching pair of long fake-grandad shirts she'd bought from Parafanalia and which he hated. These were beloved times, in fact, despite the shirts. They had the whole apartment building to themselves. By the time they'd settled on the roof, all their neighbours were already sitting at their desks or standing at their tills or setting tables for lunch, 'earning corns'.

Alicja had planted up some heavy grey pots – to match the roof tiles – with mints, marjorams and balms, and four or five fessandra shrubs. They flourished there, with the help of coffee dregs, abandoned cereals, and bowls of used, soapy water, and – once in a while, when Lix was on his own and too idle to go indoors – urine. Otherwise, they had the sweetest-smelling roof in town. The foliage provided a civilizing fringe of green along the roof parapet, muffling much of the traffic thrum from the Circular but still allowing Lix with his binoculars – the householder at last, the lord of everything in sight – to study the hats and shoulders of passers-by, the roofs of trams and cars, the shadows and the silhouettes in adjacent attic rooms, the ornamented summit of Marin's Finger, and anything that moved between the city and the hills.

Except he could not see the hills in early May.

Rain had fallen on the prosperous and slanting plains that embraced the city in a semicircle of shale-on-clay-on-sand and the grand estates of manacs, vines, and tournesols, which kept the owners rich and their tenants busy. Rain had fallen in the far-flung hills and stripped the valleys of their oaten topsoils and their undergrowth. The fields were silver and the rivers bronze. Nine days of it. Rain had fallen every-where it seemed, except on us. We had blue skies. The whole of May was mocking blue for us, disdainful of the countryside. The city's blessed, we told ourselves, in shirtsleeves, eating out in pavement bars, getting tanned, getting over-confident. We have the nation's summer to ourselves.

So the hills were virtually invisible to Lix and to Alicja, from their high and costly patio. A heavy mass of slaty clouds had gathered discreetly in the first few days of the month like a sieging army, patient and bullying, softening the countryside with rain, but still just far enough away from the outer suburbs not to appear too menacing. No wind. The clouds just seemed to darken, breed amongst themselves and fatten on the washed-loose produce of the plains, reluctant to depart, unwilling to invade the determined patch of urban blue that kept our weather fine and caused the Dern rooftop to snap and crack unseasonably with heat. Their true horizon had been smudged away by clouds, and so even in the rain-free city, untouched it seemed at first, the days were shorter than they should have been. The dawns were late and dusk was early. A sweating wintertime in May. The rising and the setting sun, to use the finest phrase of a newspaper columnist, was 'smothered by a black-brown shawl and swathed in widow's cloth'. Wet wool!

These were dramatic days for Lix and for Alicja. The weather made them feel grandiloquently loving. The fitful romance and the ecstasy of early married life can only benefit from breakfasting amongst the rooftop pots under such sensual, operatic skies. By chance, they'd rented happiness. Their mid-morning light was startling that May, low and sharp enough to give the clouds – especially in the photographs they took – their own ravines and cols and peaks and scarps that seemed as permanent and sculpted as the granite ones which they'd obscured. These were clouds you could trek in, ski down, climb. You'd think that you could mine in them for tin and silver, sink great shafts through fissures, plates and strata to haul up spoils of solid oxygen and fossil rain.

The clouds were full of riches and rewards.

Lix and Alicja watched an aircraft fly too close to that great granite cliff of wet suspended atmosphere. They watched it disappear, illogically intact. They watched through his binoculars the flocks of geese and plovers, displaced by rain, the jazz quintets of buzzards extemporizing on the thermals against the backdrop, blackdrop of the clouds, the labouring of herons, and, closer, with the naked eye, they watched the resigned and stoic flight of crows, forced into town for once. They were puffed up themselves like clouds, puffed up with massive confidence, with everything-is-possible, with an affection that Lix at least had never felt before. The weather was a prelude, so they thought with all the arrogance of newly weds, to something grand and memorable for them.

Lix was mightily relieved to find that three months after their hasty and impulsive marriage – no church, no Lesniaks, no honeymoon, just three good friends as witnesses, a short state ceremony, two shaky signatures, and a bottle of Spacchi – he was growing more attracted to his wife. More sexually attracted, that is, less fearful of the lovemaking. He'd always liked then loved her gentleness, of course, her quiet efficiency, her many skills, her pluckiness, her company. His fixed vision of happiness had encompassed her. Her mood was not tempestuous. She was not cruel. But he had doubted in those early days whether he was truly passionate for her. He'd found with Freda, all those years before – and barely for a month, it's true! – that they'd possessed a kind of private ideology, beyond the politics, a set of common condescending principles and prejudices, a shared vocabulary of phrases and signs that they regarded as superior to anybody else's. Oh, pity everybody else; those diminished, longing looks when he and she walked past, those dull and compromising lives. Not so with Alicja. She did not make Lix feel superior. She might love him more than Freda ever had, if such a thing were measurable, but somehow, so far, all her love seemed lesser than the passion he had felt in 1981.

It worried him at first, of course. Love minus true sexual desire is little more than friendship, he had thought. It's a lager without gas. Preferable in a marriage to true desire without the friendship, of course – a marriage such as that could not survive the honeymoon. But it was still not total love, still not quite the brimming litre. He understood only too well whose fault it was. He dared not say this even to himself –

but his new wife was not his type. Not the type he'd dreamed of sleeping with, still dreamed of sleeping with. In those days he liked a woman who was tall, bony, small-breasted, unconventional, and slightly and capriciously cruel. A woman just like Freda, actually. Alicja was none of these things. That made her good and chastely lovable, of course. But not desirable. Not arousing. He did not feel a hero in her company. Her qualities, he sometimes felt, especially her homeliness, her cosiness, her patience, were sexual liabilities. They blunted his desire. She was not the actress he would cast to play his wife in his stage fantasies. That part belonged elsewhere.

She'd surprised him, though. She might not turn as many heads as Freda on the street. She dressed too casually and too timidly, neither elegant nor Bohemian, neither striking nor mysterious, and wary of adornments such as jewellery or hats. Her underclothes were functional. She wore amusing T-shirts – perhaps the only way in summer that she could draw attention to her breasts. Lix was not amused. An entertaining T-shirt was not a flattering accessory, in his precise opinion. Also, she was too plump and healthy to be anything other than agreeable to the eye.

But naked she was beautiful. Plump's only plump in clothes. Released from her unexceptional garments, her serviceable shoes, her sensible pants, Alicja was curved and silky and irresistible. Solid, comely, yes –

but not unpleasingly overweight, at all. If only every-body knew how beautiful she was with nothing on, and how substantial.

Naked she was unpredictable. What greater stimu-lation can there be than that?

THE ONLY PROBLEM with the weather and the out-lying storms was a pretty one, at first. Within a day or two, the city's river was engorged. It heaved itself out of its bed. It didn't break its banks exactly. It merely ventured here and there into a waterside parking lot, cleaning tyres, activating litter, or nosed across the running track to show its idle interest in the bird pavilion and the children's climbing frames.

Alicja and Lix, like almost everybody there, enjoyed the city's altered forms. At lunchtime, when the roof and their apartment were too hot for comfort, they would cycle down to the wharfside market for their vegetables and bread, then sit out on one of the commemorative benches in the Navy Gardens to watch the river's latest exploits. They were amused at first to see the ducks and water doves quite at home in gentle shallows where just the day before there'd been a lawn and shrubbery.

The pedestrian underpasses were unusable, as well. Nobody would attempt to wade through their wet history, the discarded bottles and cans, the antique, subterranean, water-activated smells of urine, cardboard, and tobacco. (But nobody used the underpasses anyway, wet or dry, except prostitutes and drunks – and men with urgent bladders.) So city shoes and socks were not yet getting wet. Except children's shoes and socks, that is. The children went out of their way to paddle home from school. The placid flooding was a treat that they'd remember till they died.

The city centre was more humid than it should have been, and smellier, and tempers were more frayed than usual. Trade and business is impatient with the slightest inconvenience. No one likes to break routines. But still it felt, in places, as if the countryside had come into the city with no intention more malign than to lap affectionately against our verges for a day or two, provide some gentler contours to the over-managed waterside, and then subside with no harm done.

One or two of the lowest streets down on the wharf and behind the boat and ferry yards were ankle deep in river by the third day of the rains, but who minds that? You seek such places out. It's fun to carve up water with your bikes. It's fun to wear your boots in town, and splash about, dispersing all your troubles and anxieties with whooping loops of water. It's better fun than Dry and Safe and Unremarkable. Odd weather stimulates. Such days are dancing lessons from the gods.

By the fifth day, a Sunday, the river had grown more impudent and menacing. Lix and Alicja could finally see water from their rooftop patio. Not moving water yet. Not quite a river view. A sheet. The great cobbled Company Square, where the old town market halls and narrow Hives abutted the theatre district, was oddly brilliant with colour from the reflected buildings and reflected sky. A rectangular expanse of water, hardly more than ten centimetres deep, architect-designed, it seemed, had turned the square brown-blue, with undulating fringes of marble grey, brick red, and stucco white. The sun, for once, was mirrored and disintegrated on the surface of the city, an idle, rippling shoal of golden fish.

The flooding was an unexpected wonder, too rare and beautiful to miss.

Alicja and Lix hurried out of their apartment to join the paddlers and the watching crowds, and to enjoy the latest dispositions of the streets. You'd only need a pair of skates and freezing temperatures, Alicja said, once they had waded to the dry, raised stand in the middle of the square where once there'd been a statue, already crammed with willing castaways, and 'this could be a Dutch masterpiece'.

'Except for the hills,' somebody said. 'No hills in Holland.'

'There are no hills here, either. The hills have disappeared.'

She felt absurdly privileged to know so much. Nobody else amongst that crowd could boast such thrilling rooftop views. She felt absurdly privileged as well to be the wife of Lix. She stood behind him on the plinth, her arms wrapped round his waist, her thumbs tucked in beneath his belt, her cheek pressed up against his back. Love is enacted by small things. Love is what you do with what you've got.

Lix was admitting to himself with some relief that he had at last become seduced by her. While Freda, really, had only wanted pseudoLix, the fearless and obliging activist – and only for a month! – Alicja provided her husband with moments of true value and true grace as they walked arm in arm around and through the floods. It wasn't that her every pat and tap, like Freda's every touch, seemed to settle with a fingertip the riddles of existence. It was rather that his uncruel wife was generous with her caresses, conferring unsolicited gifts, and not simply taking pleasure for herself. Her embraces acknowledged Lix's bloated self-image but recognized as well his hidden but more plausible self, his shortfalls and inadequacies. She welcomed all of it, it seemed, and wanted all of him, peel to core.

On Monday, it was far too deep to paddle in the square. By lunchtime, when Lix and Alicja finally went down to the old town, only a handful of young men had been conceited and foolish enough to wade in up to their knees to reach the central stand, their office trousers ruined but their sense of self enhanced. The sheet had spread beyond the square and was lapping at the rising ground around the narrow, medieval side lanes. Basements had been lost already to floodwater, but none of these were residential streets. Only storage spaces had been breached. Cellars full of laundered sheets and laundered banknotes, clamps of vegetables, catering cans and imported wine below the many restaurants and tourist hotels were underwater. Expensive labels had peeled off. Good unidentifiable wines, which would only sell off cheaply now, were bobbing free just centimetres from the ceiling in the democratic company of tonic water, lemonade, and Coke.

One of the little brasseries, the Fencing Shed, where Lix performed his unaccompanied songs on those evenings, such as now, when he was not working in the theatre, was unreachable by anyone who wanted to keep their toes dry.

The Debit Bar just around the corner, another of Lix's occasional venues, was already closed. It would be on the rising shoreline soon, a waterfront cafe. The day-shift Debit waiters were stacking chairs and lining all the entrances with makeshift flood barriers. Short-tempered policemen, armed with batons and whistles, were turning vehicles away. The ancient drains were overwhelmed. Instead of swallowing the floods, they were regurgitating. For the first time since the rains began, nerves were being lost in our normally lacklustre city. The mounting waters were now regarded not with smiles but with shaking heads, and everybody had begun to calculate the cost.

That evening, when Alicja returned from her late shift a little before midnight, she and Lix almost made love. It would have been the first time they'd made love since the weather changed. She wanted to. Making love had been implicit in their holding hands all day as they'd splashed through the town. A flirting conversation she'd had that evening with an older colleague had made her feel desirable, something she was too often missing in her marriage but that was essential for her self-esteem. Lix had had a flirting conversation with himself that night as well when he'd come back much earlier than usual from his shrinking, drowning round of busking venues. Performing, singing, had always made him sexually provoked. On stage he was a Casanovan balladeer – love songs and songs of loss, intended to arouse. He'd masturbated in their tiny bathroom, dreaming first of one or two of the well-dressed women who'd come into the restaurant in cocktail dresses and knee-high rubber boots, then of Freda, then of a new waitress, scarcely seventeen, and then – a triumph of the married will – of his own wife. It made no sense, to climax thinking of his wife, bringing to mind a body that was not wholly present when she'd be home and completely tangible within the hour. He was impatient, though, and tense. Uncertain anyway if she would share his mood when she returned. He had not been strong enough to stop himself.

So by the time his wife walked through the door, kicked off her shoes and put her arms around his waist, her thumbs again beneath his belt, his appetite for her or anyone was blunted. He'd make amends, he told himself. He'd truly make amends, some other day. For marriages are rich in other days. He made excuses for himself, sat in the toilet for a while, busied himself preparing coffee, talked too little and too much, and only joined her on the bed when he was sure that he was irritating her, that he had driven her away. Chatter is the cheapest contraceptive.

Instead of making love, then, they lay apart in their twin shirts, not even holding hands, and listened to the radio – the midnight news, the weather report, and 'music from the studio' – in their dark attic room. Between a polka for accordions, some jailhouse jazz, a French chanson, and music from Alfredo Busi's *Tamborina*, the weather pundits and one of the city senators warned that people ought to stay away from the floods (and from the riverside especially). Matters would get a little worse, perhaps, before they could get better. We should not panic, though. Talk of cholera was wildly mischievous. No one would drown if everyone was sensible. The easterlies would soon dislodge the distant rain.

Anyway, according to an expert from the university,

the worst would pass us by. The towns and villages downstream might soon be underwater, though, she said. Floods always find the lowest ground. The farmers could expect widespread waterlogging in their fields, a decimated harvest, and costly winter vegetables for us. 'Everything invades the purse.'

The city itself, however, was not vulnerable, she added. No need to construct an ark or walk about with flotation jackets on. Or drag your mats and furniture upstairs. No call for goggles yet. The streets would not be jammed with snorklers or bathyspheres instead of cyclists and trams. We'd not have ducks indoors. The dictates and principles of urban geography would keep us almost dry. If you build a city on a river's floodplain and then defend yourself with embankments, as our ancestors had, as the local governments had continued to do for the past four hundred years, replacing, adding, and extending until the only open ground was parks, she explained, then the floods would be rebuffed by 'solid surfaces' and hurried off elsewhere by drains and conduits and canals. These were the benefits of cobbles, asphalt and cement, especially in gently sloping cities such as ours. The rushing river always rushes to the sinks and basins of the fields where the hospitality is softer and the waters more at home.

Alicja and Lix, though, were young and free enough not to be discouraged from an adventure by the advice of senators, geographers, and forecasters. Next morning, they did not feel intimate enough to breakfast on the roof. Indeed, Alicja was beginning to fear that Lix was not the moodless paragon she had hoped. Instead, they walked in silence down to the river's edge, soon after eight o'clock, turned their trousers up above their knees, and, carrying their shoes in knapsacks, waded through the thigh-deep and now traffic-free streets – streets where the Lesniaks had wanted their daughter to rent some rooms – six blocks below their own apartment building to reach the stairs of the flimsy wrought-iron walkway that ran alongside Deliverance Bridge onto Navigation Island and then across the further stream into the campuses. They had to see for themselves what all the excitement was about and walk off their ill-temper.

There *was* excitement. A city's seldom livelier than when things are clearly going wrong. At dawn, all five of the east–west bridges across the river had been closed to traffic. Some brickwork on a single central pier had been dislodged by the force of the flooding. The mortar pointing in the stonework of the oldest bridge below the wharf was being washed away. The engineers detected shifting in the wider spans. So there was very little choice but to put up traffic barricades until the floods retreated and repairs could be carried out.

Half of the city's drivers couldn't get to work, unless they were prepared to travel out of town up to the high suspension bridge and its high tolls. Or else they'd have to dump their cars and walk between the eastern and the western banks by joining Lix and Alicja on the wrought-iron walkway, which, as yet, had not been closed. Anybody with any sense – that's everybody not desperate to work – would see this as the perfect opportunity to shrug their shoulders, phone the boss, and thank the gods of mischief that dangerous bridges stood between their workplace and their home, and that the sun was shining in a kind, blue sky.

Here was an unexpected holiday. They could take pleasure in the drama of the streets with all the other addicts and devotees of the flood, with Lix and his Alicja, with all the ne'er-do-wells who'd never done a decent hour's work but saved their energies for days like this. With good advice to be ignored ('Stay away from water. It is dangerous') and nothing else to do till after dark except to witness the more expensive parts of their home town submerge, how could they not enjoy themselves?

As Lix had suspected, though, the warnings on the radio that they should stay away from the river itself had been alarmist. Appeared so, anyway. The flooding waters, viewed from above on the walkway, did not seem so threatening. They were more beautiful than threatening. The crowds of pedestrians trying to get to work were much more dangerous and unpredictable. The two impatient counter-flows made it almost impossible to progress on the walkway except by taking risks, except by leaning out, and squeezing past, and shoving. But the progress of the swollen currents speeding only metres below their feet seemed unstoppable and satisfying. So, despite the urgency, the atmosphere was festive on the footbridge. There was good reason to rejoice. It seemed as if the problems of the world were river-borne and would be swept away and out of view. Any true disasters would only manifest themselves in someone else's neighbourhood, too far away to count, everybody said, repeating the good news from the radio. No cost to us. Besides, the river was far too spirited and glorious that day to seem anything other than a brief and welcome visitor. It was the placid uncle who'd suddenly turned hilarious and boisterous with drink. How could anybody – in this regular and regulated city, suppressed by laws and protocols – not enjoy the drama of the freshly sinewed river, its inflammation, its chalky, swept-up smell, its shots of clay-red colouring and the unexpected noise it made, thunder rendered into skeins, a din made muscly and physical?

By eleven o'clock, Alicja and Lix had crossed to the east side, bought breakfast at the Campus Café as they'd done so often as students, attended an exhibition at MeCCA, and started on their journey back to their apartment. Not touching yet. Not holding hands. The great panicking throng of workers had dispersed to work. The pedestrian bridge was still busy, though.

The walkway was a perfect gallery for the city's *enfants du paradis* to observe the drama, feel the spray, even, watch the rare and disconcerting spectacle of traffic-free bridges. These were images of old. Pre-motor car. The walkway's ironwork, which earlier had groaned almost silently from the burden of so many workers, now creaked and grumbled out loud as it shrugged itself back into shape. It had never carried such a weight before or hosted such a cheerful party of sightseers.

No one was glad to hear the bullhorn of the police instructing everybody on the wrought-iron bridge 'to come ashore', an inappropriate but thrilling phrase. The walkway was 'unstable' and would be closed. Anyone who'd walked to work that morning would not get home that night. So, finally, the city had been sliced in two, disunified by water.

'Evacuate. Evacuate,' the bullhorn said. But no one wants to be the first to leave the spectacle. A fire, a crash, a flood – we want to be the last to stay and watch the world go wrong. The crowd of gawkers on the bridge slowed down and might have taken all morning to disperse. Except there was a little accident, a loss, which made their vantage-point seem unreliable and fragile. A woman's hat fell in. Her immediate cry gave everybody time to spot it tumbling, halfway down between her stretched hand and the flood. Its fall seemed glacial, a lifeless flight of peaked denim.

Its disappearance in the water, though, was instantaneous. It vanished like a slug in a frog, as they say. Then seconds later, fifty metres downstream, it showed itself again, blue cloth against the white-grey-green.

'It makes you want to jump in yourself,' said Lix. 'Or give someone a push.' Alicja held him firmly by the arm at last. She felt the pull of drowning, too.

Before they'd seen the disappearing hat, Lix and Alicja had not noticed all the detritus. What city-dweller ever does? You close your mind to it, or else you have to walk with fury as a constant at your side, offended by the woman and her discarded can, the small child and his lolly stick, the thoughtless driver, cleaning out his car, the tissues and the cigarettes, the paper bags. But finally, as everybody pushed and pressed to reach their own side of the river, Lix and Alicja took refuge on an observation deck and leaned out over the water to let the more impatient and the more fearful squeeze by. Then they could not help but notice what the muscle of the river had swept up. The sticks and paper first, the evidence of living rooms and kitchens, the tossed-up hanks of hay and rope, the bottles and the cans, the sheets of farming polythene and plastic bags. A book. A hollowed grapefruit half. A little wooden figurine. A smashed and empty produce box. Vine canes. Bamboo. Nothing large.

Once the crowd had cleared, though, and they'd reached the west side of the bridge, where the river was at its (so far) mightiest, the detritus was weightier. Stripped trunks of trees, their branches knocked off by the journey from the hills. Container pallets, lifting up and ducking in the torrent. Sides of boathouses and sheds. A roof. And borne along, as blithe and cheerful as a toy tossed blissfully into a stream, what seemed at first to be a bungalow. It was, in fact, a houseboat still afloat but desperate, its curtains more like flags than sails.

That houseboat silenced everyone. It even silenced the policeman's bullhorn for a moment. 'Evacuate' and 'Come ashore' would be no help to anyone. The houseboat seemed alive with possibilities. You could not help but people it. You could not help but think of children sleeping in its only bed, restless with nightmares that could never be as terrible or hopeless as what awaited them when they woke up. You could imagine making love in it, in that sweet wooden house, and never knowing that your moorings had come loose. You'd think the world was twisting just for you. Or, perhaps, you could enliven the houseboat with one old man, too frail and rheumatoid to get up from his deep and ancient chair to save himself. He'd feel the helpless flight of his frail home. He'd see the landscape hurtling by. Perhaps he'd even spot the *enfants* on the bridge and think the world was coming to an end.

Just as the houseboat swept away, quite disappeared below the swell, just as the call to 'Come ashore' resumed, somebody said, a lie perhaps, an honest error, or the truth maybe, we'll never know for sure, 'I think I saw a cat on board.' They all turned round to face downstream and hope to catch a final glimpse of the children and the lovemakers, the old man and his cat, in their houseboat on its mad and bundling emigration to the sea.

ON THURSDAY MORNING, no one was surprised to wake to havoc on our streets and the din of rescue boats and helicopters, winching busy people from their penthouses and from their balconies. Flood depths downtown had almost trebled overnight. It was the city's turn to be submerged. The waters had ignored the basic dictates of geography. Although the distant mocking clouds had finally dispersed, the widow had tossed off her shawl to reveal the sodden, sunbaked shoulders of the hills, Navigation Island was now invisible. Only the tops of tarbonies and pines bending in the flows and disrupted by the weight of squirrels, the green clay roof of the bandstand with half its tiles removed, street lamps, still lit and sending orange streaks of light downstream, and sodden flags on three-quarters-submerged poles, revealed that this had once – a day ago – been land and home to weasels, rats, and foxes, all long since drowned because they'd never learned to swim or climb or fly.

The campuses across the bridges were standing in a

glistening lake. The MeisterCorps Creative Centre for the Arts was closed. The utility corridor where once a-Lix-in-love had planned a kidnapping was little more than a cloudy sump. A brown-grey river ran where they had waited in their hired van. It ran and spread into the banking district and beyond, into the army barracks, even, and the zoo. The one hundred famous green koi carp in the open pool escaped. One ended up – or so the story goes – in an eel trap a hundred and fifty kilometres downstream. The zoo's three missing Nile crocodiles, four metres long and volatile, were never found, however, although they gave the city much to talk about. As did the mosquitoes.

On the west side, all the old parts of the city, the valued and expensive parts, the tourist sites, the markets and the galleries, the narrow medieval squints, were flooded and cut off, and blocked by tumbled and abandoned cars. Even Anchorage Street was under four metres of water.

Alicja and Lix had river views at last.

It was approaching midday and they were on the rooftop, still in their grandad shirts and nothing else, when they heard the shouting from the street – the new canal – below. A voice they recognized. Her father's voice. A voice they did not want to hear, not when they were almost making love, nothing spoken yet but certainly implied when Alicja had dropped her head on Lix's shoulder, misunderstandings of two nights before forgiven, and pulled her shirt up above her knees to sun herself. He'd said she had attractive legs.

Reluctantly, she got up from their breakfast spot and found the space between the pots where they could look down on the street, where normally they could drop their key to friends or call out to acquaintances.

'It's my father,' she said. 'He's in a boat.'

'Is it a gondola?'

'A motor boat.'

'Ignore him. Come back here.'

'He's seen me already.'

'What's he selling? Has he got bananas? Ask him to sing some Verdi. *Bel canto*, Signor Lesniak. Ask him to dive for coins.' Lix was in the best of moods. Their decision earlier that morning not to get on evacuation boats like every one of their neighbours from the more vulnerable lower floors of the building but sit the crisis out had made him almost joyful. He and his wife would stay exactly where they were, at home, and watch the river from their windows and the roof, the entertainment of the unexpected regatta, the kayakers who'd waited all their lives for this, the uptown fishermen turned ferrymen who'd find that people were a better catch than perch, the firemen in their dinghies fighting water for a change, and looters with their craft tied up to balconies that now were jetties. They wouldn't miss such mayhem for the world.

Clinging to their own nest like breeding grebes was not the timid thing to do, Lix thought. Staying put was a risk, surely. His choice had been adventurous for once. No one could tell how long the floods and their supplies of food and clean water would last. No one could guarantee, indeed, that the river would not sweep the street away, like it had swept away the little houseboat and (as it had turned out, overnight) every strut and stay of the wrought-iron walkway where they'd chanced their lives the day before. Perhaps that's why Lix felt so weightless and alive.

'Ask him to call someone to have the flood removed within the hour.' Lix spoke in perfect Lesniak: '"Dry streets are just a call away. I'll put some pressure on someone in Forecasting. I've got some favours I can cash. I only have to whisper in a friendly ear and there'll be drought. I only have to say our name. The Polish parents are the very best."'

Alicja did not allow herself to laugh. Lix's imitations could be wearying, she thought. She'd always thought. She did not like to hear her father so accurately mocked. 'Stay out of it,' she said, in a voice that warned a steely afternoon if Lix did not comply, and felt guilty straight away. When it suited her – she never moved until it suited her – she would apologize. First she had to see her father's back. She formed a tranquil face, leaned out into the street, and listened to his lecture and advice.

Mr Lesniak, it seemed, had borrowed someone's launch and had come to evacuate his daughter, drawing up like a Venetian merchant against the balustrade of the second-floor apartment. He was determined to call out until she showed herself, and then stay until she did what he asked. He could not understand why the couple had not moved out of their apartment the night before, like everybody else with any sense. 'You don't play games with water,' he said, gnomically.

'We've made our minds up anyway,' Alicja shouted to him, cupping her hands around her mouth and trying to ignore her husband's running commentary. They'd considered all their choices when the hastily appointed flood wardens had directed them to leave and take their allocated places and their allocated camping beds in the Commerce Hall with all their neighbours, she explained. At least that would have been amusing and sociable, she thought but did not say out loud. More fun than moving out to the bone-dry suburbs and her parents' over-furnished house, where gated entry kept everything at bay, including the unruly river, probably. 'No Floods, Except by Appointment.'

No, their own home was best by far, she said. The floods would never reach their attic rooms, which were too high even for the mosquitoes, she'd told the warden earlier that day and repeated to her father now. 'That is not guaranteed,' the warden had said. 'I'm not responsible for you, if you don't come. You might not drown, but you'll be stuck indoors until the floods go down. We won't come back.' Her father said very much the same except he thought he was responsible for her. It was possible that he'd come back, again and again, until his daughter did as she was asked. 'You think I'm going to let you starve?'

'How can we starve?' Even if their food ran out, she said, hoping to amuse her father and disarm him, they'd swim for bread like spaniels or dive for vegetables like ducks or hunt for fish with barbecue forks.

'That's being childish, Alicja.'

Exactly so. The prospects of having the building all to themselves for a few days seemed irresistible, a private island where they could be kids again. Juveniles had all the fun. The trick for adults, then, was to act like juveniles. 'Walk naked if we want to,' Lix had said. That was a more appealing prospect, to him at least, than eating and sleeping in a hall with ninety other refugees or living with the Lesniaks. What could be safer than their Private Patio?

Alicja called out to her father, trying to suppress her irritation with the man, all men: 'Stop fidgeting. We'll take good care of ourselves,' she said again. 'I'm twenty-nine, for heaven's sake!'

'I'm sixty-nine, for heaven's sake. You think I don't know best by now?'

Lix listened to his wife discussing safety with her father, three storeys below, occasionally lapsing into

Polish when Mr Lesniak was irritated or baffled. 'We'll be all right,' she said again, leaning forward over the barricade. 'Go home. Don't worry. We'll not drown, you know. We'll not even catch a chill.' And, then, a daughter's tease, exasperated, though. 'I'm a married woman. I do not need the inshore lifeboat, thank you very much, Captain Lesniak.'

Her sensible and knee-length grandad shirt had ridden some way up her thigh as she leaned forward to shout down to her father. Lix shuffled forward on his haunches, ducking down below the balustrade, and sat amongst the pots beside his wife. He did not want to be seen by Mr Lesniak. Being charming and polite was wearying. And Mr Lesniak was more successful at bullying his son-in-law than his daughter. Before they knew it Lix would have agreed to pack a bag and climb out the window on the second floor into their rescue boat. The flood would be an opportunity lost.

So he hid himself and concentrated on his wife. He concentrated on the naked contours of her legs, the dimpled hollows behind her knee, the flexing ligaments, the moles and veins and creases. She liked caresses – who doesn't like to be caressed? – even when her father was standing in a rocking boat and talking to her as if she were still a teenager. 'Be sensible,' et cetera, when she was anything but sensible – and hoping never to be sensible again.

This was not yet a sexual act between the two of

them. They'd often lain together on the bed, tweaking toes or massaging the other's neck and back, without it ending as intercourse. Marriages would combust if every touch were sexual. Caresses of fondness and affection are only little, passing gifts, the fleshly version of a word which gives reassurance to your partner that everything is going well, that no one's cross. The fingertips convey no message other than the whispered tenderness of skin on skin.

For the moment Lix's fingertips were restricted to her middle leg, the knee, the calf, the upper shin. Alicja welcomed this as just a simple intimacy, an unspoken symbol of support in the war amongst the Lesniaks. But tender touching never lasts quite long enough with men. They seek possession. They want to occupy the land and harvest it. They want to plunder it. They have to stretch and reach – as Lix was doing now – out of the realms of charity, beyond the zones of tenderness.

He pushed a hand under her nightshirt and began caressing her behind, a tactic that had succeeded several times before. He pushed her shirt tail up to her waist and she could feel him breathing on her naked skin, could feel his face too close to her. She did not like that quite as much as massages. A parent's presence made her feel unwomanly. If she allowed her husband to proceed, she understood he'd slip his finger into her, while she was talking to her father. That was some-thing she did not want. Not yet. Her head said no.

Indeed, she shook her head. Yet instinctively her body, her grander, baser biological self, was already preparing for the possibility of sex, the likelihood that her husband would not despair of her, not give her any guilt-free peace until they had made love. Her vagina had already softened and lengthened for his stiffening erection.

Alicja knew what was expected of young wives, that she was expected to feel excited beyond recall. Those were the footnotes to Lix's script – and she was cast to be the active and obliging star, being intimately touched by a lover crouching in the hems and shadows of her clothes, with nothing on beneath, but seeming to the world below the apartment as if she were simply chatting like a less than sensible daughter but with an inexplicably thickening voice.

Alicja would not accept the role. She pushed her husband's hand away, coughed, and persevered with her assurances until her father gave the order for the engines to be started and for the launch to go back where it had come from. She felt infuriated with the pair of them – her father for his bullying, her husband for his fickleness. Two nights before he'd been too distracted even to notice that she wanted to make love. Now, because he'd changed his mind, she was expected to respond to him like some trained horse. She shook her legs until he moved his hand away.

That might have been the end of it. Another

moment lost. No unplanned pregnancy. No ill-timed son. But Alicja was more dutiful by temperament than resentful. She got her way by giving way. Besides, the weather was disarming and liberating and the circumstances of the flood so bizarre and stimulating that it would be a shame to punish the whole day by not responding to her husband, a husband who could sulk for a week if he so chose.

She watched her father's launch proceed along the street, sending wakes of water up against the windows of the ground-floor rooms and rocking all the floating debris that had surfaced in the night, the plastic dustbins and the furniture, while Lix sat at her feet and persevered.

Finally, of course, she warmed to him. She put her hand back on his head and gripped his hair. 'No need to stop,' she said, in case he thought she was rebuffing him again. Actually her first rebuff had quietened him, reminded him how single-minded she could be, and how resistant to his bullying. He tried to be more tender and more circumspect. He pulled a leaf off one of the fessandra bushes and ran it down the back of her right knee. He'd never really paid much attention to the smell of fessandras before, but the pressure of his forefinger and thumb had bruised the leaf and let the odour out. It was oddly pungent, like cough lozenges with lemon undertones, bitter-sweet and cloying like a teenager's perfume. He smelt his fingertips and was aroused by what he smelt. Physically aroused, that is, and – unlike an animal – imaginatively aroused as well because it was not hard to imply and to anticipate what might ensue, this moment rushing forward to the next at his behest but out of his control. The busy fingertips, at first, but then the lips and tongue. The gentleness, at first, but then the gripping and the biting, the fingernails. The man, at first, and then the beast.

Let's not forget that Lix, indeed, was just an animal, compelled by base impulses to spread his seed in his selected mate so that his species could, in principle anyway, negotiate from eighty thousand genes an offspring more efficient than themselves. He was content to be 'just an animal' on these occasions in his married life, to be instinctive and unambiguous in ways he couldn't be when not aroused, to be unembarrassed by his irrational self, to be unselfconsciously brave, patient and cunning.

So Lix, the mating mammal, folded the fessandra leaf and rolled it up and down her leg, perfuming her, a ruminating little courtship play that would not ill suit gorillas or baboons. His wife stayed at the balustrade and let her husband put his leaf to work. She knew the smell, of course. She often rubbed the shrubs and brushed up against them, and she'd always found the odour stimulating, half kitchen and half dressing table. Someone ought to bottle it, she thought. An aphrodisiac. An aphrodisiac that at that moment truly worked. She felt her flood of irritation seep away, and then the swooning shift of mood that tossed her inhibitions to the far side of the roof. She felt intensely physical, exactly as she should, for her body was in free fall, in a kind of benign but toxic shock.

Her skin was turning red. Blood was pumping to the surface of her face and chest. Blood congested in her lips and nose, her earlobes and her nipples, her breasts and genitals. The arteries were working faster than her veins. Her pulse had passed the hundred mark. Her blood pressure was up. Her lungs seemed hardly capable of reaching for breath. She was sweating visibly. You'd think the woman was not well, and that she should be hooked to sugar drips and heart machines and monitors.

Alicja was concentrating now. She had to draw the moment in. She stood a little straighter to allow the released odour to reach her nose directly. Her legs were buckling. She had to rest her hands on Lix's shoulders for support. 'Fessandra,' she said, as if this were an identification test. Lix took her comment as a cue. He snapped off leaves from balm, much damper leaves, more succulent and ticklish, and rolled them once again on Alicja's lower leg. This time the odour was much fruitier and clogged, the smell of bed and sweat and oranges, as pungent as a pot pourri and heavier than the fessandra perfume. It didn't float as readily, but gathered in the curtains of her shirt. 'I can't smell that.' Again an invitation to move up. Again, he pushed her shirt aside and tested out the balm on the softer, plumper skin between her bottom and her waist. And then some marjoram. 'It's balm,' she said, a little late.

Lix still had one hand free to pluck some mint for her. But he'd stood at last and now was pressing against her back, a little buckle-kneed himself. If anyone naive, some passing boatman, or a marooned neighbour on another roof, had seen them there, they might just pass for a couple looking virtuously at their flooded street, as innocent as pigeons, but only if you took their swaying and their twining, their sudden shakes, to be a childish, clinging dance and their contorted faces – their mouths agape, their nostrils flared – to be a game of Visages.

When they had finished and were able to stand tall again, Lix rubbed the mint into the nape of her neck, a freshener, a waking tonic for the nose. It was a smell that she'd associate for ever with the advent of their son. Mint would remind her, too, of proper love, because their midday breeding on the roof (that's what it was), their mating in the time of floods, had also been an act of fondness and affection. Everything they'd done and seen in those nine days of rain had led as surely as water runs downhill to lovemaking. Everything had proved to be a prelude to the kisses and embraces, and the child. There'd be no grander day than this.

This couple, these rooftop newly weds, shipwrecked above the flooded streets, had done two things at once, two things connected and discrete: had sex, made love. What better way to start a life? What better way to start an afternoon?

A CHILDISH question now. What happened to the clouds? What happened to the clouds once they'd peeled off to give us back our hills, their scalped-to-the-bone maturity? They'd spread out as evenly as oil. The blue skies lost their pure edge, as well. The wind picked up. By June, it was another summer just like all the others we endure in this safe city on the water's edge. Not fine, not wet, but hazy and exhausting and unkind. Our world regained its shape. If we were hawks, if only we were hawks once in a while, we'd recognize the city patterns had returned to normal, the river flowing in its place, observing man-made banks, the traffic moving freely in the dried-out streets and on the mended bridges, no sheeny parks or squares to paddle in, the bipeds as busy as they ever were, observing pavement rules.

And, as hawks, we'd spot an unexpected confluence one afternoon in July, beyond glass roofs. Not such a rare coincidence. For cities like ours where people move around on tracks, meetings such as this are inevitable: Alicja and Lix have gone down to the Palm & Orchid for a late Saturday-afternoon treat. They've something to celebrate and think about. Something both pleasing and unnerving for Lix: his children stretch behind him and they stretch ahead. Her pregnancy's confirmed.

Unluckily, for this should be a blissful, undiluted time, Freda's already in the Palm & Orchid Coffee House with her small boy. She's sitting almost hidden by a plant, facing out across the room disdainfully and being watched by half the men. When she sees her ex-lover, her very best RoCoCo Renegade, and the father of her son with his fat Polish wife at the entrance desk pleading with the maître d' for an unshared table, she's tempted first to stay where she is and ignore them, loftily. He'd not dare bother her.

They are being led to a table far too close to hers. So she gets up from her seat, brushes all the crumbs off her black skirt, and hurries out without a glance but only once she's sure that Lix has noticed her, seen not only how grand and beautiful she is, but also how she's still *concerned*, *involved*, *engaged* (and if she still is beautiful then that's a beauty that stems not from her genes but from her seriousness). She wants the man whom she possessed for more than thirty days to take the blame for everything, the child, the kidnapping, the ever-growing problems of the city and the world.

George had not been pleased to be there in the first

place, in such a disappointing restaurant. Now he is furious to be dragged away before he's even despatched his cake or had a chance to feed the finches with his mother's crumbs. He drags behind his mother's arm, afraid to make a fuss, and as he drags, he catches for an instant the eye of a man he cannot recognize but knows, a hypnotized and startled man who's staring at him with an open mouth.

4

ALICJA MUST HAVE known as soon as she opened her mouth that risking such a joke in front of her husband's most recent friends might be an error – and a costly one, because, as any Lesniak could tell you, 'For every pair of Ears, there is a set of Teeth.' In other words, if anyone can hear what you say, then anyone can repeat it, and anyone can sharpen up the most blameless banter to give it a damaging bite, especially if the object of the joke was an as yet unrevealed public figure.

So, despite the ingenuousness of Alicja's blunder, the word went round that Lix, for all his money and success, was not much good in bed. That would always be the sweetest rumour of them all, to hear that even a celebrity could fail between the sheets. Not fail to procreate, of course, he'd not failed that, but fail to please. The word spread fast. By midnight all the dogs were barking it and all the owls were hooting it.

Alicja by now was not the woman of the roof, a little overweight, ill-dressed, too eager to comply, dismissive of her parents' wealth, in love with Lix. She

had become the woman that she'd planned, free at last
of her lesser, deferential self, impatient to move on.
She was a working mother, hardly slimmer than she'd
always been, but grand and smart enough these days to
'carry it'. Mrs Lesniak-Dern was the new Director of
the Citizens' Commission and also a district senator,
elected by the waitresses and office workers of the
Anchorage quarter because three years before she'd
done so much – without success – to fight for flood
repairs and compensation for the neighbourhood. Her
little kindnesses had paid big dividends for her, exactly
as she'd thought they might. The Quandary Queen
had been the local heroine for several months, long
enough to offer herself in the elections – and to win.

It didn't seem to matter to the Anchorage voters
that nowadays their senator mostly lived elsewhere. In
Polish luxury, Beyond. What mattered was that she
and Lix had kept the little apartment-without-a-river-
view as their city centre pied-à-terre, no longer their
rented rooftop happiness, perhaps, but somewhere for
Lix to sleep after a late curtain, somewhere for Alicja
to meet with her constituents – and with her lover.
So – democracy! – their homely representative could
sometimes be caught walking in their streets with her
little son in his stroller and could be greeted by her
Christian name. Alicja could still be thought of as a
neighbour and a fixer, the ear to whisper in. She was
their woman to admire and claim to be their own.

Though her husband Lix was not so patient when they greeted him, just the presence of his familiar face was further evidence that even people who had once inhabited cramped apartment rooms, even people who'd been marked at birth, could make successes of themselves. Though two successful people in one house, as everybody knew, was one too many. Successful people are too busy, as the saying goes, to take care of the chickens. So it was with Lix and Alicja. They hardly seemed to meet these days. Even their photographs appeared in separate sections of the newspaper. They lived in different and divergent worlds.

To celebrate his first contract with Paramount in Hollywood (he'd co-co-star with Pacino in *The Girder Man*) and the outstanding reviews and ticket sales for his *Don Juan Amongst the Feminists*, Lix had decided to blow some of the profits from the album sales of *Hand Baggage*, the 'Travelogue of Songs', which he had tested out so many times in restaurants and bars when he was still unknown and hungry for loose change and cheap applause, by hosting an Obligation Feast to prove his gratitude to thirty or so good friends. These were the actor colleagues, musicians, the journalists and slighter celebrities with time to spare who clung to him now that he was recognized and famous in the city. He could not expect them to drive out to his and Alicja's new village-style house in Beyond (as the New Extensions on the east side of the city were known dismissively by those who did not have young children or money and did not value privacy, security, and lawns). These men and women were either too busy or too grand to make the forty-minute trek. Anyway, he'd rather keep his private house – with its seven private trees – secure and secret even from them. He'd not been truly happy there. Beyond had ruined everything. Besides, he did not want his name to turn up in a tittle-tattle diary piece in the newspaper, ridiculed for having – what? – the wrong-shaped bath, a bourgeois sofa set, last year's shrubs, or mocked for having in-laws like the Lesniaks who could both buy then give away to their daughter such a fine and current building.

Beyond was not only *beyond* the old suburbs but *beyond* the means and wildest dreams of anyone in Lix's lunch party. 'Grand and busy' is not the same as rich, not in the Arts. It was never wise to make your comrades jealous or resentful or scornful. Best that they were kept away and not invited to inspect what tainted Polish cash could buy. Childless people never understood how costly – to your purse and principles – parenthood could be. 'Blood before Ink' was Roesenthaler's mocking phrase for it. Nor do they understand – the never-married ones, at least – how quickly love gets washed ashore and beached. They'd see the evidence themselves if they came out to Beyond: the shallowness, the elegance, and the formality.

So Lix had hired the Hesitation Room (as the

windowless private cellar beneath the Debit's public areas was known). Perhaps it was the lack of natural light on this aggressively bright spring day that caused the diners to behave more drunkenly and less cautiously than they should have done at lunchtime. Once that baize door – with the high flood mark of May 1989 recorded just a centimetre below the lintel – was closed and all the meals had been served, it must have seemed like night down there, late night, with hardly any traffic noise and just occasionally digestive rumbles from the nightmare trams reminding them of city life. Time, then, to pop a pile of corks, and throw discretion to the many cellar rats, even though, out in the world, the sun had hardly passed its highest point.

More often than not Alicja would have used their son, Lech, as an excuse for not attending Lix's 'self-celebrating' meal. Lech had to be collected from his minder. Lech had to be delivered to his grandparents. Lech had to be adored and fussed and indulged on any day that Lix would like Alicja to be his public wife. There were other useful excuses, of course. Her public duties were the perfect alibi. Sometimes she simply said that it would not be politic to be at his side at this event or that occasion. The company was not discreet, there were too many journalists, her presence might be misinterpreted politically, et cetera. It wasn't hard to fake an alibi. She and her husband led their own lives, neither one of any interest to the other. The senate and the theatre were ancient enemies.

There were no convincing reasons, though, not to join his private gathering in the Hesitation Room. It was taking place in daytime after all. Lech was at the Polish kindergarten until late afternoon and then he had a Toddler Party to attend. The district senate was not due to meet for two more days. The Citizens' Commission provided an income but, since its quan-going, few responsibilities. And Lix would take offence – quite reasonably – and sulk like a carp if his wife was absent from the Feast. My God, the man could sulk the juice out of a lemon. In less than a week he would be leaving for LA and then the film set in Nevada and not returning home for two sweet months. Surely Alicja, he had said, could make the effort just this once and smile upon his friends.

So she'd dressed up in her ComPoneau suit, deter-mined to enjoy herself, despite the immodest and undiplomatic company of Lix's 'limpets'. Luckily, there was one of his newly minted friends she was keen to share a table with – and the Debit food was always interesting, even in the Hesitation Room where the lighting was so blunt.

Alicja had seemed, Lix thought, almost enthusiastic at the prospect of spending lunchtime with her hus-band for a change. She'd had her hair styled early in the morning and had then spent an hour at home on clothes and make-up. Lix had been a spectator, more disarmed by watching her than usual. He'd always liked to watch his wife prepare herself, a homely version of the many times he'd spent in theatre dressing rooms talking to half-dressed actresses in mirrors, addressing their bare backs, their pins and zips and straps.

Yet in the past few months his and his wife's physical intimacies, the social glue of lovemaking, had become so infrequent and fraught, and so inconclusive, that even watching her dress had become a bitter pleasure, especially as recently – and this was pitiless – Alicja seemed to have discovered a new interest in her appearance to match her status in the Senate and on the street. She'd never dressed so sexily before. She'd always thought his occasional gifts of clothes hilarious and 'fussy'. Now she'd taken to wearing skirts and well-cut suits and shoes with just a tiny heel and did not seem impatient as she once had at the mindless waste of time of putting on make-up and coordinating her colours and fabrics and her jewellery. Clothes, at last, were fun for her, it seemed. Her mother's influence, possibly. Mrs Lesniak had always thought her daughter dressed 'like an English dumpling', just to prove herself a rebel. This was one rebellion that even Lix – ashamed of all the other compromises they had made – was glad to see the end of. What happened to the plump, quiescent girl, he asked himself, the woman eager to appease and please? He blamed the Lesniaks. He blamed the stultifying culture of Beyond. He blamed democracy for voting his Alicja away from home. He faulted himself as well – and he was justified – for letting his ambitions on the stage become more vital and consuming than his marriage. His wife could not be blamed for seeking spotlights of her own. He'd mend his ways.

Alicja's more yielding attitude to clothes, Lix understood, was just a happy product of her age but he also hoped that she was doing what she could to rescue their relationship as well from its ever-present anxiety and its heartless determination to be civilized. She wanted to display a livelier, more seductive version of herself because – the Poles, as ever, had a mordant phrase for it – 'A dab of rouge resuscitates the dead.'

Relations between Alicja and Lix – *dealings* might be a better word, these days – had become if not quite corpselike then stiffly formal. Not just in bed, where, truth be told, stiffness was not always guaranteed. No, out of bed as well. They had turned into little more than domestic colleagues, starched and polite but unengaged. A child and minder in the house did not encourage intimacy. Neither did the late nights that they both kept nowadays. Nor the increasing number of occasions when they slept apart, whether divided by an angry hollow in the bed, or marooned in separate rooms, in different parts of town, the Anchorage apartment or the family house Beyond. She told her mother that Lix snored. That's why she ended up so often in a different bed. He never snored. Nor was he a restless night companion. Much worse. Her husband sighed while he was sleeping, as if even his dreams were flat and saddening. To share a bed with Lix was to wrap yourself in sheets of woe. How had the man become so wounded by success? Alicja's dreams were livelier and full of hope and opportunity. She'd dreamed, just the night before his Obligation Feast, that he was in the flood-tossed houseboat, and lost downstream amongst the missing crocodiles and koi. She understood her dream to mean their marriage was, well, waterlogged, too swept away to save, and that this was an opportunity for her to be an adult finally, liberated from the Lesniaks and Derns.

Lix himself knew no such thing. He thought the new blouse she was putting on for him that day suggested a rapprochement of a sort, a signifier that there could be (before he fled to Hollywood) a renewed alliance between old friends. When she'd returned from the hairdresser's, looking like a mature bride, Lix had sat in the wicker rocking-chair on the bedroom balcony with his coffee and a play script he had to consider and witnessed her undress, throw her clothes over the back of a chair – so many layers, so many unexpected and alerting loops – and then bedeck herself before the mirror in recent purchases. A woman is renewed by clothes. Perhaps a marriage could be, too.

The blouse was beryl green, short-sleeved and halter-cut. It seemed to make her nakeder. Alicja's spine, so girlish and inexpressive when innocently unclothed, was not removed from sight when thinly covered by the blouse and underclothes but, rather, emphasized and sexualized by new and displaced vertebrae, where the clasps and buckles of her brassiere showed up as petite bony studs against the cloth. Her back became a pattern of raised signs.

Lix considered getting up at once to read the message of her Braille. Yet again – the story of his life – he lacked the courage and he lacked the confidence. He knew that if he stood and moved towards his wife, then she would close herself to him. A woman dressing does not welcome damp fingers or damp lips. Lix would be left – as ever when he took chances, in love, in business, on the stage – standing, swaying in a fug of vertigo, that familiar nausea and loss of balance that had always made him take descending steps away from risk.

So he stayed where he was, behind his play script, making marks on the page and imprinting marks into his own back, from the pressure of the wicker chair. He'd wait for a better opportunity. Patience is a dignified form of cowardice, that's all.

If he waited till the evening, Lix thought, there would be other marks for him to ponder and enjoy. Throughout the day, her underclothes, mediating between the naked and the dressed, the hidden and the visible, would press their tender traceries not only on her outer garments, but on her naked body too. When she undressed again, then he would find – if she allowed, if she came home with him and did not spend the night in Anchorage Street – indentations and elastic imprints across her back and shoulders, round her waist, around her upper thighs.

The very thought of these brief naevuses, which could not last beyond the hour, which were so innocent and yet so rousing, made his throat go dry. A hint of vertigo. It was not only fear of contact with Alicja but also the opposite, the shocking prospect of his fingers never touching her again. For a man who no longer had the habit or the self-belief to cross the room and hold his wife, there was something heart-wrenchingly tender, too, about the vestigial rectangles of ridge and furrow from her pressing and her folding of the blouse. Those creases and impressions were eloquent and sad, and so domestically nostalgic. They were the marks of married life – a shelf of clothes, a cupboard and a room, an ironing board, the smell of bodies and cologne and steam.

Alicja, unexpectedly, was not in the least discomfited that her husband was watching her and that – she knew the man of old; men were so *visual* – he was sexually aroused. She was aroused herself, but not aroused by him. Not making love to him empowered her. It was satisfying. She watched herself pull on her tights. She did not think that she was showing off, although she knew she would have dressed herself more hurriedly if Lix had not been watching from the balcony, behind his cursed script. The man was always buried in a script. It seemed that everything she'd ever said to him had been filtered through a script or blocked by one. The pages of dialogue were the shield with which her husband rebuffed conversation, consigned her to the wings. He'd lost the knack of being normal and offstage. Alicja was coming round to her father's view of theatre.

Once she was fully clad in shoes and skirt, her suit jacket folded across her arm, she pirouetted for the mirror's sake, but also for the audience of one. Now that she was dressed and safe, she didn't mind that Lix had got up from his chair and was standing at the balcony door, openly admiring her, with that weasel expression on his face.

'Smart,' he said. A safe remark.

Her shorter, razored hair was indeed smart and flattering, Lix thought, flattering to him as well because there is nothing more supportive of a vain and famous man than to have a wife who merits the admiration and desire of friends, a head-turner. The new cut made the most of Alicja's Polish cheeks. Her hair seemed mischievously springy and boyish once the gel had been applied. Surely Lix could reach out and feel. Surely he could touch his wife.

Sadness made Lix almost brave. He had the pretext of his empty coffee cup, which needed putting on the breakfast tray by the bedroom door. He squeezed between his wife, the mirror and the bed and, as light-heartedly and as drained of meaning as possible, he ruffled her hair as he might ruffle little Lech's head except that he was careful not to dishevel hers. That's all it was, a manly reassuring touch, no threat to her. Her responding smile emboldened him. What other manly, reassuring contact could he make, drained of meaning, now that he was standing by her back?

He spotted his pretext almost at once: the blouse's white label showing at her razored neck, both a spillage and encroachment, something public, manufactured, but meant to be concealed. He'd not resist just dipping a finger below her collar to poke the label back in place and steal his second touch that day. It should have taken just a moment, but he left his finger tucked inside her collar, freeze-frame, enjoying both the fabric and the skin. He was too bold, perhaps, and certainly too obvious, but he leaned forward over his much-shorter wife to kiss the nape of her neck, his lips brushing both her newly shortened hair and his own fingertips. Her perfume almost made him weep.

It didn't matter that she pushed his hand away and said, 'Not now.' *Not now*, indeed. *Later, later* was implied. He could proceed with his used cup and take the loaded tray downstairs. She had invited him to live in hope.

When Lix returned five minutes later, already anxious that they would be late for his Obligation Feast, Alicja was sitting at their dressing table. 'Just touching up,' she said. She leaned towards the mirror, pouted her mouth and coated the pink-blue of her naked lips with fashionable and less alarming plum-red lipstick. She cleaned away the residue with the edge of a tissue. Sprayed a little extra perfume on her throat and wrists. Then, despite herself, or else because at last she approved this risky, finished version of herself, she air-smacked a kiss towards the mirror and her husband's reflection. He smacked one back, with sound effects, an actor's *mwah*. They routed smiles into the glass.

Did Lix have reason for some optimism, then? Certainly their drive to town was comfortable, their conversation was affectionate. She wanted him to have a successful lunch. Their sexual drought was coming to an end, perhaps, Lix thought, although he was not mad enough to stretch his hand and grasp her leg. The drought might end that day, if they survived the company of friends. Fortified by alcohol and panicked by the prospect of two months apart, on different continents, once they got home and in the hour or so before Lix had to leave again for that evening's performance, they could perhaps begin to mend some fallen bridges.

'We're running short of time,' Lix commented out loud, not wanting to explain, or needing to. Alicja just raised a brow.

AT FIRST THERE had been too many of her husband's crew crowded round the bank of tables in the hired cellar, too many for concentrated conversation, too many for any indiscretions or any intimacy. The ordering, the serving and the eating had been intrusive and disruptive. But by three o'clock only the dregs were left, the dregs of wines and spirits, that's to say, and the dregs of Lix's new acquaintances, those who had no desks or families to return to, no stories to file, and no higher priorities than to keep the party going till the waiters chucked them out. The Debit waiters never chucked you out. The only time the Debit Bar was closed to customers was when the police or the river took charge.

There was the little dancer from *Don Juan*, intense and talkative in a way that Alicja could not admire, despite the woman's obvious desire to draw attention to herself and despite the dancer's admiration, many times repeated, for people such as 'District Senator

Lesniak-Dern' who'd invested so much of her energy in civic life.

'Dance never, never does a bit of good,' she insisted, and Alicja had felt obliged to disagree, saying – lying – that politics was not as good at bettering the world as politicians wanted everyone to believe, and that dance, at least, provided uncomplicated joy.

'Perhaps you're right,' the dancer said, 'in both respects.'

To Alicja's left – ignoring her – there was the fussy trumpeter from Lix's recording group whose flattened mouth and hamster cheeks, especially when flushed with drink and two desserts, made him look like a cheery doll. A cheery doll that liked an argument.

Further up the table, engaged by a cigar that would not draw, there was an actress who had once been as celebrated as Lix but had lost her passion for theatre and had turned instead to poetry, which she had published at her own expense while neglecting to renew her wardrobe or her anecdotes. To Alicja's right, beyond the dancer, there was the undernourished couple who owned the studio where Lix had recorded his LP-cassette; the dishevelled husband scarcely able to survive three minutes without tobacco or a cough; the wife scarcely twenty-two years old, and drunk and bored and sitting next to Lix with her hand on his shoulder and her chair turned sideways to the table so that she need only talk to him and no one else could talk to her.

On Lix's other side was 'Joop the Scoop', Jupiter the columnist, a man who would never give his proper name but everybody knew to be the embarrassed but untouchable younger brother of the garrison commander who, more than any dancer or district senator at that time, the spring of 1992, controlled the city's destiny, controlled the bettering, controlled the joy. Alicja would have much preferred Joop as a neighbour at the table, of course. Any woman would. He had the chiselled Roman face to match his name, though on the evidence of his own newspaper column he was hardly the celestial Guardian of Honour or the God of Oaths, Treaties and Marriages. His pen was cruel and snobbish, perhaps, his politics unworthy of a citizen his age, but in person he had shown himself to be attentive and a little shy, a man who was not disposed to flirting openly, who hardly raised his voice, who rationed and so enhanced the value of his studiedly melancholy smile. He seemed exactly the opposite of Lix and not a bit like Mr Lesniak.

Alicja had wondered when she first encountered Joop, while waiting for Lix in the lobby of the theatre some months before, if he was a homosexual, besotted with her husband. She'd asked. She had to know at once. No, not homosexual, he'd said. He was simply so self-conscious about his early baldness that he thought it best not to bother bright and pretty women such as her. She'd told him he had no reason to be self-conscious, actually, touching him for the first time on his forearm. The baldness made a handsome, intellectual monk of him.

'Your skull is sculptural,' she said, longing not so much to touch it as to smell it.

'I'll have it cast in bronze, Senator, and give it to the city. I'm sure that you can find a plinth for it. The empty plinth in Company Square, perhaps.'

'Amongst the cobbles, yes.'

They had embarked on an affair. Alicja and Jupiter.

So now she listened to the dancer's anecdote about *Swan Lake*, Nureyev and the bearded French Ambassador and watched her lover paying polite attention to his host. Any moment he would catch her eye, and she would smile for him, the risky smile that says I'm Yours, the risky smile that can't suppress the showing of the tongue.

What if Lix looked up and caught her eye? Well, let it be. That evening, when they were home, or preferably as they were driving home protected by the darkness in the car, while he was trapped behind the wheel, she'd find the courage to talk to him. She owed it to the man who'd been her husband for more than three years, the father of her child, the first who'd ever earned her love, to be direct with him, to send him off to Hollywood understanding that everything would be rearranged while he was gone. More than that, she owed it to herself. She'd got a career. She'd got constituents. She'd got the promise, if she watched her step for a year or two, of joining the executive and making history. No other woman in the city had ever gone so far. She'd got a well-connected lover, too, whose appeal included a vasectomy. What she didn't want was a husband or another child to hold her back. The time had come, the time was good, for the City Senator and Celebrated Lix to separate.

So Alicja can surely be forgiven for her nervousness at lunch, the shrill and wine-fuelled conversations that she held, her unexpected gaiety, her robust appetite, her pleasure in the word games that were passing round the table, and then the risqué games of Dare and Truth, and Ultimatum.

Perhaps it was because playing Never was her lover's suggestion, his way of flirting with her across the table, she imagined, that Alicja joined in too readily and so incautiously. The game was this: each diner at the table had to admit to something they'd never done that everybody else there most certainly would have done. If it proved that you were not alone in your humiliation then you were out of the game, and could not join the second round when further admissions of inexperience were required. 'You have to use the word Never in your confession. And lying's absolutely not allowed,' said Joop. 'This isn't journalism.' It was an invitation to disclose failings, cowardice, defeat, and limited horizons. The prize? 'The mocking disrespect of all your friends.'

'It's your idea. You first,' Alicja said to Joop. Already she had persuaded herself – or else his roguish grin persuaded her – that his own contribution would convey a private message. Almost everything he said turned out to be a tease. He kept her on her toes. 'I've only ever loved one person in my life,' he'd say. 'I've never loved another.' Or (a confirmation of a trip they'd planned) 'I've never shared a hotel room. Not yet.' Instead he disappointed her. He said, 'I've never been on a motorbike or scooter. The very idea terrifies me.' But he was out of the game at once, because it seemed that the dancer had never risked a motorbike either.

So now the dancer's go. She claimed for herself that she had never seen the sea. No one could rival that. How was it possible to reach your thirties and not have seen the sea, especially when travel was so easy during the Big Melt?

'Not even from an aeroplane?' Lix asked.

'I've never been on an aeroplane,' she replied. Three goes in one. No motorbikes, no aeroplanes, no sea.

The trumpeter went through to the second round with his 'mortified' claim never to have swallowed an oyster, an embarrassing and squeamish admission, he said, because he'd spat one out one evening in New York when his bass player had drawn attention to an oyster's semen smell. 'Tasted, yes, but never stomached one, never passed one through.'

The twenty-two-year-old had never had sex with a person younger than herself, she claimed. 'And never will.'

'So I'm in with a chance,' the trumpeter said, parping out his cheeks.

'Hardly. I've never had sex with a hamster either. And absolutely never will.'

The actress-poet's contribution was, 'I've never smoked a cigarette, not one. Only my cigars.'

'Not even after you've made love?'

'When I've made love I always take a shot of peppermint liqueur. To take away the taste.' Their laughter bounced around the room.

Now Lix's turn. He lied. He lied because he wanted Alicja to challenge him and be reminded of their early married days. He claimed, 'I've never had sex standing up.' No challenges from anyone. Surprisingly, he went through to the second round unopposed, even by his wife.

'Too drunk to stand up, Lix?'

'Or wasn't the goat tall enough?'

Lix had chanced a glance in Alicja's direction and he could not mistake the look of embarrassment on her face. He'd meant the claim as a joke, a challenge, a hasty response to the raised sexual playfulness of the twenty-two-year-old's boast never to have had sex with a younger person and the actress-poet's unexpected indiscretion. It was only an invitation for his wife to contribute some mordant reply of her own and to remind her of a happy afternoon with river views.

He'd also expected Alicja to say either, 'Well, if he's not had it standing up then I've not either, of course. So he's out of the game.' Or, better, she might say the truth, 'He's lying actually. We had sex standing up during the floods. On the roof of our apartment. At least, I think it was Lix. I couldn't see his face. I was looking in the wrong direction. Disqualified!' Then his trap, his joke would be pleasingly rounded off by her.

She should, as well, have challenged and matched the earlier winning claim 'never to have had sex with someone younger than myself', he realized. Lix was eight months older than his wife. She'd been a virgin almost to their wedding day. She'd said nothing then, and she said nothing now. She only frowned and reddened and let her fingers gallop on the tabletop. She evidently didn't want to enter into the spirit of the game. Because, he thought, matters sexual were not to be discussed at table with people she hardly knew. It wasn't 'politic'. It wouldn't do for Madam Senator L-D to let her hair down for a change amongst his friends. Oh, well, her loss. The Lesniaks were famous for their prudery and fear of fun. The Papal Stain. 'Your turn,' he said to her.

Alicja was annoyed with her husband, but mostly

not for the reasons he suspected. Social proprieties and reticence, especially with a newspaper columnist at the table, should be sensibly observed, she'd always thought. But she was more embarrassed than irritated. He should not have reminded her of their lovemaking on the roof in such a crude and clumsy way. She remembered most the massage of the herb leaves and the blessing of her pregnancy. He remembered best the unromantic standing up. Men were the enemies of romance. The sex gets in the way of loving.

Joop had said that 'absolute truth' was essential to the playing of Never. Well, her husband had not been absolutely truthful. Then neither would she. She could not ratify or challenge Lix's Neverness without betraying herself. For, within the last three weeks, Alicja had also had perpendicular sex – quick sex – with Joop more than once while she was standing. In the vestibule of his apartment house; leaning on the sink with the taps running in the Anchorage Street apartment; at his office desk one evening, her back to him, her nose pressed up against the window blinds. She'd smudged her lipstick on the blinds. Here was a lover who always took his time, who never let her off lightly. The absolute truth? Well, now was not the moment to tell her husband that she'd been sleeping – standing – with another man. The truth would have to wait.

'Come on,' he said again, an impatient, disappointed

edge to his voice. He panicked her. Otherwise she'd not have made her great mistake. The consequences of this moment were immense. She was suddenly the centre of attention for the first time that day. She'd show them she could be as mischievous as anyone. She shelved her boast that she had never learned to swim. Too dull. The dancer, probably, had never learned to swim either. She pushed aside the claims that she had never once been drunk, had never worn high heels, had not so far attended the ballet or a football match, had never had a filling in her teeth, could not remember ever having had hiccups, even as a child, had swallowed oysters but never semen so couldn't be put off by the smell. Her shocking, teasing boast was shouting at her from a poster twenty metres high: 'Take risks. Surprise them all. Be truly mischievous.' Bring back the roguish grin to Joop's fine face. She only meant it as a private joke. It wasn't absolutely true. She said, 'I've never had an orgasm.'

THAT AFTERNOON when they got home, they saw at once that there'd been burglars. Their house looked out of sorts, as if it had been caught out cheating on its owners. The outer gate was open, upstairs lights were on, someone had dropped a duster and length of haulage twine on the drive, no one had bothered to wipe their dirty feet on the porch mat, and there was a dry rectangle of driveway by the front door where something large had parked but which the recent rain had not yet had a chance to wet.

Had Alicja and Lix arrived back in Beyond just a few minutes earlier they would have caught the three young men in overalls loading everything expensive, imported, and electric into their van; the two television sets, the video, the emptied refrigerator, the new computer system and printer, not yet even installed, the hi-fi tower, the three telephones, the answer-machine, the radio alarm, the Italian stove, the PowerChef, the washing machine, even the vacuum cleaner and Lech's toy console. Trading debts and import taxes had turned anything foreign with plugs into liquid currency and anyone too impatient to endure low wages and late pay into an Appliance Bandit. Only last weekend there had been a cartoon in a newspaper showing someone in a mask paying for a tube of toothpaste with an electric toothbrush and getting a socket plug by way of change.

It was a near escape that stayed with Lix and haunted him for many months, how close they'd been that afternoon to driving through the garage gates, into the shadow of their private trees, before the men in overalls had driven off to deliver that day's 'imports' to their clientele. Then what? What kind of heroism would have been required of him, the man who'd never satisfied his wife, to rescue their appliances?

The Lix we know would not have challenged any

burglars. He might have hovered at the shoulder of his braver wife, muttering his cautions, if she'd been mad enough to get out of the car and battle with the thieves. He might have locked the car doors and blared his horn at them, the car hovering in reverse gear. He might have driven off at once, fled the scene, to call the local police from the nearest bar. On this day of anger and resentment, however, there was another possibility. A murderous one.

It was, then, just as well, perhaps, that Lix would never have the chance to find out if his anger was more brutal than his fear. The traffic had been locked across the bridges to the city's eastern banks since mid-afternoon and so their drive out to Beyond had taken more than an hour, an hour in which the weather changed to drizzle and the dusk set in. What began in sunlight ended in darkness and in rain.

FOR AN ACTOR, trained in faces, Lix was surprisingly readable when he was in a temper. His muscles tightened and his eyes went watery. Anger, was it? Embarrassment? Hurt? During their journey home he needed to identify the exact nature of his distress; then he'd know what his reaction ought to be to what Alicja had claimed. *Never* is the cruellest word, beyond negotiation. He understood that he was the resentful victim of a joke, the rough-and-tumble of the tablecloth, and that his rage would appear – had appeared – paranoid and feeble to outsiders. But there was also something dark behind his wife's disclosure at the Feast that needled him and panicked him. It had left him cold and cruel.

The driving home was difficult. Lix squinted back the sunlight and the tears, and then he had to peer through heavy rain – two films of water then – which made the road seem remote and hazardous. Lix had imagined earlier that day that they'd be heading home for sex. Now he wanted to get home only to shout at his infuriating wife if he could find the pluck to shout. Lix, to tell the truth, the shy and celebrated Lix who'd never done much harm to anyone despite his curse, despite his fame, was in the suburbs of a breakdown.

So, trapped in the traffic in the inner parts of the city, he set his jaw against the world. He would not speak to Alicja. He would not even look at her until his mind had cleared and he had formulated sentences that would repay her, punish her, match her indiscretion with some bruising indiscretion of his own. He would not grant her a single nod or shake of the head, not even when she tried to thaw him out with her calm voice and then her tough one. He silenced her with his own heavy breathing and exasperated sighs, and then with music. He put on a maddening jazz cassette, a tinkling trio of New Yorkers – string, skin, and ivory – chatting amongst themselves through their fingertips. He added the percussion of the windscreen wipers. He banged his hand impatiently on the steering wheel, pretending to enjoy the jazz. He drove the car erratically, on purpose.

Even that could not shake off his irritation. The last ten minutes of their meal, before the sulky settling of the bill and the awkward farewells, played through his mind in an uninterruptible loop: the malice of everybody laughing, the grateful gape of pleasure on Joop the Scoop's normally disdainful face as the scandalous material for his next Diary piece dropped into his lap, the clumsy comment from the owner of his record company that 'Never Had an Orgasm' would be the perfect title for a song.

'What never, Alicja? Not even almost? Not even on your own?' the actress-poet had asked. Then everybody else – his colleagues and his friends, so-called – had felt obliged to add their ridicule.

'Not even on an aeroplane?'

'Try riding a scooter or a motorbike. That ought to do the trick.'

'Go home and hug the washing machine. Super-spin cycle.'

'Poor Lix.'

'No, poor Alicja! We ought to order her a plate of oysters. Waiter! Bring on the aphrodisiacs.'

'One for me, one for you, and one for the chicken.'

Lix's Obligation Feast had been humiliating.

Alicja had been humiliated, too, of course. But she

was used to it. Her husband's friends had never been the subtle sort, especially after so much wine. She shrugged their comments off. What she could not shrug off was Lix's hurt. She had not meant to hurt him; she did not want him to be hurt. It was inconvenient. What she had planned – a tender, loving telling of the truth to a man for whom she still had feelings – was now impossible. He was bound to ask, 'Is the sex better with Joop?' So the orgasm quip had been a big mistake, because it would appear that the affair was only about sex. Then Lix would think that better sex would rescue it. Sex with Joop was better, as a matter of fact. Your neighbour's fruit is always sweeter than your own. But it wasn't about sex entirely. It was about marriage and freedom. Making love to Lix, between the household chores and work and being a responsible senator and taking care of constituents and finding time for Lech, had come to feel like just more wifework.

She'd meant the passion of their marriage to endure, of course. No one's to blame, but passion is not intended to endure. The overture is short or else it's not the overture. Nor is marriage meant to be perfect. It has to toughen on its blemishes. It has to morph and change its shape and turn its insides out and move beyond the passion that is its architect. Falling in love is not being in love. Waiting for the perfect partner is self-sabotage. Alicja knew all these things. She still wanted, though, to be womanly, not wifely. Lix had failed her in that regard. Yet saying so was difficult and cruel. She'd spent the month since she'd accepted that their marriage was in ruins running her wedding ring up and down her finger and practising how she should phrase the uncomfortable news of her infidelity. Now, as they crawled through the traffic in the suburbs and the rain, all she had to practise was an explanation and an apology.

Lix had not been such a dreadful lover, mostly. He'd been attentive, regular, prepared to act on her advice. What more could any woman want? Nobody could expect a faultless performance every time. This was not the theatre. She felt no grievances. But repetition takes its toll, she supposed, as did parenthood. Habituation dulls the soul. She would not have been the first woman who had become bored after three years of well-rehearsed routines or who had lately much preferred those tender contacts that were neither sexual nor time-consuming. To want your husband as an undemanding friend and a reliable relative but not a lover, was that the first sign that their love was lost? She'd been a fool to let him think she'd never had an orgasm with him. She'd undermined their three not unhappy years together. Marriages consist of more than orgasms, of graver spasms and contractions. She'd had a child with him, for heaven's sake! As soon as they were home, she thought, she'd sit him down and make him talk.

THEY WENT THROUGH the house from room to room, tiptoeing almost, careful not to make a noise. Lix's fists were clenched and his toes were rolled inside his shoes ready to run or kick if anybody was still inside their home. Alicja was trembling.

The ornamented metalwork on the window by the lobby door had been chiselled out of the holding mortar and bent back enough to let a small man, hardly bigger than Lech, it seemed, clamber through the broken glass. That was the only damage, though. Thank goodness the thieves had been professional. There was no soiling and no gratuitous mess, apart from the contents of the fridge and freezer, which had been tumbled onto the kitchen floor and were already weeping icy water. There was, though, evidence of disregard. Lech's toys, always neatly kept in boxes, had been tipped out on the rugs and pushed about the floor either by somebody who believed that toys were hiding places for jewellery and cash or else was young enough himself not to resist the invitation of a plastic car, with a friction engine and flashing lights.

One of the taps was running in Alicja's bathroom. Someone had used the lavatory – the seat was up – and rinsed their hands: the soap was wet. The upstairs curtains had been drawn halfway across their windows. The burglars had not wiped their shoes between each trip out to their van. Nor had they, thankfully, paid much attention to the cupboards and the drawers. A wallet was missing from the mantelshelf but their passports and the family papers had not been touched, and Lix's acting memorabilia had been ignored. Nothing had been spoiled or damaged out of spite. The thieves had not been desecrators, just hasty businessmen.

'It doesn't matter, does it?' Alicja said. 'It's only machines. No one's hurt.' She didn't say, as she was tempted to, 'I'll not be hugging my washing machine today.' Another joke would not be wise. Nor did she say, 'We'll get new stuff, within a week or two. My father only has to say his name in certain ears.' She didn't say it, because in fact she thought, We won't get new stuff, actually. There'll be no need. The cargo of their marriage was already shipping out, and though she was not exactly pleased, the burglary seemed meaningful. Beyond the shock and sense of violation there was a sliver of elation as they toured their perfect and expensive house, noting all the spaces. Rid yourself of chattels first, and then the man.

The man was by now almost in tears again.

'What should we do?' She had to put her arm

around his waist. Today was not the day, she realized, for admitting her affair. It would have to wait until he got back from America.

'What can we do? They've taken everything and gone.'

'We ought to call the police. We'd better not touch anything. I'll telephone my father . . .'

'Call the police? Call the police on what? They didn't leave a telephone,' he said. 'Let's leave your father out of it.'

'Go to the neighbour's house and call from there.'

Lix did not want more invaders yet, tramping through the house, unnerving him with questions. And Alicja preferred to deal with problems in the order they arose. So they did not tell the police or call for help for twenty minutes more. Instead, she suffered him. She had first to restore at least one of the orgasms that she had denied in front of all his friends downstairs below the Debit Bar. She had to make amends and reassure her failing husband. That was only fair. A marriage should be straightened out before it's pulled apart.

HE MADE HER pregnant again, of course. The contraceptives, not much used in recent months, were kept in Lix's missing wallet. Thanks to burglars, perhaps, their second son was taking shape. Thanks to the purchase of a blouse. Thanks to the risky game of Never. Thanks to the guilty fondness that endures, survives the break-up of a marriage, she would have a second son.

By ill-fortune and good luck, Lix had done as much as any man could do in natural history to see his scoundrel rival slink away, his tail and nothing else between his legs. Vasectomized Jupiter, the columnist, would speedily lose interest in the senator when he discovered she was pregnant. So Lix would never have to hear the truth about his lunch pal, Joop – because by the time he got back from Nevada, his wife's new relationship would be over and she'd be two months pregnant.

We should not, though, expect a reconciliation, for this would be the last occasion Lix and his Alicja, his plump and much improving wife, would ever kiss, embrace, make love. For it was love, this final time. Not perfect sex. Not orgasms and passion such as she would have with Joop and with the fellow after Joop or with the man who'd be her second husband and the father of her only daughter, but tender love nevertheless, two bodies being thoughtful, being kind and fond, and being slightly desperate because at moments such as these the truth is always on display.

Alicja had not admitted anything just yet, and Lix had not dared to ask. His cowardice was without boundaries. Besides, her beryl blouse was lying on the bed, and her indented body was so engaged with his, that he could hardly think or grieve. Perhaps it was just as well that when the sex was over and before they called the police they could lie in bed and not feel obliged to talk. Talk at that time was dangerous.

Then Lix was in the car again, the smell of her not quite removed by showering, not quite hidden by his spray cologne. He'd have to be *Don Juan Amongst the Feminists* at eight o'clock that night, and if he didn't hurry he'd arrive too late for staging notes and make-up calls. It was as dark by now as it had seemed when they were dining in the Hesitation Room. He was heading into town while traffic from the offices and shops was heading out. The actor's face was flecked and flashed by lights and indicators, profile, profile, then full on.

He parked his car behind the theatre, depressed, elated, but relieved to have the pressure of the sex removed. The anger was reduced as well. He'd been a fool. He was resigned to what the future held if it held anything. He was content to be back in the ancient town, amongst the places that he loved. The buildings seemed to shimmer in the shifting lights, as offices winked off their lamps, and bars and restaurants and clubs sprang into life.

Lix waited for a bus to pass, its windows full of backs and coats, before he crossed to the theatre and made it to his dressing room without needing to exchange a word with anyone. He closed the door and he was Don Juan.

An hour later, costumed and made-up, he stood at the window with his play script looking out on the heads of the first arrivals at the theatre, his captive audience. The building shook a little to the digestive rumbling once again of the nightmare trams that didn't suspend their timetables for mere theatre. Instead they did their best to remind his audience every night that they were watching an artifice and that only one street away the city's aged transport laboured on, taking uninvented people to their uninvented homes.

There was a point in Don Juan's last speech each night when Lix could almost guarantee a tram. Some of the audience would laugh. Such incongruity, a tram. Others, though, would look alarmed as the auditorium amplified the rattle of the carriages into something that might be the distant and approaching earthquake that the city had been promised by geophysicists 'within a hundred years'. Then the theatre would shake with nervousness and they would ask themselves, Will we survive? What will survive? Uncannily, the answer came from off the stage. 'Of all the edifices in our town,' Don Juan explained, as trams passed by, 'no one can doubt, not anyone who's lived at least, that love's the frailest tower of them all, meant to tumble, built to fall.'

5

THEY'D NEVER TRULY kissed before, Lix and An. It was undeniable, though – there had been nine thousand witnesses, so far – that their lips had touched, and had done so every night for fourteen weeks, in character, in costume and on stage, abetted by their scripts. They were obedient professionals. The play demanded that they fall in love, so they obliged convincingly. They were old hands at that.

They'd been respectful colleagues, yes, cheerful and supportive. Yet nobody could claim that they were even friends offstage. If they ever coincided in the Players' Easy Room or in the bar behind the theatre, they were polite with each other but uninvolved, the lively little actress, not so young and not so pretty any more, and Mr Taciturn who'd led God knows what kind of life since his divorce and his success. The gossip columns couldn't even guess, beyond the rumours circulating still that he was either egotistical in bed or impotent. The evidence was thin, either way. Lix had no public life, no politics. 'Reclusive' was the word the papers used these days to describe the actor. Or, better, 'secretive', because that suggested he was concealing something. You'd not expect a man like that to couple up with An, for whom concealment and reclusion were anathema. But this was the break of New Year's Day, New Century's Day, and both of them were lonely, and exhilarated by the date, 01/01/01. Conception day for Rosa Dern.

THE THIRD MILLENNIUM for us started one year after everybody else's, because some bored and playful speculators from the Tourist Bureau had decided and decreed that the City of Balconies and the City of Kisses could now be marketed for a lucrative month or so as the City of Mathematical Truth, the Capital of Calendar Authenticity, and would thereby reap and thresh the ripest crop of revellers from abroad who'd want a replay of the false New Millennium they'd already celebrated so memorably, so profitably, one year before. We'd be the only place where you could observe the Accurate Millennium, they said. We'd be the only town where you could mark the Advent of the Future twice. Sudden fortunes would be made by hotels, restaurants, and breweries, normally run down for the winter, and by the opportunists from the Tourist Bureau who'd put in place some subtle private deals.

So, in expectation of fifteen thousand out-of-season visitors, all eager to procure a night of pleasure, the bunting and the streamers were prepared. The historic city centre was closed to traffic. The whole of Company Square was equipped with braziers and licensed for the sale of alcohol. The airport lobby was emblazoned with the banners THE TIME IS RIGHT (AT LAST!) FOR HAVING FUN, and WELCOME TO THE CITY THAT TRULY COUNTS. Prostitutes took rooms downtown and women hoping to be wifed abroad bought new, provoking clothes and carried their Final School Grades in their evening bags as 'proof'. And a midnight firework show, which would be 'visible from the moon', was readied on Navigation Island, in the mud.

The foreign revellers, regrettably, were sick of new millennia by then. The disappointment – and the hangovers – of the first would last them for a thousand years. One anticlimax was enough. Therefore they did not come to us in their expected droves. Instead, our hotels were half filled with maths curmudgeons, mostly male, Dutchmen, Scandinavians, and Yanks, academics, intellectuals, and bachelors, who'd refused the year before to recognize the numerically premature end of the millennium but now had got an opportunity to demonstrate their bloody-mindedness and learning. Imagine it, on New Year's Eve, our city full of nit-pickers, hair-splitters, pedants, and rationalists, and local women dressed like queens scaring them to death, with their grade Cs in science, languages, and art. And what did these maths curmudgeons want to do to celebrate the passing year? They wanted to avoid the crowds.

In fact, the streets were full enough that night. With citizens. We've always liked a firework show and alcohol and women in provoking clothes. 'There is, indeed, good cause for all of us to celebrate,' Jupiter wrote in his Sunday column on New Year's Eve. 'Contrary to the evidence of our own eyes, we are making measurable progress in this city. Now we are only a year behind the rest of the world. Let's see if we can close the gap by 3001.'

Lix had been on stage till ten in his revival of *The Devotee*, not the most testing of romantic comedies but an easy and welcome opportunity for him to sing and act and show his famous face before an uncritical audience that normally would not spend time or money in the theatre. No need to exert himself. No need for nuances or subtlety. Just be certain, he reminded himself before each performance, that the laughter clears before the next amusing line, and that the next amusing line is timed to end before the laughter starts. 'And don't forget, of course,' his stage director said, 'to beam and bounce.'

The audience did not want art at that time of the year or intellectual theatre. They'd only come, that evening anyway, to pass the time before midnight by watching two luminaries make love on stage, and then to boast they'd seen the celebrated Lix in the flesh.

They'd seen his birthmark and they'd seen his shaved and naked chest. What's more, they'd watched their television star, the man who'd made a fortune from his songs about their city, kissing Anita Julius, the actress who was equally famous for her Channel Beta talent show, her range of tempers, and for her fleeting love affairs with older men, younger men, men with chauffeur-driven cars, and then the chauffeurs, too.

So, when finally, and as the curtains closed, An and Lix reached the moment of that much-vaunted, promised kiss – the one the theatre posters reproduced, the one so many times reprinted in the magazines, the one that all the gossip columnists would use when the scandal broke on New Year's Day – the otherwise inattentive audience grew tense and quiet. Opera glasses were lifted up. People shifted in their seats to gain the clearest view. Men licked their lips and cleared their throats, as if they believed their turn would come, that An would jump down off the stage to plant her lovely lips on theirs. Not one single person looked elsewhere. They watched through narrowed eyes. You'd think that *Life* magazine had got it wrong in 1979 when it recorded so much affection on the streets and that for us public kissing was still as exotic, rare, and disconcerting as a total eclipse. Miss it, and it wouldn't come again for years; stare too long and openly and you'd go blind.

It wasn't only the actual kiss that mesmerized and

silenced them. It was also the unexpected display of what they took – mistook – as privacy, the unembarrassed breaching of a hidden world that only chambermaids and paparazzi ever stumbled on. Four famous lips engaged in lovemaking while all the world, sunk and squirming in their seats, looked on and felt the pangs of exclusion. Here was a life denied to ticketholders in the audience, a life of cash and fame and sex and unselfconsciousness. No wonder no one dared to breathe or be the first to clap.

The audience that night was witnessing something new and dangerous, however. In every performance until this one on New Year's Eve, the lovers' kissing had been a cleverly rehearsed sham. They were, to use the actors' phrase, 'kissing like puppets' or 'dry drinking', their lips stitched shut, their mouths as passionate and hard as stones, their breaths held in until the kissing was completed.

It's true, all the audiences so far had seen both Lix and An put out their tongues a little as their faces closed in, as their noses touched. A little strip of reflective mouth gel achieves that trick. The stage lights had caught the wet and fleshy tongue tips, exactly as the stage director planned. It might have looked as if the actors' mouths were busy with each other's tongue; everyone would swear to that. But they'd been fooled. They wanted to believe, they wanted to be duped. What was rolling in the actors' cheeks, convincing the galleries and the stalls that this was more than theatre, was only the mockery of tongues. Lix and An were performing in the pockets of their own mouths with their own tongues – 'playing solo trumpet' is the term – with no more sexual passion than they'd need to free a wedge of toffee from their teeth. That's showbusiness. It's trickery and counterfeit. The actors have to seem to care, when they do not.

The fact was this, however it appeared on stage: until the final act on New Year's Eve, their tongues had never touched. An did not truly fancy Lix, no matter what the gossips and the posters might imply, no matter what they did on stage. He did not truly fancy her. Yet if theatre was powerful and could transform an audience, then how could it not affect the principals themselves, eventually? How could their nightly kissing on the stage not spill over into life – particularly on New Year's Eve when all the cast and all the staff, including Lix and An (especially), had oiled the way by drinking to each other's health before the show? It isn't love that's blind, it's alcohol.

The twenty minutes he'd spent sharing wine with his co-star in the Players' Easy Room that evening had left Lix – who'd never had a head for drink – a little off-balance and even more bewildered than usual by his offstage feelings for his irritating little colleague, so lively and so noisy, so 'unstitched'. On the one hand, anyone could see – to use the idiotic jargon of our city's most expensive psychoanalyst, a man that An had 'couched' herself on more than one occasion – 'their compasses were pointing at a different north'. She might be only a couple of years younger than Lix, but she was the product of a different age. You'd think her only gods were clothiers and coiffeurs. She liked a man in uniform, she claimed. She liked him even better out of uniform. She'd never voted, never would. She dined and dieted instead. She held strong views but only about the sounds and fashions of the day, whose singing voice was sexiest, what went with mauve, how best to get away with hats. She'd told a journalist that if the Mother Nature Beauty Clinic had intended her to stop at home with a good book on a Saturday night, it wouldn't have equipped her with such high heels, such long fingernails, and 'plastic breasts that didn't jiggle when she danced'. Lix had read the press releases before *The Devotee* had opened, and they had made him blush. Bring back the Street Beat Renegades.

On the other hand, it had to be admitted that the little featherhead could act. It had to be admitted, too, that as each day and each performance had passed, his dismissal of and disdain for An had ebbed. Now when he was reminded what she'd said about her bulky, plastic chest, he was more curious and amused than irritated. She certainly had pluck. She certainly was fun. She certainly was beddable. Whereas during rehearsals and the first few days of performance their stage kissing, dry though it was, had been an embarrassment and an ordeal for him – fencing and wearing weight bags were the only things he hated more – he had since become resigned to it, and then addicted. Some things are inevitable. Once again, the old refrain, 'Such is the nature of the beast.'

Lix had discovered as each night passed in this long season of *The Devotee* that truly not wanting a woman, not in his head, not in his heart of hearts, not in his Perfect Future, was not a logic that the lower body valued much. Anita Julius might not be the kind of partner he dreamed of waking with in his own bed or – horror at the thought of it – engaging in a conversation over breakfast cups on his expensive balcony, but, lately, as the final curtain cut the audience away on their supposedly unfeeling kiss, he had felt increasingly perturbed. His face was numb, perhaps. His lips were little more than bruised by her hard mouth. The insides of his cheeks were tender from too much 'trumpeting'. But elsewhere Lix was suffering what actors call 'an impromptu', that's to say an unexpected intervention by an unpredictable performer. His cock was enlarged. His 'rubbery courgette' was ripe.

It stirred a little more each evening, a little earlier in the plot, a little more insistently. It could not help itself (the truest and the weakest excuse you'll ever hear in life). It responded to his co-star as unjudgementally, it seemed, as mushrooms react to light.

Six

By late December, Lix had become wearied by his performance, its drudgery and duplication, and only truly involved in the closing moments of the play when finally An's body crossed the boards to hold her Devotee. He was not nervous of his co-star any more. He trusted her. Her skin and hair now smelt familiar, like family. They were becoming intimates. He enjoyed the laundered and rustling contact of their costumes, the comic stiffness of her breasts, the clammy perspiration on his fingertips from her back and neck, like offstage lovers do. He prized and cursed the audience. Without the audience, he thought, his cock would not stir for her. They were a love triangle, the star, the co-star, and the crowd.

It would be ingenuously optimistic – the stuff of theatre – to hope that An herself had not become aware of Lix's extra contribution to the play. There could be no disguising what was going on from her. Their costumes were too thin and flexible. The stage directions said, 'They hold each other tightly and they kiss. The curtain slowly falls.' She would have felt the difference up against her abdomen. That's not to say that his erection was abnormally large and resolute. It was a meekly modest one, like most men's are, most of the time.

Nevertheless, An would have known exactly what it was and who was causing it. After all, it couldn't be oedema or a hernia. It came and went too readily. For her, a woman used to provoking men, the explanation would have been a simple one. Her charms were irresistible. After all, she could deliver erections to half a theatre. She'd made a living out of it. Usherettes at other shows had told her several times about the witless stiffening of men standing at the back of the gallery, thirty metres from the stage – and out of range, you would have thought. And, during her brief appearance in *Regina Vagina*, before it was raided and banned, she had heard reports of husbands who had to squirm and rearrange their trousers while their wives preferred to concentrate elsewhere. 'The members of the audience,' some wit had said at the time, 'stood up for Anita Julius.'

It would be unusual, then, and perhaps a little disappointing, if Lix, a youngish, active, divorced man and not a homosexual, so far as anybody knew, did not respond to her, especially when her body was so close, especially when her long nails were digging through his shirt.

Lix, really, was not as active as An imagined, not as busy with the women as anyone with his celebrity and power ought to be. Perhaps that's why he'd lost control with her so easily and why his penis had informed on him as incautiously as an untrained boy's. He was the celibate celebrity, unused to having women in his arms.

Lix had been divorced since 1993. He'd been physically apart from Alicja since he'd taken flight to

Hollywood and Nevada. His wife had gone. His anchor was pulled up. He was entirely – *free* is not the word – at liberty. Yet here's a truth that's hard to credit, given what we hear about the opportunities of fame, but more common than you'd think in men who are divorced and past their best: he'd not had any full sex or any romance since then, not since that afternoon of burglary, in fact, when Karol was conceived. That's more than seven years on his own. That's more than seven years' losing confidence. You'd never guess it, from the way he spoke and walked, the city's movie star, the Celebrated Lix. You'd think a man like him with distinguished looks, a mighty income, and acclaim, could have as many women in his bed as he wanted, and any way he wanted. You'd think, you'd hope, he had so much passion that he wearied of it.

Well, that's the daydream. But even if the opportunities were manifold, Lix like many actors did not trust strangers even in the dressing room. He'd not invite the audience to watch the shedding of his costume and his make-up, the stowing of his wig and sword. He'd not disarm himself in public. That's the point. That's what he studied for, pretence and privacy. So certainly he could not have much appetite for being the naked animal in bed with someone he hardly knew, that chance encounter in a bar who recognized his face and didn't want to waste the opportunity, that theatre student intent on ways of furthering her own career, or that waitress who's only there, in bed with him – oh, there'd been offers, many times for Lix from waitresses – because she'd like, just once, to squeeze up close to fame's gold ribs.

Lix had been tempted, naturally. The magnet force of casual sex is almost irresistible, like gravity. In those seven years, he had almost succumbed half a dozen times at most, but he always managed to avoid true intimacy. He did it Freda's way. No penetration, that's to say, and therefore hardly any chance of pregnancy. Heavy petting was the best he could offer. Initially his sexual reticence baffled his admirers. Then – once they had realized that here was a man unable to yield himself – it angered them. They did not persevere with him.

But mostly Lix did not engage at all. He was fearful – and, as ever, timid. Fearful of the body in the mirror. What would these conquests think when he took off his clothes to show the grey hairs on his arm, the raised veins on his legs, his paunch, his meagreness, his tremor, the telltale addition of purple tints to his skin's pale palette? Fearful also of the future and the past. He dared not expose himself again to that cruel battle-ground. He was ashamed by his near-celibacy as well, as if it were a character flaw and proof that he was insufficiently advanced for love. He'd never been – not even once, he judged – much good with love or sex, except on stage. (And in photographs, of course. Freda and Alicja were always smiling for him in the photos that he kept.) Certainly he'd not impressed the three women he'd slept with so far: one had only stayed the night, one had only stayed a month, and one had told the world she'd never had an orgasm, so packed her bags and left. His was a history of love rebutted and love devalued. Besides, the poor man felt the force of his unfortunate fertility. Three children were enough, he judged: two children he rarely saw, a son he'd never loved or met, and more calamities attending in the wings, no doubt. He was, he understood too well, best left alone: the unshared frying pan, the undivided loaf. He'd turned into a reluctant kind of man, disconcerted, hesitant, persuaded that he had little future as a lover, except the futures he dreamed up alone, and hardly any past.

Yet Lix had gained contentment of a sort. Desire was like a plant, he'd found. The more you watered it, the bigger and the thirstier it became, the more demanding and dissatisfied. When he had had a woman in his life, then Lix's sexual frustration had not diminished. Rather it had escalated. To have removed himself from the cycle of demand was for Lix a release into a long, flat period of calm.

Yet an understanding of oneself, a well-earned dread of strangers, children, love, is no defence against the concentrated moment in the arms of someone of the other sex: her textures and her odours and her voice are

old and powerful. There comes a point where everything is lost, where self-control becomes abandonment,
and man becomes – it's glib to say but nothing else is
true – as mindlessly and helplessly fixated as a beast.

Lix, then, can be excused by his biology? Well, yes.
So can An. Biology's the victor every time. It's only
natural that she would want to fool around with Lix,
provoke him more and more. She could not help
devising ways to fit her body just a shade more snugly
into his when they embraced before the spellbound
ticket-holders any more than a bee could fly away from
honey. My God, the play was tedious, she thought,
but new distractions such as this at least added spice to
their performances.

As the days passed and their stage kisses multiplied,
she began to choose her underclothes and body scent
more carefully, and even to make her bed before she
left her studio for the theatre each evening and to spray
her mouth with TobaGo if she'd smoked in the interval
before the final act. She understood ahead of Lix that
it would only be a matter of time before the two of
them were having sex, and so she might as well prepare
for it – and so they might as well get on with it. Let's
eat the porridge while it's hot.

On New Year's Eve, the last performance of the
year and stoked up by the wine she'd drunk a little
earlier and by a lack of partners for the Night of
the Mathematical Millennium and by the evidence that

pressed against her abdomen, An ditched the usual protocols and when they kissed, the scripted Widow and her Devotee, she popped her tongue into his mouth, just for a second, a warm and playful sortie into perilous domains. She dipped it in and out so swiftly that his own tongue did not have the chance to mate with it, although it tried, instinctively. Both tongues briefly caught the lights and for half a second a string of glistening saliva unified their lips.

Now everybody in the theatre could swear that absolutely they were making love. The only one in any doubt was Lix himself. All An had to do, she knew, was wait. Do nothing more, she told herself. Act normal during curtain calls. Be cool. Enjoy the moment while it lasts. If he's as weak and predictable as all the other men she'd poked her tongue into then he'd come running to her dressing room with some excuse or else he'd hang around outside the theatre for her, and she could celebrate her New Year's Eve in company.

NOT-SO-LITTLE George had witnessed all of this. He was sitting in an aisle seat on row H on New Year's Eve, next to his mother Freda and her cousin Mouetta, when he encountered Lix for the second time. Was this the weirdest evening of his life? His mother had promised him four months before, on his eighteenth birthday – but only after years of secrecy and cussedness and argument – that she would 'set up' a meeting with his father, 'if you really have to persevere with this'. He was prepared. He'd always thought and hoped his father was the bare-chested man whose picture his mother kept in her wallet. The Czech. They would go to Prague and meet the hero in a gas-lit restaurant. Freda had only laughed at the idea. 'Your father's not a hero, that's for sure.'

'Just give me his name and his address and leave it to me,' George had said. 'It's time! You don't even have to be involved.'

But she had always insisted, 'If we have to do it at all, we'll do it my way. You owe me that. He hasn't shown a hint of interest in you, by the way, in eighteen years. He hasn't contributed one single bean. So don't expect some paragon. But still I want to make it memorable.'

'Memorable for whom?'

'For him and for you.'

She'd kept her word.

George had waited for the 'set-up' that she planned with (his genetic inheritance from Lix) timidity and fear. His mother's set-ups always took an age to organize and, usually, another age to disentangle. Perhaps his father would prove to be less militant and complicating, and there'd be explanations, too, for why he'd never tried to get in touch himself.

Then finally, a week before the end of the millennium, she'd said, 'We'll take a look at him on New

Year's Eve,' and handed over tickets for *The Devotee*, a play that normally she'd mock as bourgeois and offensive.

George knew better than to spoil her plans by asking for some details in advance. Had she arranged for him to sit next to the man, perhaps? That seemed the likeliest. Was there some lobby rendezvous designed? Was he an actor, maybe, or one of the musicians? The possibilities at least had narrowed from the thousands he'd considered all his life: his missing father was a foreigner, a gigolo, a member of the government, an anarchist, a colleague at the university, a criminal, a beggar on the streets, a lunatic, a priest, a man too dull to care about, a man she'd hired to fill a tube with sperm. There'd always been a silence and a mystery. The only clue was that once or twice she'd described the man, dismissively, as Smudge. Then on New Year's Eve itself when George, Freda, and Mouetta had been sitting in their seats, before the curtain rose, his mother had taken out a marking pen and ringed a name on the cast list. A famous name he recognized but could not yet quite put a face to. 'That's him,' she said. 'Starring Felix Dern.'

The play itself, he thought, was a bag of feathers. What interest could it hold for anybody there who'd not come to be united with a parent? The music was ill-balanced and predictable. The script was far too nudging. The female lead, an actress almost as old as his own mother, appeared a little drunk. But everybody in the audience, including Freda – and especially Freda – seemed amused, vindicated, even. His mother's was the loudest laugh, and not a mocking one.

When, halfway through the opening act, his father first appeared on stage and the spontaneous applause of recognition had abated, George himself burst into tears that, luckily, he could disguise as laughter. That face was so familiar, of course. The celebrated Felix Dern. The photo in the magazines. The birthmark on the cheek. Now that he saw the actor in the flesh, animated, George was not only sure he'd already met the man some years before – he racked his brains, but couldn't say exactly when – but also he was certain that he'd seen him, a younger version, a thousand times, in mirrors every day. George had his hair. George had his walk. George had his father's mouth.

If George had hoped *The Devotee* would offer hidden messages to Lost Boys in the audience, then he was disappointed. The drama was not relevant. Or only relevant to simple and romantic souls. George was mesmerized nevertheless, but as the evening progressed and as he weathered the two intervals, preferring not to join his mother and her cousin in the bars, but rather to remain exactly where he was, in row H, studying that one name on the cast list, his exhilaration at being George Dern turned into embarrassment. Watching a father you have never known playing the part of someone who's never existed, and speaking his invented lines, was bound to be a disconcerting experience for an awkward eighteen-year-old. In the last few moments of the final act, the boy's embarrassment was total. Even Freda had been silenced by the kiss.

'Now do you remember where you saw him once before?' his mother asked after the final curtain call, when everybody else was hurrying off to start their celebrations for Millennium Eve.

George did not want to say, 'The mirror.' He said, 'His face rings bells. But, no . . .' He shook his head.

'The Palm & Orchid,' his mother said. 'When you were a kid. You saw him there. Do you remember it? I wouldn't let you finish your cake.'

He shook his head again.

'Well, then, so now you know,' she said. 'Your father is revealed. Exposed! You even look like him a bit. I'd never thought of it before. Don't *be* like him, that's all I ask.'

Mouetta raised her eyebrows, shook her head. She seemed, as usual, slightly shocked, and disapproving of Freda's modern motherhood. Jealousy, Freda always thought. Her cousin hadn't got a lover or a son. 'Well, we have an hour or so before the fireworks,' she continued. 'What shall we do? You want to eat? Go to a bar?' More shaking heads. 'Or do you want to wait and say hello to the star?' No nods. Not quite. Freda was only teasing, anyway. She knew that meeting his father, offstage, was inescapably what George would want to do.

We must consider Freda's smile, and judge if it was cruel or only happy for her son. To tell the truth, she didn't know the answer herself. She only knew that she could not contain the smile. It took possession of her face and would not shift, although she tried to shift it. She was less handsome when she smiled. Partly she was glad to have Lix off her conscience, finally. Partly she was excited by the date and by the promise of a long, amusing night. Also she could not dismiss the compelling prospect of Lix's face when they ensnared him in the theatre lobby and finally he understood that this young man who'd seen his bloodless play was blood itself. She wasn't truly cruel or vengeful, just certain of herself and unafraid. Whatever her more tender cousin Mouetta might believe, Freda always wanted what was best for George, despite herself. She loved dramatic times. She thought they made the world a grander place. That's why she smiled and smiled. 'I've come to introduce you to your son,' she'd say. He'd never dare reply, 'The child is yours, not mine. Your pregnancy. Your body. Your responsibility. Your private life. Your kid!'

So this was how Lix met his second wife.

AFTERWARDS, Lix did not have the nerve or even the desire to go to Anita Julius's dressing room where, surely, she'd be waiting for him, if what she'd done on stage meant anything, if that warm tongue had been an honest messenger. He was shaking badly, for a start, and feeling old. He was the father of a fully grown man. How could he concentrate on casual sex when every chamber of his head was crowded out with sons?

Nor had he got the heart to go back to the too-neat bachelor apartment on the embankment as he had originally intended. For True Millennium Eve, he'd planned to sit out on the enclosed balcony, with a glass of good red wine, something comforting on the stereo, and watch the fireworks. On his own. For Lix was not a man with many friends. He might not have a glamorous life offstage but at least he had the best view in town that money could rent, directly across the river to Navigation Island and then beyond into the proliferating towers of the campuses. He had to count himself as blessed, that whatever might be wrong with his first years of middle age, his isolation and his longing, he was living exactly where he wanted to, had always wanted to. Not Beyond where everything was new and compromised, but in the city's ancient heart of squares and stone, and narrow streets and balconies.

On sunny days, with his binoculars, he could watch the couples walking on the island amongst the tarbonies and candy trees, the tantalizing world of hand-in-hand; the cyclists, the picnickers, the teenagers in noisy groups around the lido. Scenes out of Seurat and

Renoir. Even on busy days the only traffic he could see was on the bridges heading to or fleeing from the eastern side. At night, when all the bars were closed and all the lights were off, he could lie in bed and listen to the scheming of the wind and the sleepless shifting of the river, a lonely sound that sometimes made him glad to be alone.

His encounter in the theatre lobby had shocked and shaken him. Of course it had. Shame and embarrassment had been delivered publicly and unexpectedly. It didn't help to tell himself that he had merely been a victim of one of Freda's vengeful schemes. As he'd expect from her, the whole ambush had been meanly staged, he thought, and damaging for everyone involved, except, of course, for the Lovely Neck herself.

Lix had played this scene one time before, for film, in a policier, *The Reckoning*. He'd been a politician, newly elected and, of course, dishonest and corrupt. It's still available on video. In the final scene, he comes out of his offices, surrounded by a clamour of supporters. He shakes a hundred hands. He issues platitudes and thanks, and smiles his practised smile towards the ranks of cameramen, so many more than he had ever dreamed of. Out of the corner of his eye, while he is being loud and false with everyone, he spots his peasant father, and the police inspector. Behind them, waiting on the far side of his limousine, is the widow of the brother he has cheated. The cameramen move in. The screen goes white with flash. Then the soundtrack becomes silent. Regrets are deafening. All you can see, as the credits start to roll, are his admirers, clamouring.

It appeared to him, this night of the Millennium, that he had strayed into a mocking version of that bad film – except this time the formula was not the Unmasking of the False Prophet but the cliché of the Lost Child. Once he'd shed his costume and removed his paint, Lix had, as usual and despite the lure of An, come down into the lobby of the theatre to meet his more clinging admirers. It's duty, he always told himself, not vanity.

So it was duty that made him pause on the bottom stair and patronize the gathered crowd of twenty or so with his best beam so that anyone with cameras could get a decent shot and so that anybody wanting auto-graphs could form a line. Quite soon, out of the corner of his actor's eye, he would spot the tall young man, blond-haired but unmistakably a Dern, a perfect speci-men that any mother, any father should be proud to have, a young man not quite knowing how to shake his fear off with a smile.

However, it wasn't George whom Lix noticed first, or even Freda – though, Heaven knows, Freda was immensely noticeable that night. She'd pulled out all the stops for this encounter. She'd piled her hair with careful randomness, as unignorable as a wedding cake. God help the man who'd sat behind her in the theatre, though he might be glad to miss the play but have the opportunity, instead, to study Freda's nape and neck, her swinging silver earrings, the tender intersection of her hair and skin, the little golden zip-tag peeking from the collar of her fine black dress.

No, it was Mouetta whom Lix first noticed, an unembarrassed woman, not too young, her raincoat collar up, simply standing by the furthest exit door and staring at him blatantly as one might stare at the photo on a playbill or a film poster. She was clearly not the usual shy but awestruck fan. He'd always say he fell in love with her at once. But he felt next to nothing at the time, except uneasiness. He took the woman's stare as evidence of something that he'd learned to run away from: the colonizing attentions of a stranger who – wrongly – thought that actors were as interesting in themselves as they seemed on stage, the sort who would never settle for a signature and a handshake or a photograph but wanted to be taken home and wanted to be listened to and loved, the sort who never joined the noisy queue but waited at the exit door to join him as he fled the theatre. He'd steer well clear of her, he thought, until she smiled at him, returned his stagy beam with something much more genuine. And he was lost. And so were any plans he might have had for meeting up with An.

He'd understand later that the smile was only meant to offer a little sympathy. Mouetta knew her lovely cousin's ways. She knew that Freda had been selfish with the boy, and secretive. She knew that Lix would be appalled, discomfited, by what was planned for him. Most of all she smiled because she loved her second cousin George as if he were a younger brother and she wanted this first encounter with his father to be memorable. A pleasant memory. Her smile for Lix could only help to pave the way.

Lix stayed on the bottom step and stooped to do his duty. He thanked his fans, signed the last few programmes and a couple of CDs, made his final practised quips, turned up his collar too, like her, the woman at the door, and glanced again across the room to take a second look at that nice smile. He wouldn't mind it, actually, if the woman fell in beside him in the street, if she came back to share his good red wine, his balcony, his firework view, his life. He'd be better off with her, surely, than the waiting tongue upstairs. So many opportunities.

Finally he spotted Freda standing at the woman's side, clearly not a fan of his, not wanting autographs or photographs, but smiling too in his direction and nodding her hellos. And then the young man whom he knew at once to be his son. Real life, at last: the curtain down; the clamour and the silence and the flash. 'You've dined, old man – and now it's time to face the waiter and the bill.'

*

THAT FRIENDLESS DRINK he'd planned on his veranda, with his privileged outlook over the island and his prime view of the fireworks, was not now, Lix realized at once, the wisest way to pass the first few moments of the new, true, mathematical millennium. He was too excited, overwhelmed and horrified to be alone. He had intended being calm and almost sober, and waiting by the phone at midnight, ready for the dutiful calls from Alicja and the boys.

There was no afternoon performance of *The Devotee* on New Year's Day and he'd arranged for the children to make their weekly visit. He had the perfect set of treats for them. At ten and eight, Lech and Karol were the age when days out with their father at the zoo, with its newly opened river aquarium and its camel rides, were still appealing, despite the cold, especially if they were accompanied, as he had promised on this occasion, by a vedette ride upstream to the Mechanical Fair and permission, if they passed the height test, to ride the watercoaster, Yankee Tidal Wave.

He wondered now if it had been a rash mistake to ask this stranger, George, to join him on the trip. 'Meet your brothers,' he had said, a foolish suggestion, and many years too late. By now he should be taking George to brothels, not to zoos and funfairs. The moment had been panicky. Freda could not have staged the meeting to be more disconcerting: the fans, the lobby, the post-performance frenzy, the bustle of the exit doors, the terror that she knew the very sight of her would visit on her ancient lover.

Why had she not just brought the boy up to his dressing room? Why hadn't she just phoned to say that George, to her dismay, had reached the age when identifying his father was essential? Why, indeed, had she brought the boy to see him act in this dimwitted and untesting comedy, out of all the plays he'd been in? Revenge was not her only motivation, surely. She wanted rather to embarrass him as much as possible, to make him seem at once as weak and feeble as she would already have described him. 'He'll try to bluff it out,' she would have said. 'He'll do some actor stuff. He'll carry on as if meeting a magnificent son like you was something that he'd performed a hundred times. To mad applause, of course. Your blood father only does it for applause.'

So Lix's 'Come to the zoo!' had been a comically ill-judged suggestion. Lix had seen the smirking triumph on Freda's face. He'd also seen the look of hope and panic in the young man's eyes, and had tried to claw the offer back.

'Perhaps. We'll let you know. We'll phone,' Freda had said, evidently unable to control her smile. We'll let you know. *We'll* phone. The *we* was wounding, as she must have known, as she must have intended.

Lix should, of course, have been more spontaneous. A hug, perhaps. A firm handshake. Some tears. Or an apology. But there was still audience about. A couple of persistent girls with unsigned programmes were waiting in the theatre lobby, within hearing distance of anything their hero said. He had to be controlled, he had to be wary, at least until he could escape into the street, his collar up against the weather and the fans, when there would be an opportunity to try again, to ask this George to join him in a bar, perhaps, to be more passionate and brave, to sob and kiss and laugh with fearful joy. At once.

By the time he'd reached the street, and had despatched the two impatient girls with his worst of signatures and shaken one or two more hands, George and his mother and his mother's cousin whose name he did not catch, their duty done, were already walking off, down one of the crowded Hives towards the river front. Were almost out of sight, in fact. Were almost lost to him.

Lix followed them, of course. He needed time to think, and time to study this new son. If he hung on to them but kept his distance, then he could decide a further strategy, and one that left him looking wise and fine instead of stumbling and foolish. He could go up at any time while they were in the streets and say . . . well, say whatever he'd rehearsed while he was dogging them, say something that would wipe away the wasted eighteen years, quickly find the fine line that scriptwriters might take a week to perfect. Oh, yes, he was ashamed. How had he let the moment pass those many years ago? He should have said, 'Your pregnancy. Your body, yes. Your private life. But this is not your private kid! I have responsibilities, and needs.'

How had he also let that second moment pass, when he had first encountered George, his mouth made clown-like by the caster sugar of his unfinished cake, as Freda fled the Palm & Orchid, their son in tow? Some restitution had to happen in the next few minutes. Lix could not squander this last chance.

The city was not on his side, not on the side of courage and fine lines. The old millennium had only twenty minutes left to run, and everybody was anxious to reach the embankment pavements for the light and fire display. Revellers, dressed both for warmth and ostentation, a comic combination, shared cannabis and wine with strangers. Whole families were holding hands in comfort chains, lest anyone got swept away by the crowds. Old couples from the neighbourhood, decked out in their best suits, last used for funerals, did their best despite their bones to be young and contemporary, yet had not dared to venture outside into these unruly streets without their good-luck pebbles in their pockets to frighten off misfortune. Perhaps the foreign maths curmudgeons had been sensible to stay away from crowds. The multitude was hazardous. The Hives were one-way streets of pedestrians, too crowded for Lix to catch up with anyone. He simply had to fix his eye on Freda's unmistakable hair and follow from a distance, separated from his son by a shuffling and unnegotiable throng.

He did not entirely lose sight of George and Freda and the cousin. He lost sight of his resolve. He found a place where he could stand on the embankment steps and watch the three of them from behind. At first, of course, he stared and stared at George's hair and ears, waiting for the boy to turn his face and offer him a profile. Then, inevitably, he turned his attentions to Freda, seeing how she'd aged − not much − and whether being forty suited her. It did. She'd broadened slightly, and her hair was peppery. Otherwise, she was still young and eye-catching, still dangerous, of course, but sexier than he remembered her. If he hadn't made her pregnant, was it possible that they would still be together, he wondered. Fertility's a curse. He could imagine taking off her clothes and lying underneath her on a bed while she pressed down onto his wrists and made him do as he was told.

Thank goodness for the fireworks and the midnight bells: 01/01/01. The first cascade of light exploded like a drum solo. Everybody's chin went up. All the revellers, children to the core, let out a whoop a sigh a wow. Everybody smiled at once. That's what we come to cities for.

Even Lix was animated now and happy in a complicated way. Whatever his personal turmoil, the turmoil of the old town was for the moment more insistent and exuberant. Being there amongst the crowd was more cheering than any Best View from a private balcony. Nobody bothered him. Nobody seemed to recognize his muffled face. Nobody asked for signatures. If anybody shook his hand, and many did, it was just the greeting of another wine-fuelled celebrant who'd shake the devil's hand and not care less. Goodwill to everyone for this New Year. A fine beginning. Not a curse. Lix would start the New Millennium with an extra son. (An extra daughter, too.)

Then the oddest thing occurred, a piece of choreography, perfect and synchronous. Lix had dropped his chin an instant down from the fireworks just to check that his son George was seeming as happy as his father truly felt. But it was the cousin who turned her face to his and recognized that telltale birthmark on his cheek, and smiled the briefest, perfect smile again, as if she had expected him to be there, watching them. Perhaps this was the moment that he truly fell in love with her, not in the lobby of the theatre but underneath the cracking skies amongst the populace. Hers was a smile which promised that she'd let him stay undiscovered if that was what he wanted. She'd not embarrass him. She'd not say, 'See who's followed us.' It was a smile that blessed her face, that transformed her plainness into something more lasting than beauty.

And as he offered up a smile himself, secure that

there would be no betrayal, he felt a pair of arms wrap round him from behind. A pair of stage-trained hands, with digging fingernails, a scent he recognized. A chest that couldn't jiggle when it danced pressed against his back. 'I've caught you now,' she said. Here was an invitation for the second time that night to be An's Devotee.

BOTH LIX AND AN understood at once that these were kisses for a lonely New Year's Eve, a small gift for the coming century, and not the start of anything. So a visit home to her strange rooms or his high, river-view apartment was not on the cards. This encounter would be short and desperate, a firework show. They'd not repeat themselves on other nights. They'd not refer to it before their next performance when, no doubt, their kisses would once again be chaste onstage. The only wagging tongues would be the gossip columnists'.

Once they had toured the trestle bars in Company Square and lowered inhibitions round the scorching braziers with shots of aquavit, they went back to the theatre. Where else? They hammered on the Actors' Gate, relieved to be a little drunk, until the nightman came and tucked their proffered banknote in the pocket of his linen coat, as routinely as somebody who must have done this very thing before and, possibly, for An.

'I'm in my room if you want letting out,' he said. 'You know your way about.'

Indeed, they knew their way about. They ran up to the Players' Easy Room, where there were chairs and couches, and some unfinished bottles of wine and piles of unlaundered costumes from that evening's show. They pulled the curtains open so that the only light was coming from outside, from moon and stars and motor cars, and from the empty-office lights across the street.

'We have to do it in our clothes,' An said. She meant the costumes they wore each night, the clothes they acted in when they pretended love. 'Let's do it like we'd like to do it, in the play.'

'Onstage?'

She hadn't thought of that herself. But: 'Yes, on stage. In costume.'

They'd never truly kissed before, but now they truly kissed, on stage and in-and-out of character in their stage uniforms, with nothing but the borrowed light of corridors to break the darkness of the auditorium. Their tongues engaged. Alone at last – and ready to yield. An actor and an actress are most confident when they are not themselves and can inhabit places where the sound and light are trimmed and flattering, where there might always be applause and where, no matter what they do, no matter what their curses are, there'd be no price to pay, no consequences when the curtain falls, no child to bear and rear and feed for ever more, amen.

*

THERE WAS A MESSAGE on his answerphone when Lix got home a little after one o'clock, already fearful of the big mistake he'd made that night, the big mistakes he'd made for forty years. The message was from Freda, not from An as he had feared at first. She was being pleasant for a change, he thought. Her voice was light and genuine. He could hear her bangles shake. She wished him all the best for the millennium. She said how much she had responded to the play. And, by the way, oh, yes, George 'was prepared' to see his father on New Year's Day, but he was shy and just a little angry and more than normally stressed by the prospect of making contact after all this time, as surely Lix could understand. So George would not go to the zoo with his two half-brothers, unaccompanied. He'd need a friendly face. So Freda's cousin, Mouetta, had volunteered to 'chaperone'.

'Goodnight, then, Comrade Felix Dern,' Freda said on the answerphone.

'It *was* a good night,' Lix replied out loud, standing at the window high above the loyal river while the tape played on through undeleted messages until it hit the high-pitched discord of a broken line.

So NOW IT IS Mouetta's turn. She's had one hundred minutes in the city's dampest cinema, hardly bothering to focus on the film, certainly not paying attention to the subtitles, to think about her pregnancy. She doesn't much enjoy the cinema, to tell the truth. She's only there for Lix. She's been grateful for the darkness and the opportunity to rest. She's waited for *The End* quite happily, but concentrated only on herself, her unexpected joy, her hands clasped in her lap where soon there'll be no lap, she hopes. Her growing child will spill across her knees, expanding like warm dough. Her hands have formed and cupped the shape a hundred times. She's let herself imagine it: she'll never be alone, she'll never be unloved.

It's only in the last ten minutes of the film, and after the brief appearance of an actor colleague her husband says he met and shared a cognac with in Cannes, twelve years ago, that finally he is relaxed enough to take her hand in his and rub her thumb with his. Her pregnant thumb, her hand that's quick with child, does not respond to him. She'll make him wait, like he has made her wait. Mouetta feels as if she has become untouchable, beyond her husband's reach, but also untouchable in a grander sense, beyond mortality. A baby's due in May.

It no longer bothers her that Lix has yet to speak. She understands his caginess. She's used to it. She married it. Her husband's feelings do not really matter any more. His purpose has been served, she thinks. Biology has overtaken him. Now he can either be a swan and stay, or be a dog and run from this, his sixth and final child.

They are the last to leave the matinée. As usual, they've been the only ones to stay and watch the credits until the logo of the studio and the final bars of the soundtrack have given their permission to depart. Then Mouetta tucks her fingers under Lix's arm – the married grip that's far more comfortable than holding hands – and steers him into the street, past the box-office manager who always loves to talk with him, past the cab bay and the taxi touts. It has rained and stopped raining while they were in the cinema. The streets are glossy and greasy. The early evening air is washed and fresh. She wants to walk and build an appetite, Mouetta says.

You do not notice them, in this half-light, a couple almost middle-aged, not smart, not purposeful, but simply grazing on the streets with time to spare. The city's full of couples such as them at this time of the evening, too late to work or shop, too soon to eat or drink, too restless to go home. They take the tramway avenue, which leads up from Deliverance Bridge into the ancient city, crossing Anchorage Street and Cargo Street, old haunts of his, two high and fertile rooms with no views of the river, until they reach the last remaining stretch of city wall and the medieval gate. They could go straight to the cafe district. Instead they negotiate the puddles and turn into the narrow Hives to window-shop for Turkish carpets, hand-built furniture, unlikely children's clothes. Just like the cinema, the dream is lit and organized, a row of plate-glass screens. They pass a shop that only deals in cutlery, a framing shop, a pottery, an antiques studio, until they reach the cobbles of the great, cold square where commerce becomes history and where the odour of the rain is overlaid by kitchen smells and the early, flaring coals of braziers as the beet-and-kebab vendors set up their stalls.

Mouetta wants to try a new bistro she's read about, the Commerce Supper House, on the east side of the square behind the Debit Bar. It's quiet enough for them to talk, for Lix to eat unrecognized. He usually leaves the choice of restaurant to her. He chooses films; she chooses what to eat. But they have reached the terrace of the Debit Bar and the maître d' is standing underneath the canopy, smoking his cigar and curling smiles at everyone who passes. Mouetta grips her husband's arm more tightly but as soon as Lix has stooped to say hello she knows her choice of restaurant is lost.

It isn't comfortable to admit it to herself, but Mouetta is resigned to sacrificing the Commerce Supper House with its advantages because she's almost certain that her cousin will not be inside the Debit, waiting to deride her pregnancy and Lix's gift of parenthood. There'd be no risk of Freda, for a while at least.

Mouetta is ashamed to feel such comfort at her cousin's continuing misfortune: she's been in jail since that wet and riotous night in August, charged that she'd abused her public duties as an employee of the university, that contrary to Conduct Codes she'd had intercourse with a student in her charge, that she possessed a canister of Mace and documents belonging to the state, that she'd received dollars from her son in America without declaring them, that she had out-of-date IDs, and two passports, and cannabis. These are only makeweight charges, peccadilloes hardly worth a fine, although already she's been fired from her faculty and lost her campus rooms. The charge that threatens her with more imprisonment is that she'd assaulted a militiaman outside the Debit Bar, exactly where the maître d' was at that moment shaking Lix's hand.

Lix and Mouetta had witnessed Freda's arrest them-

selves, and knew she hadn't laid a hand on any militiaman. Lix had said they ought to contact Freda's
lawyers, to act as witnesses, but hadn't done so yet.
Two waiters at the Debit Bar had already put themselves forward, so perhaps there wasn't any point in
stepping into the spotlight. He cannot say how fearful
he's become that if he speaks for Freda at her trial,
then all will be revealed about how he'd tipped off the
militia that they'd find the student activist in Freda's
room that night. Such information never disappears.
It bides its time behind the scenes. So Lix gave his
practised, helpless smile as his excuse for hanging back.
And now he gives the smile again, to say how sorry he
is that his wife's choice of restaurant will be deferred
until another night. Mouetta shrugs. The Debit Bar is
home-from-home for him.

The maître d' rests his cigar on a dry sill to smoke
itself for a few moments, and leads the couple to their
preferred corner table, away from mirrors and doors.
Lix takes the seat that lets him set his back against the
room, as usual. They are, so far, the only customers.
Mouetta thinks that she has felt the first of many
thousand kicks.

THE OWLS, the hawks, and peregrines come to the
city in the colder months, as do the gulls these days,
drawn in by thermal banks and easy pickings. The
temperature is slightly higher here – our cosy, gas-

warmed rooms, the car exhausts, the street lighting, the millions of breaths exhaled each hour keep frosts at bay – and so the rodents and the beetles can earn their living for a month or so longer than their country cousins and provide the raptors with their winter meals. The daytime birds of prey prefer the riverbanks, the highway verges and the parks, but most of all they love Navigation Island with its cover of trees and its grasses rich in food. The gulls raid rubbish tips and garbage cans.

The owls, though, like the night-time hunting grounds of yards and roofs and patios where they can treat themselves to household titbits such as tile roaches, hearth crickets, larder mice, and rats.

It is a larder mouse that Rosa sees tonight. She's lined her dolls up by the sliding window to the balcony, already bored, but keen to do what her mother An has told her to – keep out of the bedroom for half an hour – because she'll be rewarded if she does. Her mother keeps a jar of chocolates. And so with the great unconscious gravity of a five-year-old, Rosa makes the minutes pass. She rearranges all her dolls, by favourites, by size, by age. She has them sitting in a group. She has them with their noses pressed against the window. She presses her own nose up against the window to see what they can see. They can see a little animal amongst the pots, a little cuddly toy no longer than her mother's thumb gnawing at a loaf of rye bread that they've thrown out for the birds. It's made a cavern for itself, so that only its grey tail hangs free. Rosa thinks she'll bring the mouse indoors and play with it. She'll introduce it to her dolls. Too late. A dark reflection on the glass, a great wide bird, flat-faced and ghostlike, hits the bread and hits the glass with its spoon wing. The noise it makes is hardly louder than a falling piece of cloth. But – a heartbeat later – the bird has disappeared, the cave of bread has rolled across the balcony, a pot is lying on its side and spilling soil.

Rosa gathers up her dolls and puts them safely on the far side of the room. She knows she's witnessed something memorable and frightening, much more important than the chocolate jar and its rewards. She doesn't know the proper words. She only knows 'a great big bird', 'a little animal'. Still, she hurries to the bedroom door, where Mother's friend has dropped his vast black shoes, and goes in. They're on the bed. Her mother is not dressed. Nor is the man. They seem to be characters from television plays, entwined and shivering and damp. But nothing Rosa can see in there and nothing that her mother says, could be more startling or sad than what has happened on the balcony. She is in tears. Her mother has to let her into bed, amid the odd and disconcerting smells, and fake belief in what she takes as Rosa's jealous lie.

The man is leaving anyway. He's slept enough. He's getting dressed. Rosa has to tell him where he's left his shoes and where the toilet is. 'Can I still have a chocolate?' she asks her mother, and then, 'Can I phone Lech and Karol?' She's sure her half-brothers will want to know at once about the death scene on the balcony.

LECH AND KAROL are not home. Alicja, their mother, has a Lesniak Trading creditors' meeting to attend. Now that her father has retired she is in charge. So she has driven her two sons by Lix out of Beyond and into town for tennis coaching at the new floodlit courts on Navigation Island. Karol is the natural sportsman of the two and already taller. He's in his college football team, has diving ribbons and vaulting cups, but most excels at racquet sports. He will be fourteen in a month and then eligible to represent the city in the junior tennis leagues. His elder brother, Lech, does not excel at anything, except the competitions of the tongue.

The tennis courts are not playable. Clay is an unreliable surface at the best of times. The afternoon of rain has left its puddles on the serving lines and made the courts too slippery. Their mother has arranged to pick them up at ten. Now they have the evening to themselves, in town, and not one single Lesniak around to stop them having fun.

Lech has the matches and the cigarettes. A girl from their tennis group has money they can spend. Her friend has tokens for the tram. The four of them walk across the river on the reconstructed pedestrian bridge, coughing from the cigarette smoke, which, oddly, makes the boys' cocks go hard. They've never been alone with girls like these before. In point of fact, it's not the girls that make them hard but nicotine. Tobacco is an aphrodisiac when you're their age.

Karol hasn't much to say. He is good with racquets, not with words. Yet Lech has found his expertise. Before the evening's out, he thinks, if he can lose his brother and the other girl, then he can try his luck with the one who has the tokens for the tram. She's prettier than anyone he's ever seen before. If he cannot steal a kiss from her before ten o'clock, then, he fears, his nose will bleed, his heart will burst out of his chest. He lights another cigarette. They cough like foxes in the night.

IT'S ONLY afternoon in Queens. George is cruising in a cab along the Van Wyck Expressway on the way to JFK International for his early evening flight back home. His pregnant girlfriend, Katherine, is at his side. She'll see his mother for the first time, at the trial, and meet his famous father, too. She's seen the videos. She recognizes George in Lix's craggy head.

She's nervous, nervous of the flying, nervous for her pregnancy, nervous of Freda, but currently most nervous of the New York cab. The driver has a brutal head. He's brutal with the brakes. She holds onto her boyfriend's arm and braces her feet against the cab floor, expecting the worst. She wishes she hadn't volunteered to go.

'Think of it as holiday,' George says. He sounds American. He has the vowels. 'There won't be proper holidays, not when the baby's small. So make the most of this.'

He tells her how they'll spend their time, the walks along the old embankment to the medieval square, a visit to the island and the MeCCA galleries, a cake and coffee at the Palm & Orchid Coffee House, some free seats at the theatre 'if Father's doing anything'. My god, he thinks, there isn't much to do if they're reduced to sitting through another disaster like *The Devotee*. His city's only worth a two-day trip and they'll be there for ten. His mother's trial will, surely, only last an afternoon. Then what? 'We could go to the zoo,' he adds, and then looks out to count the avenues of Ozone Park as JFK draws close. The zoo, in fact, is quite a good idea, he thinks. He hasn't seen the city zoo since he was eighteen, New Year's Day, 2001, when he met his father and his two half-brothers for the first time, and Father missed an opportunity by courting Mouetta instead of courting him. A disappointment, like the play.

George puts his hand on Katherine's, so that three hands are resting on her swelling stomach, and says again, 'We could go to the zoo by riverboat. We'll take the baby to the zoo.'

*

Six

Bel knows exactly who her father is. Her version of his birthmark makes him unmistakable. She is twenty-six already and has not been greatly tempted to turn up at blood's front door to claim her heritage. Her mother is embarrassed by the very thought of it. It would not be fair or just to rock the life of someone who'd been little more than shy and innocent and careless all those many years ago, she says. 'I'm sure he won't remember it. He didn't even ask my name when we . . .' She doesn't want to say 'had sex'. She doesn't want to say 'made love'.

Bel adores her mother fiercely, without reservation, like many only children of single parents do, and so will not pick up the phone to call on Lix until her mother finally succumbs to the lymphoma that has plagued her for the past six years. Bel has a daughter herself, a one-year-old called Cade. A child needs grandparents. So possibly, with Mother gone, there'll be good cause to show the child to Felix Dern. Bel has prayed that that day will never come.

Her tram, as luck would have it on this evening, is almost empty. She has space enough to leave the stroller uncollapsed on the wooden slatted floor, its wheels wedged in the grooves to keep the sleeping baby safe. Bel likes the smell and polish of an almost empty tram, the loving details of the ironwork, and the heave and judder of their progress through the town. The City Senate must be mad to try to phase them out, and build instead a rapid-transit system underground. What if the city floods again? What were the views from underground?

She hopes her husband's at her stop when they arrive. He often comes to meet them if he gets off work in time, and then they go together to the shops, then go together to the local eatery where there are baby chairs and simple food and friends with children of their own, then go together – yes, the three of them – to bed. Bel puts her finger in her mouth for luck. She lets it hang across her lower lip like a coat hanger. The longer she leaves it there, the more likely it will be that her husband is waiting. What sweeter prospect can there be than having someone meet you from your tram?

The few other passengers have other homes to think about, but one young man – the sort who wonders what the stories are that occupy the other benches of his tram, especially the stories of young women his own age – is keen to catch Bel's eye and smile at her. She's pretty in an interesting way. The smudge of birthmark on her cheek is kissable. Otherwise her face is like her baby's face, as still and innocent as sleep. She's like a little girl herself, he thinks – that girlish finger in her mouth, that girlish look of love uncompromised – and hardly old enough to be a mother. She does not look at him. She looks ahead, into the quickly gobbled streets. The tram counts off its rosary of stops. The baby sleeps.

The details of our lives are undramatic, if we're lucky, and a little dull. We hear the tram, but we have not yet heard the helicopter sweeping through the sky above, amongst the thermals that we have made with all our efforts and our industries all day. The helicopter's payload is a photographer and cameras, keen to strip us to the bone, keen to catch us at our best, at our most mesmerizing, from above at night, with all the detail washed away by distance and by darkness. It's Fifty Cities of the World again, but for international *Geo* magazine this time. *Life* has folded long ago. Our City of Kisses will become, in this aerial depiction, the City of a Million Lights, a two-page spread with staples in the sky. Our celebrated city is being photographed to be a shirt of light with its black tie of river.

Then everyone will see our slo-mo shift of moon and stars in *Geo* magazine. They'll see a thin and shaking glow, unspecified, of early evening smudged. They'll see the coloured mesh of still and moving lights, enhanced by rain – a half a million windows laying out their rhomboids of reflected brilliance, five thousand cars, ten thousand headlamps peeping at the world, a hundred bright and heated trams, six floodlit tennis courts unused, two pinprick, glowing cigarettes not quite ashore. No kissing this time. No flesh and blood. No lips. Such things cannot be spotted from afar. Still the streaks and pricks of light are eloquent. They tell of people going home. They tell of love and lovemaking, of children, marriages and lives. You think, But this could happen anywhere. It does.